Never thought I'd end up here

Also by Ann Liang

If You Could See the Sun
This Time It's Real
I Hope This Doesn't Find You
A Song to Drown Rivers
I Am Not Jessica Chen

Never thought I'd end up here

ANN LIANG

Scholastic Press / New York

Copyright © 2025 by Ann Liang

All rights reserved. Published by Scholastic Press, an imprint of Scholastic Inc., *Publishers since 1920*. SCHOLASTIC, SCHOLASTIC PRESS, and associated logos are trademarks and/or registered trademarks of Scholastic Inc.

The publisher does not have any control over and does not assume any responsibility for author or third-party websites or their content.

No part of this publication may be reproduced, stored in a retrieval system, or transmitted in any form or by any means, electronic, mechanical, photocopying, recording, or otherwise, or used to train any artificial intelligence technologies, without written permission of the publisher. For information regarding permission, write to Scholastic Inc., Attention: Permissions Department, 557 Broadway, New York, NY 10012.

This book is a work of fiction. Names, characters, places, and incidents are either the product of the author's imagination or are used fictitiously, and any resemblance to actual persons, living or dead, business establishments, events, or locales is entirely coincidental.

Library of Congress Cataloging-in-Publication Data available

ISBN 978-1-5461-1067-5

10 9 8 7 6 5 4 3 2   25 26 27 28 29

Printed in Italy 208
First edition, June 2025

Book design by Maeve Norton

FOR ALL THE PEOPLE WE MEET
IN UNEXPECTED PLACES

CHAPTER ONE

The last thing I want is to make a dramatic entrance at my cousin's wedding.

Actually, the last thing I want is to *attend* this wedding. It's not that I have anything against my cousin Xiyue; she's seemed like a lovely person from the brief times we've spoken, even if most of those conversations consisted of me communicating via elaborate gestures instead of Mandarin while she stared in faint confusion.

But that's exactly what I'm dreading.

Once she says her vows, the event will become an intensive, three-hour-long version of those awkward exchanges, with all our relatives and family friends and strangers grouped together in one hotel ballroom. There'll be small talk. Jokes. Questions—none of which I'll be able to answer without slipping into English. And while I'd been clinging to the possibility that I could keep a low profile and slide in and out without anybody noticing, those hopes have now been left to rot somewhere on the road behind us.

"We're going to be late," I warn, leaning as far forward in the back seat as my seat belt will allow.

"Nonsense," my mom says. She takes one hand off the steering wheel to point at the massive white-domed building ahead of us, rising elegantly above the rows of palm trees and picket fences. "You can already see the hotel."

"We've been able to see it for the past ten minutes," I say. When she ignores my very valid observation, I catch my dad's eye in the rearview mirror. *Help*, I mouth.

He clears his throat and adjusts his glasses, though they immediately slip down his long nose again. "We could afford to go just a little faster," he says in the gentlest tone possible.

Three cars rush past us as he speaks. Someone honks.

"I'm going very fast already," my mom snaps. To be fair, for someone who generally seems to be on a mission to prove that walking is more efficient than driving, she is. At least we're not so far below the speed limit that we're at risk of being fined, like last time.

"You've made a convincing case," my dad says at once. "There's no rush. No rush at all." He shoots me a helpless look over his shoulder, which I return with a sigh. This is about as close as either of us will ever get to arguing with my mom. He adores her too much to ever accuse her of doing anything wrong, and I simply don't like to invest energy into battles I know I'll lose.

Besides, I've upset her enough in the past week.

So I lock my jaw shut, will away the slow churning sensation in my gut, and refresh my makeup for the third time since lunch. No matter what products I use, they tend to melt off my face within an hour, and it's always worse when the air is as hot and humid as it is today. Every makeup artist I've worked with has pointed this out. That, and the "lack of real estate" around my eyelids, and the sallowness of my complexion, and the thinness of my lips.

Not that it's an issue anymore, I remind myself, feeling a pang behind my sternum. It's another reason why I don't want to draw any unnecessary attention to myself at the wedding, but there's no way I'm avoiding my fate now.

We're running half an hour late by the time my mom pulls into the crowded parking lot. I yank open the door and jump out onto the pavement in my stilettos, then smooth my dress out over my knees, ready to bolt into the hotel—

Except Mom pauses on her way to the front steps, scrutinizing me with her hand on her hip, her mouth pursed. I've never seen her in court before, but I imagine this is how she appears before her clients. Focused, serious, and slightly frightening. "You look pretty," she says.

I release an internal sigh of relief. It doesn't matter how often I hear it—I still want the confirmation that I can be beautiful. Crave it, chase it, like an adrenaline junkie seeking their next high. If too much time passes without getting *some* kind of positive feedback about my appearance, I imagine myself shriveling away, all the work I've put into my face and my body gone to waste. "Thanks," I tell her. "That's very nice—"

"It's not meant to be nice. Why are you so put together?" she demands. "You're going to upstage your cousin."

"I'm not trying to upstage anyone." And I'm really not. My goal is never to look better than other people—it's just about making sure that I don't look bad. Still, I tug the bottom of my dress even farther down. It's a fairly straightforward navy piece, with a modest collar and basic lace design on the side. A model scout once told me in passing that darker tones suit me better, and I haven't worn anything else since.

"Maybe tie your hair up," she suggests.

"Fine." I attempt to follow her advice, scraping my hair back with my nails. "Is the ponytail better? I mean, well, worse?"

My mom pulls my dad over onto the sidewalk. "What do you think? Does she look uglier?" she asks hopefully.

"Our daughter is perfect. She could never be ugly, no matter what," my dad says, which is both really moving and unhelpful.

"She's certainly suited for modeling," my mom says, then catches herself. Remembers once again. It's hard to describe the emotion on her face. Disappointment? Anger? Resentment? I feel all of it in my throat, and more, an ache I can't get rid of.

"Let's just go inside," I say, walking well ahead of them before either can continue. I could run in five-inch heels, if I wanted to. Every now and then, at my high school friends' gatherings, they'd ask me to demonstrate it as a party trick, and the response would be overwhelming.

I pick up my pace, my heart beating in sync with the sharp, satisfying *clack* of my shoes against the marble floor when I step inside.

Even though I'd much rather not be here, I do have to appreciate the venue. Lilies and violet orchids bloom in vivid clusters all the way down the wide corridor, and a six-foot-tall poster of my cousin and her fiancé is perched before the entrance. In the photo, they're gazing at each other on a balcony, both beaming, their skin near perfect thanks to some combination of the golden-hour light and professional airbrushing. There's a sign too but it's written in Chinese characters—the only one I recognize is the *Zhang* from my own family name.

Judging from the sounds of tinkling laughter and shuffling footsteps and rumbling voices, the wedding must be well underway by now. My heart rate spikes the way it always does before I'm about to enter a crowded room, and I have to consciously steady my breathing. It's an old trick, picked up and perfected two years ago at two different schools, when the simple act of grabbing a salad from the cafeteria or finding my seat in class was something I had to brace myself for.

Breathe in for four.

Hold.

Out for four.

Good.

You're good now.

Or I'm supposed to be. But when I walk through the doors, the noise drops away.

It's like I'm back at my old school again, the very last place I'd ever want to return to.

The stares. The raised brows. The exchanged glances. Even though the people here don't have a reason to dislike me the way my classmates did, there are still way too many of them, filling up almost every single table in the ballroom. Countless faces turn, assessing me, and I get that pit-in-my-stomach feeling I've always hated, this sense that I'm looming over everyone like a dark cloud, a giant in the metaphorical and, at five feet ten, literal sense, unable to blend into any crowd, incapable of fitting into any room. I can only stand here and let them stare as my face grows hot and my fingers go clammy.

There are times when I agree with my mom that maybe I *was* cut out to be a model, when I'm convinced that it's the only thing I can ever be cut out for—standing still and looking pretty—and I've wasted that, played my cards wrong. Then there are times when I'm convinced I was never suited for it, that it was ridiculous I ever believed otherwise. That the past two years were the true waste, because how can you be a model if you loathe the feeling of being looked at?

"Leah!"

More eyes flicker up as Xiyue strides over to us. The wedding poster really didn't do her justice. She's glowing. Gorgeous in her joy and in her qipao, which seems to have been designed just for her. Each delicate silver thread gleams as she moves, weaving together images of peonies and phoenixes that wrap around her shoulders and waist. She's everything you'd imagine a happy bride to be, with her red dress and rosy cheeks.

I open my mouth to tell her that I'm sorry for being so late, but the only Mandarin words I manage to recall on the spot are: "I'm sorry."

This comes out much more ominous than I'd hoped.

"Sorry?" She frowns slightly.

My mom jumps in with what I'm assuming is an explanation, and then she spots Xiyue's mother behind her. Her face tightens for just a second before her already-wide smile stretches further, into a beam so beatific it can only be fake, her arms stretching out with it.

"Jiejie," she coos, pulling my aunt into a polite hug, neither of them really touching.

I stay quiet as they exchange loud air kisses and step back to study each other. My aunt hasn't changed since I last saw her at the Spring Festival dinner a couple years ago. Same expensively coiffed, pitch-black hair, same stern, thin brows, same powdered skin pulled taut over high cheekbones. I actually don't think she's changed at all since I *first* saw her when I was a baby. The woman is walking proof that genes can only get you so far when it comes to anti-aging, because while she looks like she's been sipping from the Fountain of Youth every morning, I was helping my mom pluck out the white hairs near her temple just the other night.

The bizarre thing is that in almost any other family, my mom would be the favorite child. The success story you brag about at events like this one. Good grades, good house, good career, happy marriage. Unfortunately for her, my aunt just happens to be one of the youngest and most esteemed professors in the Department of East Asian Languages and Cultures at Stanford and a Grammy-nominated composer on the side, because being good at just *one* thing is too primitive. The family legend goes that she's so accomplished she caught the attention of NASA, who wanted to send her into space, but she declined because she was too busy. Like, too busy *for the moon.*

"Hey," I say when my aunt turns toward me with an expectant look.

My mom tugs at my wrist harder than she typically would. "You don't say *hey* like you're bumping into a friend at the mall. You say *xiaoyi hao*," she hisses.

"Xiaoyi hao," I amend, but I seem to have already failed some kind of test. And I fail it again when my aunt asks me something in Chinese. I look helplessly over at my mom, who answers for me in a strained, high-pitched voice, then waves me off to a table in the corner.

It's the kids' table, I realize. Piles of candy have been laid out around the crimson rose centerpiece: chocolates in the shape of hearts and peanut brittle and strawberry swirls and pink marshmallows. There's even the corn-flavored jelly candies I remember from my childhood, as artificially sweet as they are bright yellow, yet so good I could never stop eating them.

A few of the kids have started digging into the sweets already, the shiny wrappers crinkling in their little fists. As I sit down in the only empty chair left, I recognize two of them as my very distant cousins, but everyone else at the table is a complete stranger—

No.

My gaze catches on the person next to me, the only boy here who's also seventeen, and I feel my heart drop.

It can't be him. It *shouldn't* be.

Yet there he is, with his dark hair falling like silk over his forehead, the angles of his face so finely rendered it's almost a taunt to contemporary sculptors, the softness of his lips a lie. He looks like he hasn't smiled once in the two years since I last saw him. He's definitely not smiling right now. His eyes are pinned on me, and though they're the exact same shade of brown—the kind that turns to liquid amber in the light, and black onyx at night—there's something different about them. Something heavier and melancholy.

"Hello," he says, and his voice is different too. Low. Leveled.

I never thought I would hear it again.

I prayed I would never have to.

"Hi," I say. Or I attempt to say, the effort of that single word exhausting. My whole body is numb. The moment doesn't seem real, but I can feel moisture gathering over the bare nape of my neck.

I like to consider myself a reasonably amiable person. I've never gotten into a heated argument or physical altercation with anyone before. I have a healthy number of friends, and though we're not exactly drive-across-the-country-at-midnight-to-help-you close the way I wish to be, at least we're you-can-borrow-my-sunglasses close. And I might dislike a number of people, or disagree with them on multiple points, but I don't *hate* anybody—

Except for the boy sitting down beside me.

Cyrus Sui.

Ever since I was a child, I've had abnormally vivid nightmares. They're so believable that in those moments when I wake up in a cold sweat, I'm convinced that my life is what I experienced when I was asleep, and everything else is an illusion. I have nightmares about everything: About doing a shoot in the middle of Grand Park only to discover halfway through that I wasn't dressed. About the sky falling, about my parents turning into flesh-eating aliens, about my parents growing old, which was even more terrifying. And without fail, starting from the day of the Incident, I've had nightmares about Cyrus Sui.

Nightmares where he joined the other kids at my previous schools in making my life miserable, shrinking away dramatically every time I walked close in the corridors, flinging the ball across the court a little too hard in gym so it would hit me. Where he kept spreading rumors about the Incident, following me from school to school and shouting about it through a speaker before I could even introduce myself. Where he openly gloated about ruining my life when I was fifteen, an arsonist grinning up at the flames while I choked on the smoke.

Even though it's been two years since the Incident itself, my grudge hasn't faded. If anything, it's only festered. Strengthened like wine, grown so potent that one small taste of it is enough to cloud your head.

My part-time friend and full-time classmate, Cate Addison, accused me once of holding grudges too easily. I've been holding a grudge against her for that as well.

"Remember me?" Cyrus asks, tipping his chin up a few degrees, as if he isn't the reason my school records are permanently stained. The reason I went through hell.

My throat closes. My fists clench. How I wish this were another nightmare. "I—"

"I'm sure you do," he says. He picks up one of the chocolates using two fingers but doesn't unwrap it. Just tosses it in the air. Catches it without looking. "I remember *you* very well, Leah. Nobody else has left such a strong impression."

"What are you doing here?" I hiss, my initial shock wearing off.

"There's someone here I need to see," he says, tossing the chocolate again, then cuts me a look I can't quite parse. "Believe me, I had no idea you'd be here."

To be fair, right up until I quit modeling last month, I had no idea I'd be here either. If I hadn't quit, the chances are that I would have had to cancel last minute, and one of my parents would've also had to miss out on the wedding just to drive me to some shoot on the other side of LA. But now I have no reason to miss out on any family functions, not when my current summer schedule mostly involves me crawling out of bed at noon, making myself spicy ramen for breakfast at lunchtime, and watching celebrity documentaries to avoid my looming college application deadlines.

"Sorry to disappoint," I mutter.

"What is life if not disappointing?" he says, just dryly enough that I can't tell if he's joking or making a genuine, depressing statement.

"Well," I say, crossing my ankles together under the table to keep from fidgeting or kicking something, "don't let me ruin your enjoyment of one of the greatest joys in the world."

"Free drinks?"

"I meant the wedding."

"Oh, I wouldn't enjoy it much anyway." He makes a general gesture toward the overhanging red tassels and fake, gold-foil trees and confetti balloons floating around the ballroom. "I find these overt displays of love to be somewhat nauseating."

I must be staring, because he lifts his brows.

"Something wrong?" he asks.

"You've changed," I can't help observing aloud.

His expression flickers, but he merely tosses the chocolate again. "How so?"

I study him. It's hard for me to pinpoint myself—whether it's the alertness in his eyes, despite the insouciance of his posture; the slight pause after each sentence, as if he's assessing my immediate reaction; or even the way he's dressed, his simple button-down so crisp it must be freshly ironed.

But I remember him as the boy who would smile all the time, though it was always a crooked smile, the type that assured you he was up to no good. He was also the one who'd make sure he was sitting behind me in every class, just so he could tap my seat and annoy me. Who'd pester me during quiet reading sessions and pretend to be busy working when the teacher glared in our direction. Who'd steal my pencils. My homemade snacks. My scrunchies. My *science homework*, which is how I confirmed that he was stealing for the sole pleasure of stealing from me, because my grades were far worse than his.

He was the monster who left a real, live, buzzing bee inside my locker on Valentine's Day when all the other girls were opening theirs up to find flowers.

Not to mention that he was the culprit who got me kicked out of my old school.

He was evil. He is still evil, I'm certain, but more somber, and—if we're doing an honest evaluation—even more appallingly, unnervingly beautiful.

"Never mind," he says, setting the chocolate down flat on the crimson tablecloth, the heart pressed beneath his palm. "I can already predict the answer."

Like a fool, I rise to the bait. "How could you—"

"It's the cologne," he says. "I started using it last year. Nice, right?"

Entirely against my will, I find myself shifting forward and breathing in the clean, sandalwood scent of his shirt. It *is* new, and it is nice, not overpowering like the colognes the guys at my school seem to soak themselves in, and—I should absolutely not be smelling him right now.

I jerk back with a scowl. Then I remember the other guests in the room and stop myself. Force my facial muscles to relax. Multiple sources have informed me that I have a severe case of Ready to Kill You Face whenever I'm not making a concentrated effort to seem friendly. I blame it on my features. My arched brows and sunken cheekbones and angular chin might help me stand out in a photo, but they also make me look *downright hostile* and *unapproachable*—both quoted from other sources—in real life.

Cyrus leans over a little. "What happened to your face just now?"

"It's called disgust," I tell him, keeping my expression as serene as possible, just in case one of my cousin's maids of honor chooses this moment to glance over at our table. I must appear perfect at all times. "Something I'd think you would be very familiar with."

"It *was* disgust, perhaps. Now you look like you're about to begrudgingly embark on a journey of inner healing somewhere deep in the woods," he remarks.

"Then you're disrupting my journey," I say.

And he continues to disrupt it. "You've changed too." His

dark eyes trace my dress, my lips, then move up to my bangs, which get in the way of relatively important things like seeing, but help cover my forehead. The wedding seems to fade in my periphery, until the only sound I can hear is the strain in my own throat when I swallow. Part of me is surprised that Cyrus even recognizes me when I hardly recognize old photos of myself.

The last time he saw me, I wasn't a model yet. I wasn't pretty at all.

"Of course I've changed. It's been two years," I say, like the dramatic transformation in my style and face can be explained away by something as simple as the natural passage of time.

"I know," he says, "but you just seem really . . ."

Gorgeous? I fill in. *Elegant? Well-adjusted? Sophisticated? Glamorous?*

"Worn out."

My mask of serenity cracks, and my cheeks prickle. In no world is this a compliment. I guess I shouldn't have been expecting a compliment from someone like him, but I hadn't been braced for a personal attack either.

"How nice of you," I say coolly.

He starts to speak again, but his voice is drowned out by the most cheerful wedding music I've ever heard in my entire life. The chorus is vaguely familiar, like the particular sweetness of the corn-flavored jelly candies, something I can't name but know that I should be able to, if only for the way it creates a faint stirring under my breastbone. Familiar, but forgotten.

As I twist around in my seat to watch my beaming cousin make her way up to the front of the ballroom, I'm still fuming over Cyrus's choice of words. *Worn out.* As if even the four layers of makeup can't conceal my exhaustion. As if he can tell from one glance that I've been buckling under the pressure, pouring my tears into an industry that couldn't care less if I disappeared—and so I did. I have.

I left it all behind me, and now, somehow, I've ended up here: at a wedding I never wanted to attend, next to the old nemesis I never wanted to be reunited with, who's retained the uncanny ability to get under my skin after two years.

And I have no choice but to bear it until it's time to go.

CHAPTER TWO

I'm pretty sure my cousin gets married.

Almost certain. I do my best to pay attention as she goes through the rituals while the guests sniff into their napkins and the children continue munching on the candy. The only reason I know what the rituals even are is because my mom had been talking about them before we left the house. First, the pair must bow to the sky and the earth, and then to their parents, and then to each other.

Wine is poured into little ceramic cups. Vows are probably made, and the scene is probably beautiful, a celebration of true love and whatnot against a backdrop of brilliant scarlet and gold banners.

I would know for sure if I weren't so distracted by Cyrus and his reactions. Or, rather, his lack of reaction. He's the only person here who looks decidedly unmoved. Unimpressed. He barely seems to be paying attention to the bride and groom at all—he spends more time watching my aunt fold up her silk handkerchief into a neat square after she wipes her eyes.

"What's your problem?" I mutter as Xiyue starts to move toward one of the round tables, one hand balancing a glass of wine, the other holding on to her new husband's arm. "This is meant to be a happy occasion. They're in love."

"They think they're in love, as most newlyweds tend to," Cyrus says with a shrug. "It'll pass."

"Or," I counter, "they could grow old together in a yellow cottage with its own vegetable patch and duck pond."

This earns me a brief head tilt. "Is that your dream for the future?"

"God, no," I say. "Ducks scare me. My dream is—"

I stop halfway, reaching for something that's no longer there. My dream *was* to become a successful model, to see my face in magazine spreads, to meet the most esteemed designers and walk the most influential runway shows and get invited to the most exclusive parties. Not even because I thought it'd be fun, but just to say I was there. It used to be so simple, so clear-cut.

Now I have no idea. I imagine myself graduating from high school, and then—nothing. It's like trying to spot a distant shore through ocean fog, or recognizing a stranger's face from miles away.

"To sleep," I finish, looking off to the side. Xiyue has already moved on to the neighboring table, where all the elderly aunties take turns pinching her cheeks and showering her with their blessings. "To sleep forever."

"I believe you're describing death," Cyrus says.

"At least it's attainable."

He makes a light scoffing sound. "A low bar."

"Yes, well—" I'm distracted by a sudden, harrowing realization as Xiyue begins walking over to us. "Oh my god."

"What?" he asks immediately, shifting forward.

"*We're* not expected to say anything, are we? To Xiyue, I mean."

"Of course we are," he says, looking confused by my panic. "It's basic etiquette. You don't need to give a speech—just offer up a few congratulatory words or something."

"I—I can't—" I don't know what I'm supposed to say. My Mandarin skills are limited to simple greetings and common sayings in my household, such as "stop leaving your cups everywhere" and "clean out your wardrobe" and "math requires practice." None of them are applicable here.

"I know," one of the kids speaks up from the other side of the table. She looks no older than eight. Her hair is bunched into pigtails that bob around when she grabs another handful of candy. "Zhu nimen xinhun yukuai, zaosheng guizi."

"What—what does that mean?" I ask, tracking my cousin's movement out of the corner of my eye.

"It means you wish them a happy marriage, and hope that they start a healthy family soon," Cyrus explains.

I hesitate. "Are you sure?"

"You can look it up if you don't believe me," he says, rolling his eyes.

"Okay, thank you so much," I tell the little girl, both genuinely grateful and devastatingly humbled to be receiving Mandarin help from someone half my size. "And thank you too, I guess," I say to Cyrus with far less enthusiasm. "So it's . . . What was it again?"

"Zhu nimen xinhun yukuai, zaosheng guizi," he advises. Even though we've both grown up here in LA, his pronunciation is perfect, but I don't have time to be annoyed about it.

"Got it." I repeat the phrase rapidly under my breath as my cousin and her husband approach. *Zhu nimen xinhun yukuai, zaosheng guizi.* It's only a few words. Even though I might not understand them, I can rely on my short-term memory to know the sounds. I just have to focus and recite them until it's my turn. *Zhu nimen xinhun yukuai—*

"I thought your Mandarin was decent," Cyrus says.

Dammit.

"Please don't talk to me right now," I say, wiping my hands against my dress. "I'm concentrating."

Zhu nimen xinhun yukuai.

"I can tell. Your concentrating face looks the same." He points to the space between his brows, then to mine. "You get this little crease here."

Xinhun. Xin. Hun.

Zhu nimen xinhun—

"But really. Have you been slacking off on your Chinese studies these past two years or what?" Cyrus asks.

I glare at him. "Could you not—"

"Hi!" Xiyue appears at our table, her husband following close after her. She smiles over at me expectantly, her glass of wine refilled. And then she waits. Her husband waits too. This is my first time seeing him up close, and he has the sort of face that just belongs to a banker: a soft jaw, gelled hair, round glasses. He would look great with square frames though. I'm debating whether to offer this fashion tip when I remember what I'm meant to do.

I rise hastily to my feet and hold up my untouched glass of orange juice. "Zhu nimen . . ." As I talk, I notice that the ballroom has fallen quiet. A few people are even pushing back their chairs or craning their heads to look at me.

It's a strange feeling, but not a new one.

Most of the guests here must still think of me as the model, thanks to my mom's constant promotional-slash-humblebrag posts on WeChat. That's what everyone from my current high school knows me as too—and it's by design. After the Incident, after the first and second school I transferred into and left again because nobody wanted me there, I knew that unless I wanted to graduate a social pariah, I needed to change something. Not in an *Eat Pray Love* way, but quick, shallow changes, Band-Aid fixes to hold myself together while everything was falling apart.

So I cut my hair at a salon recommended by all the prettiest influencers. Learned how to do my makeup. Blasted songs about *loving yourself as you are* while working out to remold my body into something else. Poured my savings into completely revamping my wardrobe—out went the comfortable sweatpants and basic, faded shirts, and in came the suffocatingly tight dresses and crop tops that always left my stomach cold.

The shocking thing was that it worked. When I joined my current school mid-semester last year, I had already become the swan. Enough time had passed that the rumors about me no longer traveled faster than the transfer papers did, and being conventionally attractive changed *everything*. I was still the same person, but only I knew that. Instead of being called cold and unapproachable, I was suddenly cool and unattainable. Instead of quiet, I was mysterious. Instead of weird, I was alluring. When Cate and her pretty, popular friends approached me on the first day of school, Cate's first words to me were: *Oh my god, I love your hair.*

And when a model scout gave me her card outside a frozen yogurt shop just a month later, Cate had been even more excited than I was. Modeling, I realized, was the ultimate key to cementing my social status at my new school, the final stage in my transformation. It's just one of those jobs where there's something inherently shiny and interesting about the title. Something desirable. That's why I held on to it for so long, even when it felt like I was holding on to a jagged cliff edge: because I've never been shiny or interesting on my own.

Then someone coughs—Cyrus—and I snap back to the present.

The wedding. The blessing.

The words I need to say, but now can't remember.

"Zhu nimen xinhun . . ." Panic lodges itself in my throat. What was it? Yu? Yao? Yin? "Yiyu," I say, which sounds about right. "And, um, zaosheng . . ." I do a frantic search through my sad vocabulary bank. What's the word that usually comes after *sheng*? "Shengbing."

There's a pause.

If the ballroom had been quiet before, it's completely silent now.

Looks of horror travel swiftly from table to table. My aunt is frowning right at me, shaking her head in clear disapproval. Cyrus has a fist pressed to his mouth—either to keep from laughing, or maybe just to keep himself from making some kind of unhelpful remark. From across the room, I can see my parents: My mom is dragging a hand over her eyes, as if to shield herself from the scene, and my dad's face is twisted into a sympathetic grimace. My cousin and cousin-in-law are frozen to the spot before me. They both appear stricken, their eyes wide.

A sinking feeling rolls over my gut, even though I still have no idea what went wrong. Only that something must have.

Then Xiyue's face crumples, and the silence cracks as she bursts into tears.

I stare in stunned, confused horror as she flees from the room as fast as the tight fabric of her qipao will allow, her new husband chasing after her. "Xiyue! Xiyue—wait!" Then, as if my words have set off the world's most chaotic game of tag, my aunt chases after them too, but not before she sends me the most withering glare I've ever received in my life. It stings like a slap, and I have no doubt that if I weren't related to her, she would actually march over here to strike me.

"What . . . did I do?" I whisper to Cyrus.

"You really don't know what you just said?" he asks, pulling me back down into the seat.

"No?" Ice fills my blood. My gaze flits from the guests' appalled expressions to the open door where my cousin fled. It seems impossible that just seconds ago, she'd been happy and head over heels in love, and now, this might go down in our family history as the most disastrous wedding ever. Because of me. "No . . . What? I was just repeating the phrase—wasn't I?"

"You were *supposed* to wish them a happy marriage and healthy children. Instead," he says, with the air of an executioner right before the ax drops, "you told them you hope they have a depressing marriage, and that they fall ill quickly."

The wedding ends early.

Once it becomes apparent that my cousin isn't coming back anytime soon, the guests scatter, murmuring to themselves and eyeing me on their way out like I'm the car crash that's been blocking the freeway. Nobody's even tasted the wedding cake, which is starting to melt, the clay figurines of my cousin and her husband sliding off the top.

If the floor weren't made of absurdly shiny marble, I'd dig a ditch right this instant and lie in it forever.

My dad excuses himself to go to the bathroom, and my mom

heads off in the same direction my aunt and cousin went, her heels echoing down the corridor. Then it's just me and Cyrus left in the bloody aftermath, the crimson streamers and slowly dying flowers spilling out around us. I have no idea why *he's* still here, other than to watch me suffer.

And I'm absolutely suffering. While Cyrus has been standing by the entrance, I've circled the entire length of the room about a thousand times like a caged animal. My stomach won't stop twisting in on itself, tighter and tighter and tighter until it feels like I might vomit. How could I have messed up everything with just a few wrong words? How do I keep messing things up?

"I think they're talking about you," Cyrus says quietly when I pass him on my thousand-and-second lap.

My heart clenches. I jolt to a stop next to him and strain my ears. Sure enough, through the closed doors, I can hear my aunt's voice, rising over my mom's softer, apologetic one. It's like listening to a whole different person. Gone is the self-assured lawyer who addresses almost everyone—babies, businessmen, waiters, puppies, you name it—in the same clipped, no-nonsense tone. Right now, she just sounds like a chastened child. My aunt is probably the only person in the world who can have that effect on her.

I attempt to focus on the conversation, but I can't understand anything either of them is saying, except for my name, which pops up at an alarming frequency.

"She says your cousin is having second thoughts," Cyrus murmurs.

I turn to him, my wariness waging war against my need to know exactly what they're talking about.

"She's really superstitious, apparently," Cyrus continues translating, his brows furrowed in concentration, his ear pressed to the door. "Won't stick her chopsticks upright in rice. Hates the number four. She doesn't even like to use four exclamation points in a row. She took a trip all the way to this sacred fountain at the top of the Yellow Mountain last month, just to pray for a happy marriage, but . . . she thinks her marriage is doomed now."

I squeeze my eyes shut and wonder if it's physically possible to die from guilt. Like, maybe the sheer weight of it will crush my organs. And if not that, then maybe my aunt's disapproval will do the trick. I keep replaying the way she glowered at me before she chased after her crying daughter, like she was affronted by the very idea that we're connected by blood.

Her voice grows louder now, sharper, until eavesdropping becomes unnecessary. It would be harder *not* to hear her speaking. My name comes up again, spat out.

"She says . . ." Cyrus hesitates.

"Tell me," I say through gritted teeth. "Just tell me."

He clears his throat. "She says . . . your mother should be ashamed of herself for raising such an ignorant foreigner."

An ignorant foreigner. I try to hold the words out at a safe, painless distance, like when you have to grab something hot from the oven, careful not to let it burn any exposed skin. But my mental grip slips, and it burns me anyway, searing my face and my chest. I twist my head toward the wall so Cyrus can't see my expression.

"Leah," he begins, in a tone that sounds suspiciously like sympathy. "I think—"

"I don't care what you think," I cut in. It's almost a relief to find a target, to distract myself from the minor fact that I've most certainly just gotten myself blacklisted from every single future family function and made my mom lose face in front of the only person she feels insecure around. "What are you even still doing here?"

"Waiting," he says.

I blink. "For what? The wedding's over."

"For *who*," he corrects me. "Do you know how busy Dr. Linda Shen is? And she must receive hundreds of emails begging her for a letter of recommendation every day, so of course I had to—"

"Hang on. You're here to see . . . my aunt?" I demand incredulously. "For *a letter of recommendation*? Oh my god. Were you even invited to this wedding?"

"I have an invitation to the wedding."

I don't miss the subtle distinction. My brows rise.

"Okay, fine, a friend of a friend was invited by your cousin's husband," he admits, straightening the cuff of his sleeve. "They weren't planning on coming, so I asked them to give their invitation to me."

I add *opportunist* to the long list of names I've saved for Cyrus in my head. It's probably the most flattering one on there. I toss *insensitive asshole* in too for good measure, because when the doors swing open and my aunt steps out, Cyrus practically launches himself off the wall in her direction.

"Dr. Linda Shen," he says, and I *swear* he just made his voice deeper. "I know you're busy, but if you have a second, I wanted to—"

My aunt walks right past him as if he doesn't exist. On any ordinary day, this would be incredible to witness, but any spark of petty glee I feel is quickly stamped out by the fact that my aunt seems determined to ignore my existence too.

Then my mom emerges, and the look on her face makes everything in my body turn cold.

"In the car," she grits out. "Now."

CHAPTER THREE

My mom is still fuming when she slams the car door behind her.

I shrivel in my seat, my shoulder pressed to the window for support. "I'm sorry," I say, even though the words sound too weak, too superficial to my own ears, like trying to fill a gaping hole in a dam with nothing but napkins. "I'm really so extremely sorry. I didn't mean to curse my cousin or . . . or ruin the wedding. I just—I forgot the right words—and I feel awful."

My mom turns on the ignition and grips the steering wheel. "No, *I'm* sorry," she tells me.

I blink.

This is new.

"I should have done something ages ago," she continues. "I knew you were forgetting your Mandarin. They all warned me this would happen. They told me I should encourage you to read more books about Chinese history and culture and converse in Mandarin at home whenever possible." She heaves out a long, heavy sigh. "It's my fault my English is so good. If I weren't perfectly bilingual, things might not have turned out this way."

"Your English is phenomenal," my dad offers from the passenger seat.

"Yes, I know," Mom says. She finally starts easing the car out of the parking lot.

The constant lurching motion doesn't help the sick feeling in the pit of my stomach. It's not just that I feel guilty for ruining things—it's also humiliating. I've always made it my goal to move through life as gracefully as possible, to only do the things I already excel at, to only participate in games I'm confident I'll win. This was a major defeat, and Cyrus just had to be around to witness it.

Then again, maybe it isn't a coincidence that Cyrus is involved in two of the very worst days of my life so far. At this point, I wouldn't be surprised if in a past life, I accidentally ran him over with a horse carriage or something, and his whole purpose in this life is to bring me misery. He's definitely succeeding.

"But what's the point of speaking great English if our daughter can't speak her own mother tongue?" my mom says. "She can't even speak to her own grandparents."

My aunt's words ring inside my skull, and I wonder if my mom's thinking of them too. *Ignorant foreigner.* "I . . . I do speak to my grandparents," I venture through the lump in my throat, desperate to defend myself. "I called my nainai just last week."

My mom draws in a deep breath and sighs again, as if there's an excess of oxygen inside the vehicle. "You said *love you, dude* at the end."

"What's wrong with telling her I love her?"

"You called your nainai *dude*," she emphasizes.

"Respectfully."

"You don't even know who Tang Bohu is."

I hesitate, trying to place the name. "Who is that? One of my uncles?"

Dad makes an impassioned motion for me to stop talking.

"Look, this is a serious problem, Leah," my mom says as she turns onto the main street. "How long has it been since you visited China? Do you not remember anything anymore?"

I'm not sure how to answer that. I gaze out the window, at the smooth, winding roads and the lush lawns and the ocean simmering on the horizon, peppered with little white boats, the clear sky opening up around us. When I think of *here*, I think of LA. These are my most intimate, immediate surroundings. This is the place where I grew up, where I learned to ride a bike and spell my name and play soccer, where we buried my pet goldfish and planted a cherry tree and set up a tent in our backyard to watch movies at night. But I don't think of China as *there* either. It's not the same as when my friends talk about traveling to France or Bali for the holidays, some hazy, distant destination I know only from photos and travel brochures. Although my memories of China are flimsy, stretched almost translucent over a total of five summer breaks from my childhood, I always have this feeling that my bones will know the place, even when I don't.

"I'm not sure," I mumble.

"Well, if you're actually sorry about what happened today,

and if you'd like to prevent anything similar from ever happening again, we'll need to make some changes around here," my mom says with a terrifying note of resolve in her voice. When she decides on something, she means it. Last year, she made an abrupt announcement that she felt the house chores weren't being evenly distributed enough. By the end of the evening, she'd created a very strict roster we've been following to this day. Tonight is dish duty for me.

"I *am* sorry," I say quickly. "We can go to my aunt and my cousin right now—I can write them an apology letter—"

"In what, English?" my mom says with a scoff. "If you're apologizing to them, it better be in perfect Chinese. You should start practicing. No more English allowed in our house."

"What?"

"Starting now," she repeats. "Xianzai."

"But—that's—" I splutter. "I don't—"

"Yong zhongwen" is all she says. *Use Chinese.*

Nobody speaks again for the rest of the car ride.

All throughout the next week, my mom is in a strange mood.

She stays up in her home office until midnight; when I go to sleep, it's to the sound of the printer whirring or her computer humming. She disappears at dinner to make important calls, speaking in a hushed voice. She cancels our pizza night on Friday and cooks for the first time in a month to make sweet-and-sour pork ribs and sticky pineapple rice. She keeps her word about only speaking in Chinese; the one time she weakens is when she accidentally locks herself in the garage and I can't figure out where the key is.

Then, on Saturday, she lowers herself onto the couch next to me and holds up a document.

I hit pause on my laptop. "What is that?" I ask warily, rubbing my eyes.

I've spent the past two hours binge-watching a documentary about the career revival of a famous singer-songwriter. The last scene had been of her sobbing into a napkin in the darkness of her studio, while screenshots of absurdly mean comments floated around her like digital phantoms.

Of course, I know how things will go from here. She'll remember why she got into the industry in the first place: because of her *passion for music*. Maybe she'll receive a heartfelt message from a fan, or she'll find a video of herself playing the piano as a toddler. *This is what it's really about*, she'll say, *not success*. She'll then wake up one morning with a melody stuck in her head, and she'll hurry down to the studio, and the rough, original audio will transition into the final song, which she'll play at sold-out stadiums, having become successful at last.

"An application," my mom says.

"An application for what?" I ask. "And are we finally speaking English again?"

She ignores my second question. Just waves the document around with excitement like it's a winning lottery ticket. "Journey to the East."

I stare.

"You know, like *Journey to the West*? It's a play on words. Because this is a journey to—well, the East," she explains.

"Yeah, um, I got that part," I say, still trying to decipher what this means.

"It's a two-week trip around China's cities to really immerse you in the culture," she goes on. "The local Chinese school, Jiu Yin He, is hosting it. It's perfect for kids like you, who've forgotten their Mandarin and barely know anything about China. Studies show the most effective way to relearn a language is by being in the environment. And," she adds, like it's an afterthought, "the program is run in collaboration with the Department of East Asian Languages and Cultures at Stanford, so your aunt is the one who designed the itinerary for this year. She'll be receiving regular updates about the trip and will meet the participating students at the end."

There it is. The real reason. I can almost *see* the gears in my mom's head working. This is her big plan for redemption—both hers and mine. Prove to her sister that she didn't raise a completely uncultured daughter, that she hasn't failed as a parent.

"Are you sure my aunt will want me to join her program?" I ask tentatively.

"Yes, because you're going to commit fully to her itinerary

and amaze her with your dramatic improvement in Chinese when you come back afterward," my mom says, sounding far more confident than I deserve. There's a distant look in her eyes, like she's already fast-forwarded into the future, one where I'm probably reciting ancient poetry and pouring tea for my aunt while she smiles at me in glowing approval, the disastrous wedding forgotten behind us. "Plus, a program like this will look amazing on your college applications, which I know are currently a little . . . underdeveloped."

"Underdeveloped," I repeat under my breath. That's a nice way of putting it. I'm willing to bet that I'm our career counselor's worst headache. At our last meeting, she stressed that my grades are *abysmal*, my attendance record even worse, and that the last time I signed up for an extracurricular, it was to serve lemonade at a charity event for iguanas.

". . . even though it's last minute, one of the original participating students canceled, so there's a spot open for you, and I snagged it just in time," my mom is saying. She smiles. "Can you believe how perfectly everything's worked out?"

No. I truly can't believe this.

"Don't worry," she says, misinterpreting my silence. "You won't have to miss the start of school. You'll be leaving in a week, and you'll be back just before your break ends."

"Wait. But—" I drag a hand through my hair, my mind struggling to keep up. "But you can't just send me halfway across the world on some trip. I—I had *plans* for this summer—"

Her smile vanishes at once. "You haven't moved an inch from that couch all day. Not even to drink water."

"I had plans to rest," I elaborate.

"And that's okay." She tucks a strand of her long, always-straight hair behind her ear. "Your dad and I have been saying that you need a good, long break. But you don't seem well rested. Do you *feel* like you've been resting?"

The problem is, I don't.

After I officially parted ways with my modeling agency last month, I imagined sleeping for fifteen hours straight, without having to worry about going to the gym or rushing in for hair and makeup or stressing over how my photos will turn out, and then waking up refreshed. Feeling like a proper person again. Dedicating time to my hobbies.

Instead, when I woke up, I felt an exhaustion so heavy and bone-deep I feared it would crush me. And as it turns out, I don't have any hobbies. I never had a chance or reason to discover other interests, because modeling was an all-consuming force, coloring in every single aspect of my life, and now that it's gone, there's only blank white space.

Maybe my mom's right.

Maybe a change of scenery will help. It'd be preferable to slowly losing my mind inside the house.

Besides, after the wedding, I owe it to my mom—and my cousin and aunt—to at least *try* to make amends. Make myself better. Show them that I do genuinely care about my culture, that I'm not an ignorant foreigner who goes around dooming my family members' marriages. Learn how to hold a conversation long enough to apologize properly, in Mandarin.

"Okay, fine," I say, holding out a hand. "Let me see that."

My mom's face breaks into a wide beam as she passes me the application, and I feel a pang in my chest. It's been a while since she last looked so happy. So hopeful. Even if the Journey to the East can't solve all of my problems, at least it'll be worth this.

Later that evening, my phone buzzes with a text from Cate.

we're heading down to sarah's beach house next sat. u coming? xxx

This is how most of our conversations go. Short, to the point. Often, it'll just be a question: *Should I wear this dress or this? Is the jacket too much? Are you free tomorrow?* I understand that the vast majority of the student body would consider it a great privilege to be trusted by Cate Addison for fashion advice, and I guess I do. I just wish we really *talked*, that I could feel comfortable confiding in her about anything without worrying I'd seem too weird. The closest we've ever come to having a heart-to-heart talk was when she got drunk on a martini and told me that she sometimes feels insecure about her music taste.

But I'm not sure if she'll even want to talk to me at all once we return to school. I still haven't told her that I've quit modeling. Partly because my gut churns at the thought of her reaction—it'll no doubt be some vocal mixture of disappointment and confusion—and partly because I haven't figured out a way to do so without bringing up the photo shoot. She wouldn't understand why it was such a big deal to me, why I *had* to leave after that, for the sake of my own sanity and dignity.

At least I now have a legitimate excuse to put off telling her for just a little longer.

I'd love to, but I can't, I text back. *My mom's signed me up for this trip to China and I'll be gone two weeks. You guys have fun though!!!*

Her reply is immediate. *oh my god, you poor thing. why on earth would they send you to that place?*

I stare at the screen, my muscles tensing. I can easily imagine her petite nose scrunched up in pity, her bleached brows knitted together—just like I can imagine that if I were to tell her I was going on a trip to Paris, or London, or Italy, she'd be expressing a very different sentiment.

Why not? I respond. *It's going to be fun.*

And it will be. I'm determined to make it so, to prove her assumptions wrong. Even if it's purely out of spite, I'm going to have the time of my life.

CHAPTER FOUR

I'm still in an optimistic mood when my parents drop me off outside the LAX gates.

"Do you see them?" my mom asks, scanning the busy area. "They said to gather here—"

"That's them, isn't it?" I point at the small group standing off to the side of the bag drop counters. Even through the steady streams of wailing children and tired mothers holding neck pillows and younger guys who magically all look attractive in the airport lighting, I can spot the raised blue flag with the coiling dragon printed over it. It's the same logo that's included in the Journey to the East itinerary I'm holding and the introductory brochure my mom's shoving into my other hand.

"Yes. Perfect. You better go join them." She gives my shoulder a light squeeze and steps back. "Be good, okay?"

My mom has never been one for sentimentality. Whenever my school arranged for field trips or weeklong camps, she was always the first to say goodbye while the other parents clung to their children and wiped at their eyes.

The same cannot be said of my dad, who pulls me into a fierce hug.

"We'll miss you," he says. I'm so tall that he has to stretch his arms to fully reach over my shoulders, but I've never felt safer, more at ease. "If anything goes wrong, or if you get hurt, or if you feel sad, just call us, okay? Anytime. We'll book the first ticket there and fetch you ourselves."

"Okay, okay, stop it," my mom tells him, clicking her tongue. "You'll embarrass her in front of her new peers."

"He won't embarrass me," I say firmly, hugging my dad back tighter. "I'll miss you two as well."

When I finally let go, there's this weird, queasy sensation in my gut, like I'm already homesick. But I don't let any of that show on my face. I just smile and walk away and wave until I can't see them anymore.

Until I find myself standing in front of the group I'll be spending the next two weeks with.

There are about a dozen people here, not including the stern, gray-haired man whose faded shirt is the same shade as the flag he's holding. More girls than guys. All my age. I take inventory of each individual within seconds, something I've learned from photo shoots. When you're always meeting strangers you're about to work with in close proximity, you have to quickly pick up on the group dynamics, who you should stick to and who you shouldn't, who might be rude to you and who you can ask for help.

Already, a trio of sporty girls have formed in the corner, talking loudly and giggling and adding one another's numbers to their phones. One girl is in the middle of a serious call from the looks of it; she keeps frowning and flipping through her spiral notebook and reading out long series of numbers. Another girl stands a few feet away from them, with the bulkiest carry-on bag I've ever seen strapped to her back. It's so massive, especially compared to her small, scrawny frame, that I'm concerned it's going to crush her. She looks like she's at risk of being crushed in general; her features are soft, timid, her dark brown hair tied loosely into a ponytail that spills over her cotton dress, and she keeps her gaze lowered to the floor.

Then I turn my attention to the boys. One of them instantly catches my eye and grins at me, as if we already know each other. He has good style, which I appreciate: an oversized coat and fitted white shirt underneath, even though it's much too hot for layers. A nice face too, with a defined jaw and nose and the kind of light freckles makeup artists like to deliberately draw on. It's a shame I'm kind of desensitized to pretty people by this point.

There's only one unfortunate exception, but I've been doing my best to forget about him since the wedding.

"Oliver Kang," the boy introduces himself, then shoots me an appraising look. "Have we met somewhere before? You seem . . . kind of familiar."

I freeze as a few of the other students stop to listen. My mouth dries. He's probably referring to a campaign, or maybe he's stumbled across one of my photos on social media. But for the first time in a while, I'm surrounded by people who know nothing about my history, and I want to keep it that way. I could be anybody here. Not the weird kid in class, or the girl who was expelled from her old school, or the model.

"Is that meant to be a pickup line?" I ask mildly, feigning ignorance.

To my relief, he laughs, his expression clearing. *Crisis averted.* For now anyway. "No, sorry. I do have a few great pickup lines though. Would you like to hear one?"

"Sure," I say, unfazed by the flirting. It's what most of the bolder guys do in the beginning. They tell me I'm beautiful, and then they ask to hang out so they can show me off to their friends, and then they grow bored and come to the inevitable conclusion that I'm far more fascinating when I'm an enigma. So much more desirable when kept at a distance. If they're nice enough, I'll go along with it, but I no longer fall for it.

"Sure?" Oliver repeats. "Hey, where's the enthusiasm? I'm about to blow your mind. You should know that my pickup lines have a *one-hundred-percent* success rate."

"Right," I say.

"Okay, tough crowd, but I can work with it. Listen to this . . ."

But I'm not listening. Because in the same moment, someone behind me says: "Leah?"

I spin around, my chest seizing at the voice.

Cyrus is staring at me, a thick, blue-covered novel and boarding pass in his hand. He looks about as shocked as I feel, and after a few seconds of pure, incredulous silence, he rubs his eyes with the back of his hand, like maybe there's a speck of dust caught in his lashes that precisely resembles my shape.

The one exception. Life would be infinitely easier if I were also desensitized to his solemn, dark gaze and the visible cut of his collarbone, but my pulse rate skyrockets. The magical quality of the airport lighting seems to favor him more than anybody else.

"*You're* going on this trip too?" I demand.

An odd expression ripples over his face before he folds his arms across his chest. "Well, yeah. I never would've thought you'd be coming—"

"Hang on." Oliver steps in and looks between us, his pickup line abandoned. "Do you two know each other?"

"No," I rush to say. "Not at all."

"We know each other very well," Cyrus answers just as quickly.

"If by *very well* you mean that I have dreamed of murdering you," I mutter.

Cyrus's gaze flits to my face. Lingers an extra beat. "So you've dreamed of me?"

"Ah, I get what's going on here," Oliver says, snapping his fingers. "You two hooked up once, didn't you? Summer fling or something? Feeling kind of awkward because you've seen each other undressed and now have to travel around a country together? I get it." He nods to himself. "I've been there. Well, not this specific trip, but like. You know. The other stuff."

I fear I'm about to become the first human in history to spontaneously disintegrate. But before I can express my absolute disgust at this suggestion, I catch a glimpse of Cyrus's expression. His cheeks are flushed, his lips parted in silent protest, and the sight of his embarrassment is all too satisfying.

And that's when it hits me.

This is it. This is my chance to get Cyrus Sui back at last. He's ruined the better part of my life, so what's stopping me from ruining this trip for him? If I'm going to be stuck with him in another country either way, I might as well get something out of it. Take karma into my own hands.

He won't even know what hit him.

"Fine, you're right," I tell Oliver. In my peripheral vision, Cyrus's eyes widen a fraction, and I feel a rush of vindictive glee. Let him squirm. Let him suffer. "We did. He was *so* desperately, pathetically in love with me that I felt bad. It was only meant to be, like, a one-week thing, but then I broke his heart. I don't think he's gotten over me yet, sadly." I pat Cyrus's arm as if to comfort him, and feel his muscles bunch under my fingers.

"Damn." Oliver whistles. "That's commitment."

Cyrus appears to have been rendered quite speechless.

This is only the start of it, I promise inside my head. *By the end, you'll regret everything you've ever done to me.*

"Don't worry, bro," Oliver says, punching Cyrus's other arm. "There are other girls here. We'll have you forgetting about— Leah, right?" He looks to me for confirmation.

I beam. "Yeah."

"We'll have you moving on from her in *no time*," he says with a wink.

"Who said I wanted to?" Cyrus says flatly.

"Oh." Oliver blinks. "Uh, I mean, feel free to mope around to your heart's content if that's what you prefer . . ."

"I will, thanks," Cyrus says in the same flat, hostile tone designed to end any conversation. And it works. Oliver turns away from us, and Cyrus steps closer into the space, his voice too quiet for anybody else to overhear. "What exactly was that?"

I already have my answer prepared. "It doesn't feel great to have someone lie about something that didn't happen, does it?"

It takes only a split second for him to understand what I'm referring to. The color in his cheeks spreads down to his neck. His jaw flexes. "About that. I . . ."

"Okay, is everybody here?" the man holding the flag calls out. He retrieves a wrinkled sheet from one of the dozens of tiny pockets in his jacket and flattens it roughly. Holds it up at arm's length to read over it. "I'm Wang Laoshi, your guide and main supervisor for this trip. Shout out when you hear your name. Otherwise, no more talking, please."

Cyrus presses his lips together as the rustle of activity around us subsides and Wang Laoshi goes down the list, name by name.

"Lydia . . . There you are. Yes, I see you—thank you for raising your hand so high. You can put it down now. Oliver . . . Okay. Sean . . . Good—but please don't lie on the floor. If you want to sleep, there'll be plenty of opportunities to do so on the plane. Daisy . . . Daisy?" He squints at the students. "Is Daisy not here? Daisy? Chinese name—Daiyu? Speak up if you're here."

I glance around too, then spot her. The soft-faced girl from earlier looks like she actively wishes to sink into the limestone floor. She opens her mouth—not for the first time, judging from how red her face is—but her response is lost beneath the blare of the next flight announcement.

"Daisy's here," I say. My voice is loud enough that Wang Laoshi hears me right away.

Daisy shoots me a look of equal parts embarrassment and gratitude.

By the time the teacher has reached the end of his list, I have all the names and faces memorized, and the perfect plan for revenge devised. The best and fastest way to get under anyone's skin is to grab hold of their heart. So I'll make Cyrus lower his guard, make him think I've forgiven him at last, and when he finally wants me—*wants*, not loves, because there's a chasm between those two things, one that I've never been able to cross with any boy—I'll yank the rug out from under his feet.

I can see it play out in my head like a movie scene. We'll be walking down an alley together and he'll turn and gaze over at me, stars in his eyes, and confess that he likes me. *I want a public confession*, I'll say, smiling coyly. *Give me something dramatic, with chocolates and balloons and streamers, and then I'll consider it.*

It'll be exactly the kind of grand gesture he hates, based on his remarks at the wedding. But he'll oblige, because he's obsessed with me already, and make his declaration that same evening with everyone from our group watching, his features hopeful and earnest, arms filled with heart-shaped gift boxes. Then I'll burst out laughing, long and loud, right in his face.

Why would I ever like you, Cyrus? You ruined my life, remember? And I'll cite his long list of crimes, starting from when we were children, while the spectators shrink back from him in horror. He'll finally come close to understanding how I felt on the staircase, except he'll actually be guilty. He'll deserve all the humiliation hurtling his way.

I almost want to laugh just picturing his expression when I ruthlessly reject him. Proud, composed Cyrus, his cheeks burning with color, his jaw dropping in confusion.

"You know what? Maybe it's fate that we're on this trip together," I tell him as Wang Laoshi starts leading us deeper into the terminal, the blue flag still brandished high in the air as if we're marching off to a great battle. I actually don't think it's fate—I think it's just incredibly bad luck that I'm trying to twist in my favor. But it doesn't matter what I really think. What matters is planting the first seed of this idea that it's meant to be, that this could be the beginning of some great love story, that maybe *I'm* the girl Cyrus has been looking for the whole time—

"Yeah, I don't really believe in that," Cyrus says.

"What?"

"Fate," he says with a shrug that somehow manages to convey a whole world of indifference and disdain. "I only believe in coincidences."

Okay, so maybe it's going to take more effort for Cyrus to warm up to me than I thought. That's . . . reasonable. It's been two years, and I haven't exactly been *super* friendly toward him. It's also occurring to me that even though I endured him every day at school starting from when I was five years old all the way to fifteen, I still don't know enough about Cyrus—not this new version of him anyway, who glares more than he smiles and seems morally opposed to anything that could spark joy in his cursed existence.

"Well, *I* believe in fate," Oliver says, who's apparently been eavesdropping on our conversation. He picks up his pace to walk right next to me, forcing Cyrus to fall behind us. "It's fate that we met today, Leah, don't you think?"

"Sure," I reply in good humor, but I'm not concentrating on what I'm saying—I'm too busy glancing back at Cyrus over my shoulder. His features are set into hard lines, his lips puckered as if he's just taken a bite out of a raw lemon.

"What's his problem?" Oliver asks me, following my gaze.

I shake my head. Resist the urge to say, *Everything.* "No idea."

Whether it's fate or pure coincidence, it seems that I can't get rid of Cyrus even if I wanted to.

I stare down at the number on my boarding pass, then at the

seat in front of me, then at Cyrus, who's currently helping the old lady behind us shove her luggage into the overhead compartment. I'm not the only person on the plane who's staring. As he stretches his torso to give the bag one final push, a girl from our group nudges her new friend, and the two of them dissolve into furious, excited whispers right there in the middle of the aisle.

"You're such a good kid," the old woman gushes to Cyrus. "Thank you so much."

Cyrus merely gives her a faint nod in return, as if this is part of his everyday routine: helping the elderly and adopting kittens and planting trees or whatever. It's an act, of course—it has to be.

Then he turns his attention to me.

"What?" he says.

"This one is yours, right?" I gesture to the seat next to mine. The one he slides into as more passengers shuffle down the aisle, grumbling and squeezing their way around the line and pausing in awkward positions to let others move first.

"Evidently," Cyrus says. He's already put his own carry-on away, but he's holding a small leather bag.

"Well, I'm sitting here," I say.

"Again. Evidently," he repeats, brows raised, like it's no big deal that I'm stuck between him and a middle-aged man who's somehow already asleep, his head lolling back against the window. For some reason, this is more offensive than if he'd shrunk back in disgust or demanded to speak to the flight attendant about switching seats with someone else. It's like he couldn't care less that we'll be sitting side by side in a tiny metal cabin for fourteen hours straight. Like my presence is of zero consequence to him.

"Okay, then." I force a tight smile. "Great. I guess we're seat partners."

He doesn't even grace me with a response right away. Instead, he unzips his bag and starts pulling out alcohol wipes and tissues. The sharp, chemical scent bleeds into the stale air around us. I can't tell if it's an upgrade or downgrade from the smell of new plastic and recycled blankets and airplane food. "If you want another seat partner, I suppose you could bring it up with Wang Laoshi," Cyrus says calmly as he begins wiping down the armrests with practiced precision. "But he might think you're difficult."

I recoil from the term. It's a knee-jerk reaction, the deeply ingrained fear of being labeled as *difficult to work with*. I've always tried my hardest to make sure that I'm not. To be cooperative and flexible and agreeable, to do my job without question, without complaint. It's why I went through with the photo shoot, even though I've spent every second since wishing I hadn't.

"Who said I wanted to change?" I ask as I lower myself into the narrow seat that's definitely just one proper-sized seat split into two. Every time I fly, I'm reminded yet again of how terribly uncomfortable flying is. My legs barely fit into the allotted space, and I can't lean to either side without bumping against the stranger or Cyrus.

We haven't even left the tarmac, and I'm exhausted.

"You could pretend I'm not here." Cyrus scrubs the armrest between us as he speaks, forcing me to fold my hands across my lap. "I recall that you were good at your make-believe games when we were kids."

My face heats. "They weren't *make-believe games*." At least, they weren't games for me. I would imagine myself as anything and everything: a poet, writing to their one true love; a princess, standing up to retrieve her crown at long last; an artist, grieving over their lost muse. Back when the future felt endless, expansive, and all the options delighted rather than terrified me. Back when I still wore my heart on my sleeve, instead of carefully concealed in ten layers of Bubble Wrap.

"You were so invested in it," he goes on with the slightest smile. "You ran around the school trying to find someone to play your prince."

I suppress a wince, but the decade-old humiliation blazes its way through me again. All the boys I'd asked had either laughed in my face or simply stared at me, like I was some wild thing in the woods they hoped would go away on its own if they didn't make any sudden noises or movements. Of course they weren't interested; I wasn't pretty back then.

Cyrus was the only one who agreed to join in on my game, just to ruin it for me. He had made me a ring of thorns, a castle of clay, and stolen the school's infamous cat, Evil Whiskers, to be our royal pet. The cat had scratched me even more than the ring, and I'd ended up crying in a corner.

It's just one of the many unpleasant memories Cyrus has contributed to.

"There's really no need to revisit that," I say.

"Why not? Your games were super creative. I remember there was another one where we'd see who could find their way around with their eyes closed—"

"Well, I don't remember anymore. That was ages ago." I speak over him, desperate to change the subject. "Are you almost done with the cleaning?"

"Almost. Though I wouldn't call anything here *clean*." He picks up his blanket with only his thumb and forefinger, like he thinks it might grow teeth and bite him. I really wish it would. "Do you know how often they wash these?"

"No. But I like to trust that they do," I say.

"I wouldn't trust strangers at all."

"I hate to break it to you, but you'll have to trust the pilot not to get us killed en route to Shanghai," I inform him.

It might just be my imagination, but his face seems to pale. Or maybe it's because he's still holding the blanket he's so disgusted by.

"If you're not planning to use it, give it to me," I tell him, rubbing my bare arms. Time and temperature seem to become irrelevant the second you get on a plane: It could be a perfect summer morning outside, but they'll turn off the lights at random and turn the air-conditioning up to full blast until it feels closer to winter. "It's way too cold in here."

I expect him to refuse, just to annoy me, or to chuck the blanket at my face. But he rolls his eyes and drapes it over my legs.

"Have fun covering yourself with bacteria," he says, already slathering his fingers with copious amounts of hand sanitizer.

"Have fun freezing," I return under my breath, just quiet enough for him to miss it.

The plane soon jerks into motion—slowly at first, then building speed, the engines humming, the strange flaps on the wings opening up. All the trays and windows go up, the seats adjusted. A baby starts giggling at the jolting movement, at the same time that another baby in the first row starts bawling.

I try and fail to get comfortable, tugging the blanket higher up my legs, only to become acutely, annoyingly aware of the cheap fabric against my skin. How *unwashed* it feels, as though I can sense the presence of all the passengers who've come before me and wrapped this very same blanket around their bodies.

Covered in bacteria, Cyrus's voice says in the back of my mind, even though the real Cyrus has stopped talking. He's staring straight ahead, both hands gripping the thoroughly sanitized armrests.

Shut up, I command the voice. *Get out of my head.*

Never, Cyrus's voice replies, with the same mocking laugh I remember so well from my childhood. Now anytime I do anything remotely embarrassing, that's the only thing I hear, the only thing I can think about. I hate it.

Him.

I inhale as the plane takes off, my stomach swooping at the sudden loss of gravity, my muscles fighting for stability that isn't there. Maybe, if I were my nine-year-old self, I could really pretend all this away. Pretend the plane is a ship, and the abrupt dips and tremors are just rushing currents, buoying us up, and the boy beside me is already gone.

Or I could play the other game. The one about closing my eyes for as long as possible and praying that, when I open them, I'll magically end up in the right place.

CHAPTER FIVE

I wake up to the world falling.

My eyes snap open, my hands instinctively gripping the armrests just as the cabin lights flicker on, illuminating the shaking scene: passengers rushing back to their seats, a businessman frowning down at his computer screen as it wobbles violently in an impressive attempt to continue working, others jolting out of their sleep the way I did seconds ago, eye masks sliding up, blankets slouching over onto the carpet. It feels as if a giant toddler's fist has shot out from the clouds to shake the plane around like a rattle toy. I try to ignore the sour jump of nausea in my mouth as we swerve sharply to the left, then to the right again.

A serene male voice floats down from the speakers:

"Ladies and gentlemen, we're experiencing some heavy turbulence . . . Please fasten your seat belts . . ."

A much less serene male voice sounds right beside my ear in a hoarse whisper:

"Good god."

I turn. Cyrus is staring straight ahead, his face and knuckles white as he clasps his fists over his lap, his teeth clenched around a curse. His rigid spine is pressed so tight against the seat that it looks like he's trying to physically meld himself with the backrest.

"You're scared of flying," I say. It's not a question, but it is a revelation. I don't remember Cyrus being scared of anything: not spiders, which he would kill without hesitation whenever we found one in the classroom; not tests, which he would always hand in half an hour before everyone else; not the dark, or the horror movie the teachers showed us thinking the animated art style automatically made it kid-friendly, or the receptionist who had earned the nickname Scary Carrie.

"I'm not—scared," he says, even as a muscle twitches in his jaw. "I'm—"

The plane pitches forward again, fast enough to make my gut churn. I can hear all the heavy bags knocking against one another overhead, a woman fussing over her airsick daughter in the row behind us, the rustle and metallic *click* of seat belts being readjusted. A plastic cup rolls off someone's tray and bounces down the aisle.

"Alert," Cyrus finishes on a ragged breath, "seeing as we're about to plummet down to earth."

Finally: a weakness. Just what I need to start softening him up and reeling him in. And even though it should be physically nauseating to comfort a boy I hate, whatever my ulterior motive is, his eyes are wide with such raw, open fear that it feels almost natural to do so.

"That's not going to happen," I tell him, trying to talk loud enough to distract both him and myself from the creaking in the wings. "It's only a bit of turbulence; it'll be over soon. In the meantime, just imagine that we're already on the ground."

"Except we're not," he points out. "We're most definitely in the air."

"Sorry, are you unfamiliar with the concept of *imagining*?"

"Consider my imagination limited," he says, the words straining out through his lips, "by the very real possibility of death."

"Then try to think about something else."

"Think about what?"

"Something pleasant. Like strolling along a beach at dawn. Or coupon codes. Or dogs that can open doors. Or banana muffins—"

"Not the biggest fan of baked goods."

I will my patience to stay put. "Or fresh daisies—"

"Allergic."

My mouth drops open. "To *flowers*? Seriously? But they're, like, the symbol of romance."

"Which allergies are famously known to care about."

I ignore his sarcasm and focus on posing my next question as if it's something I just thought of, and not a sneaky way to secure vital information for my revenge plan. "What do you do if you want to buy flowers for your girlfriend?" I'm ninety-nine percent sure he doesn't have a girlfriend. Call it a woman's sixth sense, or just plain common sense, because while his face might be fine (okay, a little better than fine), he does share a personality type with most supervillains, and there's just something about his aura that screams, *I go straight home after school to mope over the state of the world instead of planning out cute movie nights with the girl I like.* Still, if I'm going to proceed, I need to first be *one-hundred-percent sure* I'm not seducing someone who's already taken.

Cyrus fixes me with a long look. "I don't have a girlfriend."

Perfect. I lean closer to him over the armrest and do my best to act surprised. "Really? Why not?"

He tips his head back and releases a quiet groan as more tremors grip the plane, his pulse beating visibly in his throat. "I can't believe I'm saying this, but I'd rather we discuss the dogs that can open doors."

"Okay, fine. No more talking about your relationship status or lack thereof, or the flowers you're allergic to, or highly skilled dogs." I filter through my memory for inspiration, any conversation topic that won't make him tense up like he's getting his molars surgically removed. The first, unexpected thing that comes to mind is: "Do you still play piano?"

Even though the sky is swaying drunkenly outside the windows, the blue horizon tilting upward with sickening speed, he pauses for a moment, some of his fear dissolving into surprise. "You remember that?"

"Only because you were being such a show-off about the fact that you'd passed grade twenty when you were thirteen—"

"Leah, there is no grade twenty."

"And," I go on, skipping right over his correction, "as long as there was a piano in the general area, you would rush over to play it like it was your own private concert."

At this, the muscles in his face relax enough for his mouth to twitch. "I had no idea that you watched me."

"Like, once." Or a dozen times. It was one of the only occasions when he wasn't pestering me at school. When he wasn't causing any trouble at all, but completely focused, his boyish features serious, his fingers elegant and swift over the black and white keys. He played piano like it was obvious, like every note belonged together in their exact arrangement the way stars belonged in constellations, and mistakes didn't exist. He made it look so easy.

He made everything look easy.

"I do still play," he tells me, his shoulders loosening a little too. "Do you? The cello? Or the flute?"

It's been so long that at first I don't even know what he's talking about. Then, between the next dip and rise of the plane and my heart, his words register. There was a very short-lived period in my life when I watched a music video featuring a cellist and felt inspired to learn the cello myself. But five lessons in, I realized that I would have produced better music by throwing plates at a wall; even the music teacher, Ms. Torres, expressed her disappointment at my inability to pick up the basics, though she'd encouraged me not to quit. *Just because you're not naturally good at it doesn't mean you shouldn't continue.*

But what's the point in continuing something if you aren't naturally good at it?

So I left my rented cello behind in the music room and never looked at it again. A few months later, I came down with the overoptimistic idea that maybe I wasn't meant for the *cello*, but I was meant for the flute. I lasted a little longer with that one, progressing so far as to play a few shrill notes of "Ode to Joy," but my practice sessions gave everyone—including myself—a headache. It was the same way with all the hobbies I tried out as a kid. I quit karate after just one day, because I injured my hand trying to chop a block of wood. I quit swimming because the chlorine made my skin itch. I quit dance because I couldn't keep up with the choreography, and the teacher yelled at me in front of everybody. I quit basketball because I kept missing my shots and I hated feeling like I was slowing down the team.

I used to think that modeling was the one thing I would never give up. That all my failures and false starts before it were simply leading me to my true calling.

"I haven't touched an instrument in years," I say, in what I hope is a flippant tone. "It's probably for the best that I stopped."

"I'm sure Ms. Torres would be heartbroken if she found out."

"Why?" I let out a huff of incredulity. "I was her worst student."

"She liked you," he insists.

"Yeah, right," I say. "What could she have liked about me?"

I meant for it to sound casual and self-deprecating, but it comes out dangerously close to self-pitying, which is never a good look.

Cyrus frowns, as if I'm asking a trick question. "Why wouldn't she have liked you?" A pause. "Why wouldn't everyone like you?"

Maybe because I have nothing of value to offer? Because I care too much about my appearance, and I overthink everything, and I can be annoying and dumb and indecisive, and I don't have the slightest clue what I'm doing with my life? Because I have no personality outside of my flaws? But I'd rather the plane disintegrate right now than ever say any of that out loud, especially to him.

"I'm just saying," I tell him, "I'd be surprised if she even remembered my name after I left the school."

Guilt flashes across Cyrus's face.

The past pushes its way into the sudden silence between us. *Well, at least he knows to be guilty.* But it's a cheap comfort, like the thin, scratchy blanket covering my legs. If he *really* felt guilty, he would have apologized long ago. No, he wouldn't have lied in the first place.

I'm so busy feeding my grudge that it takes me a minute to notice the shaking has stopped. The seat belt sign dims, and all around us, people relax in their seats, everyone's relief palpable in the cabin air.

But it still feels like the world is careening in the wrong

direction. It's felt a little like that ever since the wedding. Ever since I saw Cyrus again.

It's a relief to be back on solid ground.

After I fire off a quick text to the family group chat to let them know I've landed safely, I join my classmates in side-shuffling a couple steps at a time through the dense, jet-lagged crowds at the airport. What with the time difference, I don't expect to hear from my parents until the next morning for them, but my mom's reply comes before I've even left the customs line.

How was your flight? Did you get enough sleep? Did you eat on the plane? How's Shanghai? When does your first activity start?

All of this in one overwhelming text box, like she might be charged for each new message she sends.

Smooth, I text back, which is an exaggeration at best, a straight-up lie at worst. Super smooth, if you take away the aggressive turbulence, and the fact that Cyrus fell asleep after my distraction services were no longer needed, only for his head to keep lolling against my shoulder for the remainder of the flight.

I slept well, I continue. *Food was fine.*

Shanghai's—

I hold off on answering because I don't actually see the city until we reach the shuttle bus outside the airport, where the teacher pairs us off according to our hotel rooms.

"Cyrus Sui—I saw your special request, but unfortunately

this program does not allow for single rooms for any of the participating students," Wang Laoshi calls over the rumbling engines, dabbing the sweat on his forehead with a folded plaid handkerchief.

I kind of wish I'd brought a handkerchief with me too, or at least a napkin. Though the afternoon sky is overcast, the skyscrapers disappearing into the gray clouds, the heat is closing in fast. We've only gone a few minutes without any air-conditioning, and I can already feel the humidity sticking to my cropped shirt and slicking my fingers. Even the wind is hot, simmering off the wide road.

"You'll be sharing with . . . Oliver Kang," Wang Laoshi continues, consulting the clipboard in his hand. "Don't look so glum about it. This is as much an opportunity to make new friends as it is a chance to explore the city."

Oliver hops up the bus steps first. He's the only person here with the energy to hop anywhere right now; I caught him charming the flight attendants into sneaking him quality coffee straight out of business class. "Yeah, dude," he says with a fully caffeinated grin, beckoning Cyrus over. "We'll be bonding in no time. It'll be like a sleepover—come on, I know that very deep down, you're excited."

I catch the look of dismay on Cyrus's face before he follows Oliver into the bus.

"Leah, you'll be with Daisy Yun," the teacher continues.

More hot gusts of wind blow my bangs across my forehead

as I shove my suitcase into the lower luggage compartment. I quickly flatten my hair back down and greet my new roommate.

"Hey," I say, joining her at the bus door. "Looks like you're stuck with me."

She seems somewhat startled, as if convinced I might be talking to someone else. "Um, hi."

Inside, I drop into the window seat at the front, squeezing over for Daisy to sit down next to me. She does so very carefully, hugging her bag tight to her chest, tucking her dress around her legs. She doesn't say another word until we've left the glass maze of the airport far behind us, the city rising tall on both sides of the highway.

I'm really here.

In Shanghai. On the other end of the world, thousands of miles from all I've ever known.

My eyes drink in the views as they rush by, my lips parted in awe. It's a city made for movie screens, a city that's stepped out of history, with one foot in the future. A city big enough to get lost in, or big enough to fit in. We speed past sparkling new subway stations, faded wonton restaurants, flower shops bursting with pink tulips and chrysanthemums, chairs stacked up beneath plastic awnings, stores illuminated by tiny LEDs spelling out advertisements in characters I can't read. I try to commit it to memory, taking mental photos of everything I see: the twelve-story malls, the lush green of the parks breaking up the yards of steel and cement, the potted plants dangling from apartment windows, the groups of men playing mahjong in the alleyways, the woman walking her pet alpaca along the pedestrian crossing.

"Is this . . . your first time here?" Daisy asks. Her voice is quiet, almost hushed, like she's scared of disturbing me.

I pull my gaze from the window, flushing when I realize that I must look like a typical wide-eyed tourist. "Yeah. Is it yours?"

She shakes her head. "My dad's side of the family is from Shanghai. I come here basically every holiday."

Her Chinese must be so much better than mine. The familiar insecurity prickles uncomfortably against my skin. Even though my mom insisted the program was perfect for people like me, I'm starting to fear that everyone on the bus is better at Chinese than I am, that I'm the only tourist here. Cyrus's Chinese is perfect. Two of the girls filled out their customs declaration forms in Chinese. And Oliver was flirting in Chinese, which would require a particular command of the language. Luckily, my own flirting tricks are pretty universal, since they're limited to squinting and smiling and twirling my hair in a semi-ironic way, and hoping the other party finds me attractive enough.

"So why did your parents sign you up for the program?" I ask Daisy.

"My parents didn't," she says, picking at a piece of lint on her dress. "Um, I did. People are always telling me to explore new things and be more social and push myself outside my comfort zone—and my comfort zone is the size of my bedroom, so . . ."

"Who's *people*?"

"Teachers. Relatives. The school librarian. Whoever writes the advice columns in magazines. My neighbors. My dentist."

I bite back a laugh. "It's nice that your dentist is so invested in your social life."

"My dentist recommends that I 'put myself out there' more often than he recommends that I floss properly." She sighs and looks at my ear, which is the closest she's come to making eye contact with me so far. "It'd be so much easier if I were you."

"Me?" I repeat.

She waves a hand in a general gesture toward my face like that's answer enough. "You're so confident and just, like, composed, you know? Like you've got everything figured out."

It's not the first time someone has called me composed in recent years, though my mom prefers the adjacent, less flattering Chinese term *duanzhe*. Literally speaking, it means "to hold" or "to carry," which always conjures the image of someone balancing a bowl filled to the brim with water. One step out of line, one careless move, and everything will spill over.

I consider telling her that I'm not any of the things she thinks I am, but I don't want to break the illusion. It would be like a magician showing the audience exactly where the rabbit is hidden.

I wouldn't have the chance to, in either case. The bus rolls to a stop in the hotel parking lot, and we're all ushered through the entrance in a mess of half-zipped jackets and straggling suitcases.

"Hurry up," Wang Laoshi chides. "We have a whole evening planned out ahead of us."

The lobby is larger and more impressive than any of the hotels I've stayed in before, with contemporary sculptures rising up to the highest floors and chandeliers lighting up the space. My attention skips from the pop-up stall near the elevators promoting pretty glass jars of tomato juice to the posters advertising the hotel's afternoon tea service, before landing on the robots carrying bottles of water and clean towels and room service trays. I watch, fascinated, as they wheel themselves over to the concierge desks, their screens flashing. Nobody else even bats an eye at their presence, as if we've been living casually among robots since the beginning of time.

"We'll be meeting down here in an hour to go on the night cruise," Wang Laoshi says as he hands out our key cards. "Go take a quick shower if you must. Just don't be late."

CHAPTER SIX

There are plenty of things I can settle for, but a quick shower before a night out is not one of them.

In our lavish hotel room, I blow-dry my hair and straighten it, even though it's technically already straight, because there's a crucial difference between naturally straight hair and flat-ironed hair. Then I unpack three bags of makeup products, letting them spill onto my side of the marble counter. Daisy's side is almost empty in comparison, and much neater: just her toothbrush standing in a plastic cup, a small tube of sunscreen, and moisturizer.

Even on days when I'm not adjusting to a new country, there's something comforting about doing my own makeup. It's familiar. Requires just enough focus to keep me preoccupied without turning my mind all the way on. There's a rhythm to it too: the tap of the brush, the slow squeeze of the eyelash curler, a quick swipe of glitter here and there. And it's *effective*. I've devoted what must be hundreds of hours to figuring out the best shade of eye shadow for my skin, the most effective contouring techniques for my jaw and nose, little magic tricks for me to hide my many shortcomings and highlight my nicer features.

I'm dabbing blush onto my cheeks when I catch Daisy staring

in the mirror. Her entire shower took less time than my skin prep routine, and she's already changed into a faded pink cotton shirt and sweatpants, her hair tied into a loose braid that trails over her shoulder.

"Do you always do this before you go out?" she asks me. "Like, the whole—" She gestures to her own bare face.

"Pretty much, yeah," I say with a faint stab of self-consciousness. She probably thinks I'm super vain, or that I'm one of those girls who can't leave the house makeup-free—which is exactly what I am. I don't think anyone at my current school has ever seen my face without some kind of product plastered on it. Even on the plane ride here, I had my perfectly glued lashes and trusted black eyeliner for support.

"But . . . doesn't it take a long time?" Daisy asks in a tone of wonder, watching as I apply my favorite cherry-colored tint next. I smudge the line on my upper lip to make it look fuller, before layering a darker red shade onto the bottom, all of it done with a surgeon's precision.

"About an hour," I confirm, reaching for my lip gloss for the final touch. The sweet, artificial smell of strawberries drifts up to my nose as I swipe it on. "Sometimes two, if I want to also style my hair and look extra good."

"Two hours?" Daisy repeats, looking aghast. "What if you have school?"

"I just wake up earlier," I say, unsure if this conversation is headed toward some kind of damning judgment about how

I choose to distribute my time. "Usually around five in the morning."

"Wow," Daisy says, though she doesn't sound critical. More bewildered by my dedication and unsure about the necessity of going through such motions, the same way someone might react if you told them your morning ritual involves hiking up a mountain at dawn every day to pluck fresh berries. "And you don't get exhausted?"

"No. Not at all," I lie. Countless times, I've wished I could be naturally, effortlessly pretty, the sort of pretty that doesn't require time or sacrifice. But since that isn't an option, my only choices are to be high-maintenance pretty and liked as a result, or unpopular the way I was before.

Daisy looks like she's about to ask something else, but she snaps her mouth shut and grabs her tote bag from the table.

"I'm almost ready," I tell her. I scrutinize my reflection one last time, then set my lip gloss back onto the counter.

I feel more like myself when I head down the glass elevator with Daisy five minutes later, my face powdered smooth, my hair flowing soft over my shoulders, my black dress fitting snug around my waist and thighs. I always feel better when I look better.

"Wow," Oliver says appreciatively the second he spots me across the lobby. "And I was so sure that *I* was the most attractive one here."

There was a time, just after I turned pretty, when getting any kind of male attention was still a novelty to me, where I'd take Oliver's words far too seriously and fantasize about *what it could all mean*. Would he fall in love with me? Did he want to start something? What would we name our future children?

Now I've learned that the most it could mean is that he wants to kiss you, and chances are Oliver's used the same line a dozen times in the past week. So out of politeness, all I do is smile at him, which he returns at double the wattage.

In my peripheral vision, I notice Cyrus standing a few feet from the others. He's showered as well and changed out of his clothes into a plain black button-down. He stares at me for a second, his face impassive, then abruptly turns to the abstract art on the wall. I'm not sure what philosophical meaning he could be uncovering in those two splotches of orange, but he keeps his eyes pinned on the painting.

"Took you all long enough," Wang Laoshi barks, raising his blue flag over his head in a somewhat menacing manner. "We're running two-and-a-half minutes behind schedule. Remember, this is *not* a family trip; you can't just choose to show up whenever."

"No, because if this were a family trip, my dad would have disappeared into the casino, and I'd already be drunk," Oliver says, loud enough for the whole group to hear. "Just kidding," he amends hastily when Wang Laoshi shoots him a stern look. "Not kidding in the slightest," he whispers to me out of the corner of his mouth as we push through the revolving doors.

The smile that twitches at my lips is a little more genuine this time.

The temperature seems to have dropped a whole season within the span of an afternoon, the cool air fanning my bare arms. The city itself is transformed by the darkness. Shanghai during the day was bright, bustling, vibrant, polished; Shanghai at night is glittering, expansive, everything dialed up and eager to show itself off, like any fashion icon swapping her blazer and sunglasses for a bold red lip and shimmering dress when the sun goes down.

We walk past vendors selling roasted sweet potatoes from the back of their carts, placed strategically at the entrance of a subway station, their honeyed fragrance chasing us for yards down the busy street. There are tea shops and cafés on every block: lanterns swaying over the patios; hand-painted ceramic cups molded into the shape of cats and ducks; glass displays of butter cookies and strawberry cakes; fishbowls sitting on mahogany counters; translucent tents set up on neat blocks of grass like giant versions of the fishbowls, happy couples huddled up inside them.

Then it's a steep climb up the overpass. *Tianqiao*, Wang Laoshi says, translated literally to "sky bridge," and I can't help thinking about how pretty the name is, how fitting, because it really feels like we're crossing through the dark sky itself. An old woman sits by the railings, tiny hair clips and sparkling trinkets stretched out on a faded mat, the traffic rushing beneath her.

Everything starts to become recognizable once we reach

the Bund—not from memory, but from photos and posters. Thousands of white and gold lights glint off the waterfront like stars, the reflection of the ferry swimming over the river. We board one at a time, with Cyrus and me falling to the end of the line.

"Lukewarm warning: Be careful of your foot," I read out in bemusement from the sign nailed to the pier. The questionable English translation is printed right under the Chinese characters.

"That sounds like what you'd say when you're extremely reluctant to help someone," Cyrus remarks just over my shoulder. I startle. I hadn't realized he was standing so close behind me. "Like if your enemy was approaching a cliff."

I can't muster a reply at once; the gap between the swaying ferry and the edge of the pier is severely testing my ability to move around in high heels. I manage to put one foot over, wishing there was a railing I could cling to for support. But then I think of something even better. "A lukewarm warning," I say, struggling a little more visibly than I really need to, "that if I don't hold on to something right now, I'm going to slip and take you down with me." And that's the only excuse I offer before I grab tight on to Cyrus's arm, using him to steady myself before I can tumble through the gap into the Huangpu River.

I can sense Cyrus's surprise, feel the way his muscles bunch and his body stiffens. But he doesn't pull away until I've finished crossing over onto the ferry and both my feet are firmly planted to the deck.

"A lukewarm warning to you," Cyrus says, jumping aboard

easily after me, "that as flattering as the dress is, you should consider bringing a jacket next time. It's going to be windy."

It's already windy, the dark waters rippling below us. I have to keep patting my bangs to keep them in place. "If you can survive an entire plane ride without a blanket, I think I can survive a cruise without a jacket. But thanks," I add, flashing him a quick, subdued smile that makes my insides turn, but—my nausea aside—has the effect I'm going for.

Cyrus stares at me for an extra beat, like he's not entirely sure what's happening.

The beginning of the path to perfect, crushing humiliation, I vow in my head. *Enjoy.*

While the outside of the ferry is designed with neon signs and the carved head of a dragon, its scales glowing yellow, fangs closing around a pearl, the ferry's interior is laid out like a restaurant. Rows of round tables stretch from one end to the other, with just enough chairs to be filled by our group. The only two remaining empty chairs are by the open windows in the back.

Which is how I find myself sitting next to Cyrus once again.

I glance over at the papers already set in front of us. I'm really hoping it's a menu—I haven't eaten anything today except the stale bread rolls handed out on the plane—but then I realize it's actually—

"A test?" Oliver demands from the table next to ours. "We're on this cruise to take a *test*?"

Not just any test. It's written entirely in Chinese, most of its meaning obscured by all the lessons I skipped over the years. And here I thought I had found a way to escape anything academic-related.

Wang Laoshi claps his hands. "Listen up," he says, raising his voice over the whispered complaints. Well, *most* are complaints. One of the girls—Lydia—looks genuinely excited by the prospect of schoolwork on a ferry. She's already whipped out a sharpened pencil and eraser and has her curly hair scraped into a bun, as if she's been training her whole life for this. I've never related to anyone less. "The test is to help gauge the extent of your Chinese abilities, including your reading and writing proficiency. I'll give you half an hour to finish. And if you have any questions," Wang Laoshi adds, "please do hesitate to ask me. It's best you work it out yourself."

I end up stuck on the first question.

We're meant to construct sentences using different vocabulary words provided at the top of the page, but I barely know enough words to string together a sentence to begin with. The only characters I can write with reasonable confidence are *I, horse, mother, you, have,* and a few numbers. This works out well enough for a couple sentences, but I run out of variations pretty quickly:

I bought ten horses.
The horses have fruits.
I have a horse in my sink.

The horse is suspicious of my mother.

My mother is a horse.

The horse is my mother.

"What do you mean by *despite the horse, my mother can still have ten sinks?*" Cyrus asks, shifting forward to read my answers.

I quickly hide my paper with my elbow, but it's harder to hide the heat flooding my face. "No cheating," I tell him.

"I don't think you have any reason to worry about me copying you," he says, resting his head on the table like it's the perfect pillow, his face angled toward me. He put his pen down before I'd even flipped the page. "Though I definitely couldn't have thought of that sentence by myself. The teacher should give you bonus points for creativity."

"You can stop now."

He regards me with an expression of well-feigned innocence. "Stop what?"

"Talking," I say. *Looking at me*, I add mentally. *Breathing.*

"I really enjoy the implication that the horse poses an obstacle to sink ownership," Cyrus continues like he didn't hear me, his mouth curving with quiet amusement. "And that the mother can only have ten sinks, specifically. Eleven would just be too many."

I put my head down, committed to tuning out his existence. But the next few questions are even harder than the first, almost impossible for me to decipher. Out of desperation, I start drawing wonky circles in place of characters I don't know, hoping I might remember them later, but then it just looks like I'm doodling eggs all over the page. Before Wang Laoshi comes up to collect our tests, I already know that I've failed mine.

Well, the good thing is that it's over, I comfort myself. Until we get the results back anyway.

Most of the other group members have left their chairs to walk back and forth along the ferry, chatting and taking photos of the stunning night scenery, their voices rippling over the rhythmic splash of water. Shanghai lies before us in all its magnificence, with its laser lights and soaring skylines. It's still hard to believe that I'm *here*, when only a day ago I'd been packing my pajamas in my bedroom, with my familiar view of the cherry tree and picnic table in the backyard. Now my views include the Huangpu River, curving out for miles and miles like a giant serpent, and, farther down the banks, the gleaming domes and rooftop bars and art museums and cinemas, the places where the city's past clashes with the present in a jigsaw of neoclassical architecture and ancient bell towers and soaring skyscrapers. Animated hearts pop up over screens that stretch wide across the sides of buildings, beckoning to tourists. *Welcome to Shanghai*, the massive text reads, appearing for seconds at a time, then vanishing like an enchantment. *I Love Shanghai.*

I take it all in from my seat, massaging my sore fingers.

It's been an embarrassingly long period of time since I last attempted to write anything in Chinese. At this point, I have to wonder if it's too late for me. If I'm a lost cause. Everyone says that there's an ideal period of time in your life to pick up or retain a language, and I stumbled past that deadline ages ago. Maybe I'll never be fluent like Cyrus. Never speak my mother tongue without it getting tangled in my mouth. Maybe my aunt was right, and I'll never be anything more than a foreigner in this city.

The thought weighs heavier than I expected. It wouldn't have bothered me as much in LA, yet it's different to physically be here, surrounded by sights I should understand but can't. I can barely read the advertisements flashing on the sides of buildings and the ships gliding by.

To his credit, Wang Laoshi finishes marking our tests before we've passed the Oriental Pearl Tower, cutting short the life cycle for my dread. After ushering everyone back to their seats, he stands up at the front of the ferry, holding the papers in his hand like they're criminal evidence.

"A few of you did *exceptionally* well on this test," he says, putting his grimace on hold to smile down at Cyrus, before switching back to it in a blink. "There were, however, some shocking answers—or rather, a lack of answers." He doesn't look my way directly, but I can feel his disapproval blowing toward me like the cold breeze off the river. "In the interest of fairness for the upcoming competition, I will be pairing you off into teams based on your scores. Those who received high marks will be put together with those who are struggling. With someone to help you, and your natural immersion in the environment, my hope is that by the end of the trip, you will all see remarkable improvement in your Chinese—even if you're practically illiterate at present . . ."

He *definitely* looks right at me this time.

"As for the specifics of the competition," Wang Laoshi continues, "it'll be running throughout the trip in every place we visit: first in Shanghai, then in Anhui, then in Guilin. Based on previous student feedback and lively discussions among the coordinators behind Journey to the East, we're changing it up a little this year to encourage more participation. You won't just be sightseeing—you'll be engaging, interacting, cooperating, absorbing. The first activity will officially begin tomorrow."

"Excuse me, Wang Laoshi?" Lydia—the same girl who looked ready to perform happy cartwheels when the teacher handed out the tests—raises her hand high in the air, her voice climbing an octave with excitement. "Will there be a prize for the winners?"

"The ultimate prize, of course, is knowledge," Wang Laoshi says very seriously.

Oliver lets out an audible snort.

"In addition," Wang Laoshi says, "there'll be a small prize for the winners of each activity. At the end of the competition, the team who performs the best overall will be selected to deliver a presentation about the trip at a special afternoon tea event held by Jiu Yin He. There, they'll have the opportunity to meet Dr. Linda Shen, a renowned Stanford professor who's helping oversee this year's program. I'll be emailing her updates for each activity, as well as the test scores from today so she can see where you're at."

At the mention of my aunt's name, my stomach drops. If my goal is to impress her, I'm off to a horrible start. I can only pray Wang Laoshi doesn't plan on sending her our test *answers* too; she might actually burn my name off the family tree if she reads my horse-and-mother series.

Beside me, Cyrus sits up straighter, and a faint suspicion stirs inside me.

"Don't tell me you joined this program just for another chance to kiss up to my aunt," I mutter to him out of the corner of my mouth.

"I was never planning on kissing up to her," he mutters back, but I notice he doesn't deny his motive. "I don't need to. She just needs to speak to me to be impressed by me, and since her mood was ruined by *someone* at the wedding, this is my only other chance before our college apps are due. My last chance."

"Seriously?" I realize I'm probably staring at him the way Daisy was staring at me earlier when I described my lengthy, multistep morning beauty routine. "You want a letter of recommendation from her that badly? You couldn't just ask someone else?"

"You don't understand. It *has* to be from her," Cyrus says, his eyes blazing with rare emotion. Then, as if catching himself, he pauses. Dials back the intensity in his tone. "It's just that a letter of recommendation from her would basically guarantee me a spot in Stanford's Chinese Literature program—"

"You're set on studying literature?" I ask. "What about piano?"

"I'd thought about it," he says slowly. "I love both—I was actually really torn between the two, and all my teachers were trying to persuade me to do one or the other. But I don't *need* to study piano the way that I need to study literature."

What a nice problem to have, I think to myself, biting back a surge of jealousy. *I'm just too talented at too many things, god help me.* No matter which option he ended up choosing, he would have a dazzling career to look forward to.

Still, I have to admit that literature suits him. Actually, a program on ruining other people's lives would suit him best. Second to that, though, he belongs in a world of quiet libraries and gold-soaked classrooms, tea steaming in his hands, books piled up on desks, the margins inhabited by scribbled epiphanies.

"I can't imagine doing anything else," he's saying. "I don't believe that books are the cure to everything, necessarily, but it's like—when you're feeling unwell, and you receive a diagnosis, and you're so relieved because now you realize that it wasn't all in your head, that there's a name for what you're experiencing. On a bad day, books offer a language for your pain, and on a good day, books remind you just how precious your life is. A program devoted entirely to books feels almost like the stuff of dreams . . ." He trails off, a hint of self-consciousness creeping into his voice. But there's no uncertainty, no doubt. That *is* his future. It's clear, tangible, achievable. He can see it lit up ahead of him, like the shining banks of the river, and now he just needs to take the necessary steps to reach it.

Meanwhile, I have zero idea what school I should be applying to, much less what program I want to do. The career counselor recommended that I try a process of elimination until I found the pathway that *spoke to me*, but I'd made my way down an entire list of possible degrees, and none of them spoke at all. None of them even spluttered at me. And at the end of the day it just felt pointless, silly, what with my horrible academic record, as if I were inspecting million-dollar castles and debating which one to move into when I couldn't even afford to rent half a bathroom.

"What about you?" Cyrus murmurs. "I would've thought that with all the modeling you've been doing—"

I almost flinch out of my seat. "How do you know about that?"

"What?" he asks, confused.

"How do you know I . . ." *Modeled*. The past tense threatens to slip its way into the sentence. It's bad enough that he's the only person here who knows about my modeling career. I can't have him finding out that my modeling career failed before it even properly took off. That as of now, I have no future plans, no known talents, no useful connections, no marketable passions, no projects in the works, not even a regular sleeping schedule. I have basically nothing except a nice wardrobe and a strong dose of existential dread. "I don't remember ever telling you I became a model."

"I mean, it's all over your social media," Cyrus says like it's obvious.

I blink. "You follow me?"

Before he can reply, a shadow looms over the two of us, and we both look up to be punished with a terrifying angle of Wang Laoshi's scowling face.

"While it's nice to see you already bonding with your new teammate, it would be better to wait until I'm finished talking," Wang Laoshi says.

"New teammate?" I repeat.

"Yes, and if you'd been paying any attention, Leah, you would have heard me announce all the teams based on your test scores," Wang Laoshi says impatiently. "If you have any objections, I don't want to hear it—all decisions are final. This trip is about opening yourself up to new places, new ideas, and new people. Most growth happens when we find ourselves in unexpected situations. And frankly," he says, raising his brows, "your Chinese skills could *really* use some help from a much more fluent speaker."

On that uplifting note, he walks off to another table, his hands behind his back.

"You should consider yourself lucky," Cyrus tells me.

"Why?"

"I mean, I'm obviously your best bet at winning," he says, arms folded across his chest, the wind tousling his hair.

He might actually be right, I conclude as I look around the ferry at the other teams: Oliver, who's eagerly waving Daisy over to take photos of him pinching the Oriental Pearl Tower as if he's a city-sized monster; Lydia, who can be heard very clearly saying, "Make sure we complete these fifty practice papers every day, and memorize this map of Shanghai . . ." to her teammate, who's taking slow steps away from her the way you would from a bear in the wild; Sean, who's dozed off so close to the edge of the ferry I'm concerned he's about to fall into the river.

With Cyrus there to help, my odds of winning the competition will increase exponentially. If we *do* win, I'll finally be able to prove to my aunt—and to myself—that I'm more than just her uncultured niece who ruined her daughter's wedding. For a few seconds, I let myself imagine the shock on her stern, ageless face when she sees me delivering a speech in Chinese at the afternoon tea event.

And being on Cyrus's team means I'll have more opportunities to uncover and exploit his weaknesses. Better to have your enemies closer and all that, especially if you want to steal their heart in order to break it.

"All right," I say. "Let's do this."

He simply nods, expressionless, then leans his head against the window, his back turned to me. But in the reflection spilling over the dark glass, I think I see the faintest of smiles tug at his lips.

CHAPTER SEVEN

"Wow, I can tell you've got a lot on your plate, Leah."

Oliver doubles over laughing at his own joke, almost knocking into the elderly woman trying to squeeze her way through to the bamboo steamers behind him. Even though it's only been open for half an hour, the breakfast buffet is already swarming with people. Tourists and smart-looking businesswomen and students from our own group wander between all the different counters, opening and shutting the large metal lids, reaching awkwardly around one another for the tongs while balancing their half-filled plates.

I give Oliver an unimpressed look as I follow him over to our table for four by the floor-to-ceiling windows. There are more diners seated on the outdoor patio under the pale, sleepy sunlight. One man in the corner is alternating between long puffs of his cigarette and bites of his cucumber salad. "That's hilarious," I tell Oliver. "You're hilarious."

"I know," he crows, setting his plate down across from me. It's stacked with bacon and hash browns and scrambled eggs, which he scoops onto his toast. While everyone else took some time finding their way around the cold meats and porridge sections, I saw him make a beeline for the right counter in the back with the familiarity of someone who frequently eats at five-star hotels. "Hey, no judgment or anything. The food here is pretty great—not Michelin star level, of course, but, like, decent."

I roll my eyes, but I honestly don't care if he *is* judging. I'm too eager to sink my teeth into everything: the sautéed beans with minced beef; the silky tofu pudding piled with chili and coriander and chopped mushrooms; the blueberry pastries; the slices of scallion pancakes; the fried pork buns sprinkled with sesame and wobbling soup dumplings.

Back when I was traveling for my modeling gigs, I was always too scared to eat what I wanted. At breakfast, I would spend ages eyeing the cinnamon swirls and crisp strips of bacon, my mouth watering, and then settle for a few cubes of watermelon.

It was strange, because nobody had ever explicitly told me that I needed to watch my diet. But so much of the pressure I felt was silent, unspoken, like being trapped inside a submarine thousands of miles underwater and feeling the oxygen slowly run out. I hadn't even realized how hungry I was—how hunger had become my usual state—until the day after I parted ways with my modeling agency, when I walked to the closest In-N-Out and wolfed down two whole cheeseburgers. That was one of the most immediate, tangible joys of quitting modeling: the realization that food wasn't meant to be an enemy or a rare treat or some kind of twisted test. And with every full meal I've had since, I can feel my body replenishing itself. My hair is so much shinier, and walking long distances is so much easier, and now, at a buffet like this, I don't have to think about anything except how rich the food tastes.

"So. How's your first night with the roommate?" Oliver asks, already moving on to his second slice of toast. "You're with Daisy, right? She's pretty quiet, isn't she? I was, like, kind of concerned she just wasn't going to talk to me at all, but she's actually been chill. She even helped take photos of me yesterday—but you should've seen her face when I started singing on our way back to the hotel. She literally turned red and ducked behind a wall because a few people were staring at me in admiration . . ."

I let him talk until he's physically forced to take a breath. "Be nice to her," I warn him, jabbing my chopsticks in his direction like they're a weapon. It's hard not to feel a little protective of my new roommate, who's currently waiting in line for the congee. Every time someone shows up, she steps aside and smiles to let them go first. I think she's been in the same spot for the past ten minutes; she might have actually moved farther back in the line.

Oliver follows my gaze and snorts. "Well, *she's* definitely nice. A bit too nice, I would even say—a problem that my roommate doesn't have."

I bite carefully into the top of my soup dumpling, sipping the hot, savory juice until only the minced meat filling is left. "How's that going, by the way?"

"Amazing. Spectacular," Oliver replies, flicking his dark brown hair out of his eyes. "He told me his whole life story and we cried over a movie about a dog together and woke up early to watch the sunrise. We're practically best friends now."

"Please don't spread such appalling lies."

We both glance up to see Cyrus standing there, brows faintly furrowed, a glass of water in one hand, his plate in the other. His breakfast is as healthy as I would've expected: fresh fruit, shredded lettuce, whole wheat bread, sliced chicken and ham in perfect proportions. It could literally be used as a model of the food pyramid.

"Ah. There he is," Oliver says with a wide, exaggerated grin, and yanks back the chair next to him. "My best friend. Please, come join us."

Cyrus eyes the chair warily, like he thinks it might be pulled out from under him at any second, but then he catches me staring and sits, rolling up the long sleeves of his white hoodie. "Good morning," he tells me, his voice quiet and still slightly thick with sleep.

Oliver's eyebrows shoot up. "He didn't say good morning to *me*, and I greeted him, like, twenty times."

"You woke me up by jumping on my bed like it was a trampoline," Cyrus says without looking at him. He spears his fork through a single piece of spinach. "That immediately disqualified the morning from being a good one."

"Okay, bro, in my defense, you were *completely* still. Like, I've never seen someone sleep in such an uncomfortable position before without moving an inch. I was starting to think you were dead."

"In the event that I do die in the middle of the night, I beg of you to not react by jumping up and down around my corpse," Cyrus says flatly.

Oliver heaves a long sigh. "See what I have to put up with?" he asks me, pointing at Cyrus with a piece of bacon. "I don't know how you hooked up with him. He doesn't even seem like he'd be open to a high five, much less a fling."

I feel my brain malfunction for three solid seconds before I remember my little white lie from the airport. With feigned calm, I reply, "Well, his attitude was a lot better when we were making out."

Cyrus chokes on his water.

I smile as Cyrus continues coughing violently into his elbow, his whole face flushed. "He was actually really thoughtful. Eager to please . . ." I'm ready to go on inventing the sort of sweet words Cyrus whispered in my ear, the way he held me close like I was the only person who mattered, when I see Daisy wandering around nearby, her wide eyes uncertain as she looks between the crowded tables like a kid on her first day of school. I stand up and wave her over. "Daisy! Come join us."

Her face melts with relief as she hurries toward us. "Hi, hi. Oops—sorry," she mumbles, flustered, raising her plate high to avoid bumping into anybody on her way to the seat.

"Now that we're all here," Oliver says, leaning forward in a conspiratorial fashion, his hand shielding his mouth as if there are professional lip-readers squatting behind the potted plants just to spy on our conversation, "I have the inside scoop on the first part of the competition today."

"Aren't we competing against each other?" I point out.

"It can't hurt to form an alliance, can it?" Oliver says. "We can take down all the other groups first—"

"I don't want to take anyone down," Daisy says quickly.

"Are you interested in the inside scoop or not?" Oliver demands.

I nod for him to go on.

"*So*," he says, "I hear it's going to be an escape room. Haunted teahouse themed."

"Wait. Really?" I'd been afraid that all the activities would be like the test Wang Laoshi gave us last night, but an escape room—that sounds infinitely more fun, not to mention more manageable. I feel a thrum of anticipation, my feet itching to get on the bus and begin the competition. It's been so long since I was looking forward to something instead of dreading it that the sensation is almost foreign to me.

Daisy doesn't appear to share my excitement. "Haunted?" she echoes, her shoulders tensing. "Why—why does it have to be haunted?"

"I mean, it's an *escape* room," Oliver tells her, popping the last of the bacon into his mouth. "If it were a room filled with flowers and puppies, you wouldn't be very motivated to escape, would you?"

"Don't worry, it can't be that scary," I reassure her. "The ghosts from the escape rooms I've been in before were pretty polite. And they're legally not allowed to hurt you."

"And if they *do*," Oliver adds, "I'll fend them off for you. My dad made me take a bunch of self-defense classes when I was a kid—I'm honestly kind of upset that nobody has ever tried to start a fight with me before. I feel like my martial arts skills are going to waste, so if I get to punch a ghost—"

"Which isn't going to happen," I emphasize. "Nobody's punching anyone."

"Right," Oliver says, holding out his hands in a placating gesture. "It'll be very peaceful. Nothing to be nervous about. I bet the ghosts will even be all talkative and friendly."

"Um, I don't want to make small talk with them either," Daisy says, looking faintly alarmed. "I'm awful at small talk."

"The ghosts will be *mildly* friendly," I settle on. "And Oliver will look out for you."

Daisy swallows but sinks back in her seat.

"Just how accurate is this information?" Cyrus asks.

Oliver winks at him. "You'll see, won't you?"

Shockingly, Oliver proves to be pretty reliable.

Two stone lions snarl at us from the gates as we follow Wang Laoshi in, weaving our way around the red-painted, zigzagging bridge, over the ponds swimming with koi fish and lotus flowers. The teahouse stands just ahead of us on slender stilts, creating the illusion that the grand, multitiered building is floating above the water.

"... used to function as an actual teahouse," Wang Laoshi is explaining over his shoulder, waving to the glossy pillars and gleaming tiles like he built the place with his own hands. "It was only recently that they decided to renovate it and repurpose it as an escape room, but they've preserved much of the original architecture, and inside, you can find a wealth of information on the importance of teahouses—and tea itself—in Chinese culture. We've booked multiple rooms, so more than one group will be able to go in at once. At the end of it, you'll be ranked according to how long it takes you to escape, and the winners will receive two stunning tea gift sets of their choosing..."

"Are you ready?" Cyrus asks me as the rest of the group scatters into private conversations and preparations, the buzz of competition building in the air.

"Obviously," I say, smoothing out my bangs. "Not sure if I'm more ready than Lydia though."

We both glance at the girl, who's quite literally bouncing on the balls of her feet, as if she's planning on sprinting inside the second they open the doors.

"To be fair, I don't think anyone can be more ready than Lydia," Cyrus remarks. "That doesn't mean she's going to *win* though. We will."

I sneak a curious glance in his direction: Everything about him is serious, sharp, severe, from the hard set of his jaw to the crisp lines of his pushed-up sleeves. This new version of him is so self-reliant and self-possessed, like a lone cottage on a remote island, that he leaves no room for anyone else to come close. *What's changed?* The question nags at my mind. *What changed you?*

I can't stop myself from studying him as he's beckoned over by the teacher, and returns with two blindfolds.

"We're meant to wear these when we enter, apparently," he says.

"These?" I raise a skeptical brow as I assess the thin scraps of fabric in his hand. "Will they even do anything? I swear I have dresses made from this exact material and those things are, like, *fully* see-through."

Cyrus blinks fast. "Why do you own dresses that are see-through? Does that not defeat the very purpose of clothing?"

"The same reason I own anything in my closet: because it looks good," I say. Then, unable to resist a chance to fluster him, I add in an offhand tone: "I even brought one of the dresses with me. Want to see me wear it?"

He freezes, blood rushing to his face, the look in his eyes almost panicked. He doesn't even seem to be breathing until I burst out laughing.

"Don't worry, I won't show you just yet. I can't have you going into shock before the competition is over."

"I—" He clears his throat. "I wouldn't go into *shock*—"

"You almost went into shock just now at my mere suggestion. Also, wait, can you help me put this on?" I nod at the blindfold.

"Yes. Sure," he says, moving behind me. I expect him to be

quick with it, the way the others are—out of the corner of my eye, I see Oliver tying the blindfold so carelessly that it ends up sliding down to Daisy's chin—but Cyrus's movements are like him: deliberate, precise. As the world goes dark, I feel his fingers in my hair fastening the ends of the blindfold, taking care not to mess up my bangs.

The world stays dark for the next few minutes while I'm led forward by a hand at my elbow. In the beginning, I try to keep track of where we're going, the places where the smooth stone underfoot transitions into uneven wooden boards, where I hear the creak of a door opening and closing behind us, where the air turns colder, more compact, and the floral notes of tea waft up to my nose. But then we make one turn after another after another, and my head is spinning by the time we come to an abrupt stop.

There's a soft *click*, a lock snapping into place.

Cyrus's voice sounds from my right. "I think we can remove our blindfolds now."

I let the fabric fall and squint around the room. The details register in pieces: stainless steel counters, woks left on stoves, blunt cleavers lying on cutting boards, bottles of vinegar and soy sauce, more pots hanging in a neat row like clothes on a laundry line, flickering lights. A kitchen. It looks like the back of any restaurant, except for the fake blood splashed everywhere.

"So that's where the *haunted* part comes in," I say, leaning over with mild curiosity to inspect the dark red liquid dripping down the closest wall. "Looks like someone was murdered in here. Daisy's not going to enjoy this very much."

"We should look for a password of some kind" Cyrus is saying, businesslike. The bulbs above us flash off for three seconds, throwing us briefly into darkness, and creaking can be heard from somewhere deeper in the teahouse, like a rusted seesaw. I'm not sure if all of it succeeds at making the atmosphere eerier, but it certainly does add an element of danger; I almost knock my chin against Cyrus's shoulder as I fumble my way forward. "Any numbers or letters or diagrams," Cyrus continues when the lights come on again, like nothing happened. "Any objects that look like they've been moved—"

"There's something here," I say, pointing at the keypad lock on the back door. The numbers are already starting to fade in places. "It requires a code."

"Let me see." Cyrus steps forward and starts punching in a few numbers.

"What are you doing?" I ask. "We don't know the password yet."

"Testing to see how many numbers we need," he replies over the beeping. "Look. It only lets you enter up to six numbers. And it should involve some combination of . . ." He shifts a little closer, running his hand over the digits that have been carved into the metal. "Two, five, seven, and nine. You can tell those are the main numbers people have pressed in the past because they've been worn away the most. Of course, there's always a chance that the staff here figured it was obvious and have changed the passcode since, but I doubt they do it very frequently because it would require them to update all the clues."

"Right. That makes sense," I say, grudgingly impressed.

"Of course it makes sense, qin ai de," Cyrus says, craning his neck to inspect the dangling pots.

I narrow my eyes at him. "What did you call me just now?"

"Hm?"

"Qin ai de, or whatever that was," I say. "It sounded like an insult."

"It means *my worst enemy*," he says casually without even turning around, and proceeds to pull open the drawers beneath the stove one by one. "There's nothing here. Nothing in here either— Oh." He pauses.

"You found something?"

"Just a severed hand." He picks up the prop and waves lazily at me with it. "What do you think the story is here? They murdered one of the guests, then cut off his hand out of spite?"

"Or they cut off his hand first and then murdered him," I say, rifling through the cabinet behind Cyrus, revealing thick cakes of black tea leaves and dried tendrils of brown and green stored inside jars. There are little square notes stuck beneath each jar, all typed out in Chinese. I attempt to read them myself before giving up and turning to Cyrus. "What do these say? Are they clues?"

He sets the hand back down and reads over my shoulder. "Hard to tell—it's about the tea itself. *There are six main types of Chinese tea: green tea, black tea, oolong tea, white tea, pu'er tea, and yellow tea.* Then it dives into the history and health benefits of each . . ."

"Keep reading," I suggest. "It could be relevant."

He goes through the notes, translating each one patiently and thoroughly like a scholar showcasing his life's work, and by the end of it I can't identify anything that could help us leave the room faster, but I *do* now know that black tea is apparently super rich in antioxidants, and that according to some legends, Shennong, the second emperor of China, discovered green tea by accident when a leaf fell into his boiling pot of water.

It's the kind of thing I wouldn't usually pay attention to if I were lectured about it in a classroom, but there's something compelling about Cyrus's voice that draws you in and keeps you hooked. I'm almost disappointed when he finishes reading the last note.

"Okay, so maybe we're still not looking in the right place," I conclude. I flip open the menu lying on the counter, thumbing the laminated pages, which separate with an unpleasant sticky noise. Bloodied fingerprints have been smeared over the list of cold dishes too. "They really went wild with the blood. It's on, like, every second page."

"Hang on." Cyrus crosses over to my side in a single stride and studies the menu, waiting as the lights plunge us into darkness again before spluttering back on. "I think there's a pattern here. Look, there's blood on page two, but page three and four are completely clean. And then there's blood on page five, but none on page six—if it had been spilt naturally, then at least some of it would have gotten on the next page. These are markers."

"It's not just blood though. It's fingerprints," I realize. "There are two fingerprints on the fifth page, but four on the first page. That's not natural either; you wouldn't be grabbing the menu with just two fingers."

Cyrus's eyes light up. "That might be the order of the numbers."

"And it fits the length of the passcode," I say, catching on, excitement fizzing through me. "Wait, I'll read the pages out—"

He's already waiting by the door, his fingers poised over the lock.

"Five . . ." I almost drop the menu in my eagerness to turn the page. "Nine . . . two . . . seven . . . one."

I hold my breath as he enters the final number. There's a beat of perfect silence, both of us staring hard at the door as if we can somehow unlock it with our minds, and just as doubt starts to creep in, the lock buzzes.

"Oh my god, we are *so* good at this," I say, grinning wide as I spin around and lift my hand in the air for a high five.

He blinks in surprise. Then he high-fives me back, and for only a moment, I see an alternative history sprawled out between us, where we might have been childhood friends instead of enemies, playing made-up games under the shade of an old oak. Where he hadn't devoted his life to making mine miserable. Where he hadn't lied and destroyed everything.

The whine of the door snaps through my thoughts.

I can't see where it leads. It's pitch-black on the other side; if I weren't factoring in the escape room's limited budget, and all the potential lawsuits such a setup would invite, I'd think there was a gaping void waiting for us to fall straight in.

"Let's go," Cyrus calls. "Stick close to me—"

But he's barely spoken when something leaps out at us from the darkness.

CHAPTER EIGHT

Cyrus lets out a high-pitched, Oscar-nominated-horror-movie scream.

This is far more noteworthy than the ghosts that have surrounded us in the crimson glow of the main dining area. I only really glance at them—their blood-splattered faces; their long, tangled wigs drooping over their pale robes; their bright red contacts—out of politeness and appreciation for their efforts. Despite my complete lack of reaction, they're still throwing themselves into their performance, moving their limbs jerkily as they reach toward me.

I turn away from them to raise my brows at Cyrus, so many taunts rushing into my mind at once that I almost give myself a headache trying to decide which one to aim at him first.

"Don't," Cyrus says with a warning look before I can even open my mouth. "I was merely startled—"

"That was definitely a scream," I say.

"That was a small sound of surprise," he argues. "A stranger's face appeared out of nowhere, and I behaved how any normal person would."

"Yes. By screaming."

"You know, we should be looking for our next clue," he says, aborting his previous defense strategy—denial—and opting for the classic *let's-turn-our-attention-elsewhere* tactic instead. He steps forward in as dignified a manner as possible for someone who's just leapt back three feet. The ghosts don't block our way, but they don't disperse either. They simply continue haunting us as we study the setup.

Half the space has been dedicated to private rooms, each with their own flower and poetic name—at least, I'm assuming it's poetic, based on the calligraphy and the fact that I don't recognize a single character—printed above the carved lattice doors. The rest of the floor is taken up by round tables and silk-cushioned chairs in various colors, a few of them pushed back as though the guest had risen bare moments ago, the double-layered trays still wet with spilt tea. A folding screen has been propped up by the window, its surface overgrown with moon-white and sun-yellow chrysanthemums, their petals curling inward as if protecting a secret.

"Does it have anything to do with the flowers?" I venture. "Like, I don't know—maybe the number of flowers is important. Maybe we should be counting them, or the petals—"

"I don't think this is one of those *he-loves-me-he-loves-me-not* situations," Cyrus says.

"I wouldn't need to count petals to guess whether someone loves me. I'd know that they do," I say, the haughty coolness of my tone masking the heat in my cheeks. I immediately feel stupid for making the suggestion. This is one of the reasons I stopped answering questions in any of my classes—because most of the time, I'd say something silly and irrelevant without realizing it, and I'd want to shrivel into a ball while the teacher fought to keep their expression professional. *You don't even try*, the same teachers accused when it came time for feedback, but I had. I simply wasn't very smart, not *school*-smart, which is the only kind of smart that seems to matter at our age.

Cyrus pauses. "Well, you're right, it could be related to the flowers," he says slowly. "I'm not sure if it's a number that we're looking for though. I haven't seen anything in the room that would require a passcode."

"Hey, there's something here," I notice, pointing to a piece of paper tucked underneath the screen.

He bends down right away and picks it up, flattening it out on the closest table so we can both read the characters scrawled over it. Or so he can read it, and I can stare at it. I'd expected it to be a message, but it looks more like a riddle: The words are listed one by one down the page.

"What is it?" I ask.

"A riddle," Cyrus replies unhelpfully.

"Yes, I figured as much, Cyrus," I say, squinting harder at the note as if it's my vision that's the problem here. "I didn't think it was a love poem you'd composed for me."

"I would never compose a love poem this bad," Cyrus says with a scoff. "There isn't even any rhythm to it."

"Okay, but there has to be some—" My words are drowned

out by the incoherent shrieking of the ghosts as they charge forward again, waving their pale fingers right in our faces, their eyes rolling back dramatically, blood dripping down their chins. I try again, louder: *"There has to be some—"*

One of the ghosts breaks from the ranks and starts circling me like a shark in water, his features contorting with so much effort I worry they're going to end up permanently altered. He lets out another pitch-perfect horror-movie scream as he claws at the air.

I raise my hand like I'm hailing a taxi. "Can you please just let us talk for a second?" I say, first in English, then in Chinese: "Deng yi xia." *Wait.* The only words I can remember on the spot.

But they're the right ones, because the ghost clamps his mouth shut mid-scream.

"Xie xie," I say, smiling at the ghost.

He smiles widely back at me before his ghost colleague elbows him.

"What do the words say?" I ask Cyrus, relieved to be able to hear my own voice again. Then, because he's taking too long to respond and it seems like I'm kind of on a roll with the Chinese, I add, "Wo wen ni ne."

His complexion changes color, as if directly absorbing the light of the scarlet lanterns above us. "Do you realize what you just said?"

"Yeah? I said that I'm asking you a question."

"No." He raises his brows. "You said that you were kissing me."

This is very much news to me. But rather than letting any of my embarrassment show on my face, I decide to lean into it. "It's an innocent mistake. And I mean, isn't that what happens in your secret little fantasies about me?"

It works even better than I thought. He goes rigid for a second, his eyes widening as if someone's started reading his actual fantasies out loud through a speaker, and then he quickly busies himself studying the piece of paper again. "So the words here are: lipstick, strawberry, wedding dress, and wine."

"Those are all things you'd get at a wedding, right?" I say. "Maybe not necessarily the strawberries, but the bride could have . . . strawberry wedding cake? Or chocolate-covered strawberries? Sidenote: Now I'm really craving chocolate-covered strawberries."

Cyrus makes a face. "I used to enjoy chocolate-covered strawberries until I witnessed a couple sharing one."

"One? A *single* strawberry? For two people?" I say, echoing his disgust.

"A single, extremely small strawberry," he confirms with a grimace. "Both their mouths were on it. I've been traumatized ever since."

"Some things just shouldn't be shared. I almost broke up with one of my exes after he suggested that we try out the *Lady and the Tramp* noodle thing. Like, yeah, it's cute when dogs do it, but that's because the *dogs* are cute. For some reason, he didn't get it."

Cyrus's brows crinkle. "You almost broke up with him? I would've asked to break up on the spot."

"I didn't get a chance to, because he dumped me first," I tell him, then wish I'd just lied. You don't go running to the enemy to point out the wound on your back, even if the wound itself is more aggravating than fatal. Especially not when there's an older, deeper wound inches below it from when the enemy pressed in with a knife. *That* one had felt fatal.

"Who would dump you?" Cyrus asks. He doesn't sound like he's mocking me; he sounds like he's genuinely baffled. But for all I know, it's a trap.

I shrug. "It's whatever. I don't even remember his name." His name was Brian. He had been sweet on our first date, the perfect gentleman, complimenting my hair, my outfit, my smile. But with every date we went on after, I could feel his interest slipping away as he slowly realized, like other guys did, that I didn't have much to offer other than my appearance. I didn't have any passions, and I didn't always understand his jokes right away, and I would ask the dumbest questions when I wanted to sound smart, like, *What year was this restaurant founded?* As if he would know or anyone would care.

"We should get back to the riddle," I say, a little too loudly. "Do we think it's wedding related somehow?"

"The word *wedding* is already included here," Cyrus says. "I feel like that's too obvious."

"Well, three of the four things are red."

"No," he says, in the hushed voice of a hero from an action movie upon discovering who the real villain is. "*Four* of the four things are red."

The wedding dress. I had been imagining a white veil and white tulle, but then I remember the qipao my cousin wore for her wedding, and my mind continues racing forward, gathering up clues, leading me to: "The cushions. That one over there."

We both turn to the only red cushion on the chairs. The ghosts spring back into action, screaming and scrabbling at the space around our heads, but Cyrus dodges them and searches around behind the cushion, his features hard with concentration, then brandishes a key. It's a dull bronze, slim and barely longer than my pinkie finger, the ridges already starting to rust.

Everything is easy after that. We find the private room with a red poppy painted next to its name and enter it together, slamming the door shut behind us to stop the ghosts from barging in. The room itself is so small as to be suffocating, and I've definitely been inside closets that are more spacious, but that's all fine because the room opens up to a balcony. Or it should, if the glass doors to the balcony weren't locked. I can *see* the sunlight streaming in, the pretty rock gardens out the back, promising fresh air and freedom. I'm just getting ready to make my victory march when Cyrus spins toward me and holds his hand out expectantly.

"What do you want?" I ask him.

He frowns, like he thinks I'm picking an inappropriate time to crack a joke. "The key," he says, his hand still stretched out in front of him. "You have it."

"No, I don't," I say, wondering if he's joking. If this is one of those instances where he'll pretend to fumble around in his pockets searching for it before grinning and waving the key in front of my face. "You took the key. Come on, Cyrus."

But his expression is as grave as the ghosts on the other side of the door. "I gave it to you just now," he says. "I wouldn't waste precious competition time pulling a prank."

So it turns out that the universe is the only one joking here. *This can't be happening.* "That's just—I mean, that's simply not true. You never gave me the key—"

"I *did*," he insists. "I distinctly remember passing it—"

"You must be from another dimension, then, because that didn't happen in this timeline—"

"I'm one hundred percent certain that I handed it to you," he says.

"And I'm one hundred percent certain you didn't," I shoot back. "I guess that makes it two hundred percent likely that you lost the key."

"Okay, that is—mathematically, that can't be right. But it does appear likely that the key is missing."

I bite back a hysterical laugh and pat down my bangs a little more aggressively than I usually would, if only to do something with my hands that doesn't involve punching the doors. The glass is thin enough that it ought to shatter with one solid strike. Thin enough that it feels all the more ridiculous to be stuck here, separated by nothing except a stupid misplaced key.

"You're *sure* you don't have it?" Cyrus asks after a beat of depressing silence. "Because I recall that we were heading into the room, and I was busy closing the doors because those ghosts kept trying to stick their heads in after us, so I took the key out of my pocket and I held it out—"

"Oh my god, Cyrus, I don't have the key," I interject, raising my arms above my head like I'm walking through airport security. "If you still don't believe me, you're welcome to feel me up. Go on. Check my back pockets. See if the key is there."

He flushes. Turns away. "I—I do believe you," he says. "We should look for the key. It can't have hopped out of the room on its own."

But I'm starting to think that the key really did sprout a pair of tiny legs and make a run for it when we weren't paying attention, because even after patting every inch of the floor and reaching into every odd crack and nook, it remains nowhere to be found.

"This is the absolute worst," I declare, pinching the bridge of my nose in frustration. "I can *feel* our chances of winning suffocating slowly in this dark, cramped room as we speak."

"I can think of far worse things," Cyrus says blithely, checking behind the table for the fifth time. "The year 536, for instance."

"What happened in the year 536?" Though I'm not sure if that's even the right question here. The year 536 sounds very well like it could also be a band, or a fancy club for rich people to chat about their yachts, or one of those supposedly profound four-hour-long movies where everyone dies.

"A devastating series of natural disasters," he says. "There was a volcanic winter and major crop failures as a result. I think about that year often."

"You think about major crop failures from centuries ago . . . *often?*"

He nods. "At least three times a day."

I have no idea if he's just messing with me at this point.

"Because I often feel like life is terrible," Cyrus explains, moving on to check the porcelain vase propped up in the middle of the table. "And then I remind myself that, well, you know, looking back on the long course of human history and everything we've survived and haven't survived, I'm actually very lucky. Helps put things into perspective— Hey, I found it," he says, triumph blazing through his voice.

I jerk my head up to see him dangling the bronze key between his fingers. Forget the northern lights. Forget Niagara Falls at sunset, snow on the beach, and every Michelangelo painting— this is officially the most beautiful sight to ever exist. If I could, I'd take a photo of this exact scene and hang it up in my bedroom. "It fell into that vase?" I demand.

"It appears so."

"Well, it definitely didn't fall from *my* pocket," I can't help emphasizing.

"How about we just agree it was lost in transit?" Cyrus says, which is about as diplomatic as we're getting, even if I'm still certain he's wrong. He slides the key smoothly into the lock and sunlight bursts through the door. The open air is perfect, layered with flavors I hadn't noticed before we entered the teahouse, like the crisp aroma of bamboo leaves and the damp scent of the soil.

Wang Laoshi is waiting for us outside. My heart falls. We must be so far behind that everyone has already left.

"We're last?" I ask.

Wang Laoshi shakes his head. "No, you're first."

"Wait. Seriously?" As a rule, I don't like to gape—it's never a graceful look. But I'm pretty sure I'm gaping at him now.

"Of course. I'm always serious," Wang Laoshi says with a stern frown, which is the best kind of confirmation he could offer. "I'll be letting Dr. Linda Shen know you're today's winners. I'm sure she'll be pleased—she was the one who chose the teahouse for this activity."

Now that I think about it, I *do* recall my mother mentioning how much my aunt loves her tea.

"See? I told you," Cyrus says, nudging me with his elbow and forcing my attention back to him. "Even if one of us lost the key and caused some unexpected delays—"

"You," I cut in. I mean to say it with vehemence, but my anger evaporates before it can boil, the euphoria of our victory plating everything in rose gold. It's been so, so long since I last won anything. Since I didn't feel like I was struggling alone at the very bottom. "You lost the key."

"We would've been way ahead of the others with the clues," Cyrus goes on, grinning at me. "What can I say? We make a good team."

I'm not totally convinced that we make a *good* team—I just feel like good teamwork shouldn't involve such frequent thoughts of murder—but with our first win secured, everything is working out according to plan. And if I'm being fair, I have to give Cyrus credit for getting us here.

So I bite down on my tongue and nod. I can put up with this a little longer if it means getting my revenge and getting into my aunt's good graces, I tell myself. I can.

After all, I've put up with more in the past for less.

CHAPTER NINE

That night, while Daisy's showering, I curl up in my blankets and call my parents.

"Hello? Baobei?"

The sound of my mom's voice sends an unexpected wave of homesickness crashing through me. It's still morning on her end, and I can hear something sizzling in the background; footsteps on hardwood; the lovely, ordinary rhythm of life back home. I imagine my father in the kitchen, flipping an omelet because my mom always makes it too runny, and the homesickness crashes in harder, sweeping the shores of my ribs.

"Hi, Mom," I say softly.

"How *is* everything?" she asks. "Your dad's cooking breakfast right now. I asked him not to—I bet he's going to burn the omelet again—but he's been going on and on about how much he misses you. He wanted to call you yesterday, but I told him you'd be busy with all the activities you're doing."

"I really miss you guys too. And everything's . . . good," I say, surprised to find that it's not a total lie. The curtains are still open a sliver, and through them, Shanghai is glowing, all its magnificent buildings bathed in an array of lights. It's the kind of sight you could never get sick of, even if you stared at it every night. "I've been learning a lot. I actually won the first activity today—it was, like, this escape room thing in a teahouse—and I got this really pretty tea set for you and Dad. I'll show you when I get back."

"You won a *tea set*?" From the sheer pride and enthusiasm in my mom's voice, you'd think I'd won a whole mansion with cash stuffed into every room and our family name trimmed into the two-hundred-acre front lawn. "That's amazing. How's everything else? Did you make any new friends?"

It's an old question, a familiar one.

Did you make any new friends? she'd asked eagerly that first afternoon after I transferred schools. I'd kept quiet, my lips quivering from the sheer effort of holding back my tears, and waited until she pulled the car away from the curb before my composure cracked. *Nobody spoke to me the entire day*, I sobbed. *I—I don't know why. Even when I tried to be friendly and ask questions, they just . . . ignored me. All of them.*

Maybe it's because you joined in the middle of the semester, my mom had tried to comfort me. *They're just getting used to you.*

Maybe, I'd allowed, but I knew somehow that it wasn't so simple.

Did you make any new friends? she'd asked when she picked me up from school the next week, still hopeful. By then, the rumors had reached me. The real reason why nobody wanted to sit next to me in class. To them, I was the girl who'd pushed someone off the stairs at my old school, the freak who'd been expelled for exhibiting violent, unstable behavior, the outcast who'd lashed out at one of the most popular, beloved boys.

During those days, it felt like I would die before the rumors did.

Did you make any new friends? my mom had asked again after I moved to my current school. It had felt strange to call Cate Addison a friend, as if I were imposing, even though we did everything friends ought to: We ate lunch together, shopped together, saved each other's numbers and made plans for the weekends. But I was too relieved to have someone to eat lunch with, someone who would smile back at me when I greeted them. *I did*, I'd told my mother, and her relief was even more palpable than mine. *See? I knew all you needed was a fresh start*, she'd gushed, squeezing my hand. *You deserve one.*

Now I glance over in the direction of the bathroom, which Daisy had rushed into after I offered to let her go first, promising she'd be done as soon as she could and apologizing three times for making me wait while I reassured her, laughing, just as many times that it was fine. The shower is running loudly enough to cover my next words, so I say, "There's this girl who's really nice. Everyone's been pretty nice to me, actually."

"I'm so glad," my mom says. "It might be just what you need."

I push myself up from the pillows. "What do you mean?"

"Well, you don't have any friends who are from a similar background. Not that Cate and your other friends aren't wonderful young women," she adds quickly. "But the more friends, the better—and you know, you might find that the people you meet on this trip have a lot in common with you."

Her words are still running in a loop inside my head after we hang up.

I scroll through my phone to find a bunch of new photos posted by Cate: her and the other girls from my class tanning at the beach, their skin smooth and shiny as seals fresh out of the water, books with the same cheerful hot-pink cover placed on the sand next to them; holding up cocktail glasses with the sun setting in the background; mirror selfies at the mall; blurry, zoomed-in shots of them posing in the parking lot. Maybe I should feel left out, but I can imagine what it'd be like if I were with them right now—forcing myself to laugh at a joke I don't find funny, pretending to be invested in the gossip about some famous British actor I don't particularly like, swallowing down the expensive champagne when all I really want is a grape soda. I guess we *don't* have that much in common, which would matter less if she cared more, but she hasn't messaged me even once since I left LA.

I click away from her page, only to end up overwhelmed by an onslaught of posts from my modeling friends—or ex-friends, since I've barely spoken to any of them in weeks. Or maybe we were never really friends to begin with, but forced together by circumstance, in way over our heads and clinging to one another to stop from sinking. As soon as the circumstances changed, those ties dissolved.

I pull my bedcovers up higher, propping myself up on one elbow, and silently flick through the pictures. Magazine covers, glossy double-spreads, a huge brand deal, a new campaign, a special invitation to the fashion show of their dreams. Captions about their *whirlwind of a weekend*, how they *had the absolute best time*, how they're *so grateful for the experience*, so excited, so thrilled, so happy. A dry, bitter taste creeps onto my tongue, and I know I should stop, leave it alone, yet it's like prodding at the roots of a rotten tooth. When I first quit, I'd been afraid that the other models would be gleeful, that they would whisper to one another in lavender-candle-scented bathrooms, between quick flicks of mascara and spritzes of perfume, about how I had failed. But the reality is so much worse: They simply don't care.

It should be proof, if nothing else, that I made the right choice to leave, and I should be searching for something new by now. Another purpose, another dream, something just for myself. But I've only ever known how to want what other people want.

I let my phone fall onto the pillow and hug the blanket to my chest. The hotel room is quiet, save for the sound of distant traffic and the water running in the bathroom. Being in Shanghai feels a little like slipping into an alternate reality, but I can no longer tell where real life is: here, in this glittering city, or what I've left back in LA.

When I caught the word *shopping* on our travel itinerary, my mind immediately lit up with images of multistory malls; banner ads for designer handbags hanging from the ceiling; groups of friends sipping milk tea and swinging their new purchases while riding the glass elevator up to the next level of clothing stores.

It's not until we're walking into the thick of the market—no designer handbags in sight, but plenty of floral shopping caddies—that I realize the shopping in question pertains to groceries. If I were the kind of person with a passion for buying fresh produce, this would probably be my favorite place in the world. The market is so massive that it takes up three whole blocks on its own, its shelves spilling over with natural colors: tangerines and dragon fruit and lychees and about ten different types of apples. It would probably also be the best place in the world to get trapped inside; even with the shoppers streaming through the stalls and haggling over carrots, there's so much food stocked here that I'm sure it would last all of us well into next year.

"You'll each get two hundred yuan to spend," Wang Laoshi shouts at us, which is the most threatening way someone has ever offered me money before. He raises his voice further, straining to be heard over the vendors advertising their newly imported coconuts from Sanya. "I've forwarded a grocery list to everyone via the WeChat group—you can check it now. We've already paid for all the items at their full price, but for the purpose of this competition, we want you to put your Chinese skills into practice through the art of bargaining. Whoever manages to buy the most items with the allotted money wins this round, and you have one hour before we all meet back here. Do *not* waste the money on anything outside the list. Yes, I'm looking at you, Oliver."

I feel myself light up as I pull out my phone. The list goes on for two whole pages, and it's written only in Chinese, making it a little hard to identify what we're meant to be buying. But it is, ultimately, a shopping competition. If this were offered as an elective at school, I might get to experience for the first time what it's like to be at the top of my class.

"We should target different sections at a time so we don't have to run around the market in circles," Cyrus says, reading over the list on his phone. "I saw someone selling lettuce from his cart just now—"

"Okay, okay, let's go," I tell him, eager to get started. Out of the corner of my eye, I can already see Lydia dragging her teammate to the closest radish stall, her expression so fierce I wonder if her haggling tactics involve intimidation.

We split from the rest of the group and turn left, making a beeline for the lettuce cart.

The person manning it is more a boy than a grown-up, old enough to have graduated from high school but definitely not college. He's playing on his phone when we approach him, and glances lazily up at us without pausing the game.

"How much for two heads of lettuce?" Cyrus asks, straight to the point. A bit *too* straight to the point.

I attempt to smother my frown, but Cyrus sees it anyway.

"What?" he mutters.

"That's a horrible way to start a negotiation," I mutter back to him. "Why would you pose it as an open-ended question? You're basically asking for a higher price."

He stares at me. "How *else* would you ask for the price of lettuce?"

"I'd ask him if it was one yuan or two yuan. He'd pick two yuan, of course, and then we'd go from there." My gaze flickers to the boy, who's already returned to his game. "Just try it."

"Fine," Cyrus says with a heavy air of skepticism. He clears his throat. "Are these one or two—"

"Two," the boy says.

I don't need a mirror to know that the smile on my face screams *I told you so*.

"All right," Cyrus says in Chinese, actively avoiding my smile, and begins to reach for his wallet. "Then we'll have—"

I elbow him, hard.

"What *now*?" he says, spinning around.

"You can't just *accept* it at two yuan," I hiss. "There's definitely room to go lower."

"You bargain with him, then."

"I will. Watch. Just don't judge me for what I'm about to do."

His brows shoot up. "Why would I judge—"

I switch my smile to the other one. The one I wear way more often in public, the one I'm admittedly a little ashamed of resorting to, but not so ashamed as to stop using it. It's softer, half-sly, my chin tipping down, my eyes squinting into a smolder that's as ridiculous as it is effective. Then, after consulting Google Translate, I fluff my hair out and lean forward as gracefully as I can over the pile of lettuce. "Really? You can't go any cheaper?" I ask in a breathy voice I'm pretty sure I borrowed from a fantasy video game about sexy elves, but it's perfect for my target audience.

The boy sets his phone aside and looks up for the first time, which I consider a tremendous success. "Two is the cheapest I can offer," he says gruffly, but I can see him taking me in, his eyes wandering down from my lips to where my halter top is cropped at the waist to the slim length of my ankles, strapped into my black stilettos. This is what I'm good at. This is maybe, probably, the only thing I'm good at: fleeting impressions, tourist-attraction interest, something to admire for a minute before you start getting bored of seeing the same scenery.

"Quick. How do you say *handsome* in Chinese? Like, in a colloquial way?" I ask Cyrus under my breath.

"You don't have to tell me I'm handsome in Chinese," he replies, cocking his head. "English is fine."

There are a number of things I *would* like to tell him that are less flattering and far more menacing, but I need to act fast while I still have the boy's attention. *"Cyrus."*

He hesitates. Sighs. "It's shuaige," he says, as resentfully as if the information had been tortured out of him. Then, in a lower voice, "I can't believe I'm helping you flirt with this guy."

"You're helping me help us win," I inform him, and turn back to the boy. "Please, shuaige. Can't you be nice and let us buy the lettuce for fifty cents?" I doubt my grammar is entirely correct, but I hold out hope that any awkward turns of phrase are smoothed over by the way I'm gazing right at him as I play with a strand of my hair.

The boy blinks at me like he's only just learned how to do it and wants to keep practicing. He blinks again. Three more blinks, two fast and one slow, and I'm beginning to wonder if he's actually conveying a message in code when he nods and grabs the lettuce for us.

"Thank you *so* much, shuaige," I coo.

"Maybe take the excitement down a notch," Cyrus mutters in my ear. "Unless you want him to bring you home to meet his parents."

I ignore him, then swiftly turn to grin at the boy. "Thanks again," I say, fluttering my fingers in a wave.

I'm still waving to him as we head off to buy carrots next, with Cyrus hauling the bag of lettuce over his shoulder.

"This should be our strategy," I tell him. "Just charm the vendors, and we might be able to buy things for a cheaper price."

"I'm not sure I'm a fan of that strategy," he says, walking faster.

"Yeah, okay, but you're not a fan of anything."

His gaze slices up to my face. "That's not true."

"Sure." I let out a scoff of disbelief.

"I just don't like relying on my charm to get the things I want."

"That's not what you were like before," I say. When he doesn't reply, I quicken my steps and peer over at him, curious. "You clearly can be charming, Cyrus. You were one of the most popular guys in our class, I remember. But these days . . . it's like you're going out of your way to make sure that nobody warms up to you, and to be honest, I have no idea why."

He looks away. Switches the lettuce over to his other shoulder, conveniently blocking my direct view of his face.

"Fine, how about this," I say. "I'll do all the charming, and you help translate a few compliments and carry the vegetables. Happy?"

"Never," he says.

"Great."

Our system works surprisingly well. With the exception of one grumpy vendor who looks like he's in the business of selling leaves in another, more illegal form, I manage to charm and barter and beam my way down the entire length of our grocery list, until Cyrus has both his hands full with sacks of grains and vegetables. We must have walked around the entire perimeter of the market, because only half an hour in, my phone buzzes to let me know I've doubled my daily fitness goal, and my feet start aching. My feet are almost always aching, and it's usually mild enough for me to ignore it, but the longer we walk, the deeper the straps of my heels press into my flesh. I feel like the little mermaid walking on land for the first time, wincing with every step I take.

I'm practically hobbling as Cyrus drops our purchases down in the designated cart, where the bus is parked and waiting. Most students in the group haven't returned yet, but Lydia's already standing there with bags of groceries so close to bursting I have to wonder if she simply robbed the vendors of their entire stalls. A small, self-satisfied smile flickers across her face when she looks over at *our* bags, which suddenly seem almost empty by comparison.

"I think she's going to win this one," I worry out loud to Cyrus.

I expect a much stronger reaction, but he appears distracted. "Is that so?" His gaze flickers down to my feet, and then he abruptly twists around in the other direction. "Come with me."

"What? But we've already finished buying everything—where are you going?" I ask. It doesn't take very long to catch up to him, and it's not because I've developed a sudden tolerance for pain or my stilettos have magically reshaped themselves to accommodate my feet. Cyrus's strides are much shorter, slower than they were before, and he glances at me every few seconds, as if to make sure we're moving at the same pace.

I limp along until we've left the market behind us, the

fresh breeze clearing away the smell of orange peels and sliced watermelon.

"In here," Cyrus says, making another sharp turn toward a pharmacy on the corner of the street. He holds the door open and nods for me to enter.

The cool blast of air-conditioning hits me with full force as I hobble in, the sweat on my bare arms drying within seconds. The entire pharmacy is barely larger than our hotel rooms, but its blue-and-white shelves appear to be stacked with a bit of everything: rows upon rows of facial creams and toners and eye masks promising to reverse all signs of aging; cheap mascaras and lip tints and nail clippers; about twenty different kinds of vitamins sealed in orange jars. A gorgeous celebrity grins down at customers from a massive banner, holding up a new shade of lipstick like he's proposing with it, his name scribbled at the bottom: *Caz Song.*

Cyrus is already at the counter, saying something in Chinese to the only retail assistant in here. I pick out the words *do you* and *where* before they both turn toward me.

"This for her?" the retail assistant asks in English, stepping around to speak to me. *Two minutes*, I note to myself with a mental grimace. *I've been inside for two minutes, and that's all it took for her to deduce that I can't speak Chinese.* By this point, I doubt I could look any more like a confused foreigner even if I glued my passport to my forehead.

The jade beads on the retail assistant's bracelet clatter noisily as she reaches for something on the upper shelf to my right. "I have very good shampoo for you," she declares, brandishing a hot-pink bottle.

"Oh," I say, confused. I demand an explanation from Cyrus with my eyes—did he drag me over here to ask for *shampoo recommendations?*—but he looks just as bewildered.

"This smells like oranges," she continues, every word punctuated by an enthusiastic nod of her head, her high bun bobbing with it. "A favorite for our customers. Many girls say their boyfriends *love* the scent too—won't stop following them around just to smell their hair. Very easy to wash out and will make your hair smooth and shiny and healthy, like a mermaid. Once you start using it, I promise you will never be able to pick up another shampoo brand again."

Cyrus clears his throat. "We're just looking for Band-Aids," he says, switching to English too. "Do you have any—"

"Check the back," the woman says briskly, and waves the shampoo higher in front of my face, her eyes gleaming. "But you will regret it for all your lifetimes to come if you leave without trying this shampoo. We have other types of shampoo too: papaya, mango, cherries, vanilla. There's one for frizzing—does your hair frizz a lot?"

"No," I say, distracted, tracking Cyrus's movements out of the corner of my eye. He disappears behind one of the shelves, and reemerges seconds later with a small pack of Band-Aids. *For me?* I wonder to myself. It's the only explanation for why he brought me here, and it's surprisingly thoughtful. *Suspiciously* thoughtful. Two years seems too short a time for someone to grow a heart from scratch.

No, it must be a ploy of some kind. Another trick up his sleeve. The fact that I can't be certain of *what* he's aiming for, exactly, unsettles me. Maybe he has plans of his own to humiliate me yet again, or maybe he just wants to get to my aunt through me. Either way, I can't let my guard down around him. Not now, not ever.

"There's another one for hair damage," the woman continues, reeling my attention back to her.

"Thank you for the recommendation," I tell her, "but I really don't need any shampoo—"

"Everyone needs this shampoo," she says, undeterred. "*Everyone.* Your favorite idol uses it. Your favorite idol's idol uses it. I use the shampoo myself and it was the best decision I ever made—better decision than marrying my husband or buying an apartment in Puxi before the prices skyrocketed. If it's the money you worry about, we have discount for first-time purchases . . ."

"That's okay, but thank you," I tell her, stepping back.

"We'll just have this," Cyrus speaks up, dropping the Band-Aids onto the counter.

Her face falls with such obvious disappointment that I almost consider buying the shampoo to cheer her up.

As soon as Cyrus finishes paying, he guides me back out onto the street and gestures for me to sit on an empty bench.

"She certainly loves that shampoo," I can't help remarking.

"Maybe they sponsored her," Cyrus suggests, tearing open the pack.

"Maybe her grandparents founded the shampoo brand."

"Maybe the founder of the shampoo brand was hiding in the pharmacy and listening to us the whole time."

"Maybe the founder saved her life many years ago and asked only that she passionately promote their product in exchange."

"Maybe the shampoo saved her life," Cyrus suggests.

I snort. "How would that work?"

"Say a robber had been about to attack, but the shampoo made her hair so shiny that they completely forget what they were doing and stopped just to admire her glossy locks."

"She *did* have pretty shiny hair," I recall. "You know, I actually kind of want that shampoo now . . ." But the rest of my sentence screeches to a halt when Cyrus bends down before me and reaches for my left heel, his hand hovering an inch away from my bare ankle.

"Let me help," he offers, his face angled down, sweet and pliant, his lashes enviably long, his eyes so dark that someone less careful would go tumbling straight into their depths, never to resurface again.

I keep my feet rooted firmly to the ground. "That's fine," I try to say, but he's already untying the delicate straps of my shoe with quick, nimble fingers, sliding it off slowly and bringing my ankle down to rest on his bent knee. He sucks in a quiet breath when he sees the angry red blisters marring my heel, the skin rubbed raw and a short walk away from bleeding. There's hardly any inch of skin that isn't damaged in some way, between the mottled purplish-yellow bruises and the dark lines from where the leather edges dug in too deep.

"I know you like your high heels, and I'm not here to get in the way of that," he says, "but do you have to wear them *everywhere* you go? Don't you own a single pair of comfortable walking shoes?"

"It's a habit," I tell him.

"But it's hurting you," he says.

As if you actually care. My pain has never meant anything to him before—it's all just for show, it must be. But whatever his real motive is, he's more committed to this act than I expected. I can only stare as Cyrus Sui peels the pink Band-Aid and presses it over my broken skin, smoothing it out with his thumb, his touch shockingly tender. And for just a few seconds, I remember him from the time before he ruined my life. When he was only a boy who'd picked up a wounded bird after it had slammed into our classroom window, cradling its tiny, shivering body in his palms, insisting on caring for it even when everyone else told him to let it go. I remember the look in his eyes, concern and fear and stubborn hope. I'd done my best to banish those memories, to destroy any evidence that suggested he might not be a wholly horrible person, because then it was too confusing. It made hating him too difficult.

My confusion only deepens alongside my suspicion when he helps me slide my shoe back on like it's a glass slipper, chivalrous and fake as a fairy-tale prince. It's ridiculous behavior. Borderline disturbing. Like a murderer stroking your hair after stabbing you in the back.

"What is this, Cyrus?" I demand, unable to take it anymore. "What are you trying to achieve here?"

He blinks up at me with perfect, pretend innocence. "Preventing you from limping the rest of the trip? You're welcome, by the way."

I grit my teeth. I have no idea how to talk to him when he's like this.

Relief sings through my body when I see two familiar figures heading out of the market just ahead of us. Oliver is carrying a single, half-empty basket, which he swings about as he walks, with Daisy following after him, her head down and elbows squeezed in to move past the other shoppers.

"That's all you got?" I ask Oliver, peering around him in the very unlikely event that he might be hiding a cart of vegetables behind his back. "Did you guys lose your money halfway through?"

"Don't even," Oliver says, setting their basket down. It's so light that it doesn't even make a sound when it lands on the concrete. "Daisy refuses to bargain—"

"I didn't refuse," Daisy protests feebly, her round face flushing.

"No, no, listen to this, guys," Oliver goes on, holding up his hands as if getting ready for a dramatic reenactment. "I had just managed to convince this man to drop the price for the radish down by fifty cents—he's literally about to hand the radish over to us—when Daisy pops her head in and tells him that *it's okay*. As in, *it's totally okay* to sell the radish for the full price. Then she *apologizes*. For volunteering to pay him *more money*. Before she offers to pay him *extra*. Have we time-traveled straight to Christmas or something?" he asks, deadpan. "Because I don't recall it being the season of giving."

"He said that he had children," Daisy mumbles.

"Didn't you hear Wang Laoshi say that everything's been pre-paid for us? Plus, I'm sorry to break this to you, but a lot of people have children," Oliver says. "If you really think—"

"Oliver has no concept of money," Daisy blurts out.

Oliver's jaw drops, obviously stunned that he's not the only one doing the tattling.

"It's true," Daisy insists, her face turning almost the same red as the single tomato in their basket, while Cyrus and I watch the exchange with growing amusement. "He kept asking me, 'Is two yuan cheap?' 'Is three hundred yuan cheap?' It's like he's never been inside a market before." Somehow, this commentary is a thousand times more entertaining when delivered in her quiet, tentative voice. "He nearly had a mental breakdown when he discovered the price of an egg. There were tears in his eyes."

"Just goes to show I'm in touch with my emotions," Oliver says without any shame. "But also, like, we couldn't find half the things on the list. We looked everywhere for the jackfruit, and every time we thought we'd spotted it at last, it turned out to be durian."

"Well," Cyrus says casually, locking eyes with me, "if you're ever searching for shampoo, we know just the place."

Laughter springs out of me before I have time to stifle it. It's my real laugh—an embarrassingly loud, honking sound that would be put to better use as a fire alarm. I clamp my mouth shut, my skin heating at the slip in my composure, but Cyrus is grinning at me.

"Uh, what?" Oliver asks, looking lost.

"Ignore him," I say, but I'm talking more to myself. *Ignore Cyrus, don't trust him, don't let yourself laugh at his remarks. Only one person is going to get their heart broken at the end of this trip, and it's not going to be you.*

I look down at the Band-Aid on my heel and make a mental note to rip it off as soon as I can.

CHAPTER TEN

There *has* to be a better way to get in my exercise for the day than sprinting to catch the bullet train, my vision half-obscured by my bangs, while my luggage bumps violently along the pavement behind me and Wang Laoshi yells at everyone to move faster because our tickets are nonrefundable.

Many better ways. As we all pile into the train car mere seconds before the doors slide shut, sweating and panting so hard that the other passengers turn to stare, I manage to think of at least ten examples just off the top of my head, including but not limited to: Getting chased by the ghosts from the haunted teahouse. Washing a full sink of dirty dishes by hand. Wrestling a bear.

But I can't help laughing with Daisy and Oliver when we finally collapse into our seats, our bags dumped gracelessly into the space beneath the footrests. I'm not sure if it's the relief of catching the train in time, or if it's the unexpected happiness bubbling beneath the exhaustion and stress of the morning. That unique camaraderie that I imagine forms only when you're traveling in a tight-knit group like this, away from home and old haunts and clinging on to these half strangers who have suddenly become more familiar to you than anyone else.

And in casual, unremarkable moments such as this one, I'm gripped by the novel idea that the people around me actually *like me*, for some bizarre reason I'm still trying to figure out—if only so I don't mess it up and make them stop.

"That was *way* too close," Daisy says as a jingle ascends over the train speakers.

A pleasant, prerecorded female voice plays in the background, sounding throughout every coach. "Nü shi men, xian sheng men, huan ying nin cheng zuo gao tie dong che . . ." I don't even register that it's in Chinese at first because I'm shocked to find I actually understand what she's saying. *Ladies and gentlemen, welcome aboard the bullet train . . .* It's not the first time this has happened since I landed in Shanghai. It's as if something in the back of my brain has been unlocked, allowing the Chinese words floating around me to settle in.

"Unnecessarily close, might I add" Cyrus is saying. "Some buffer time would be nice."

We'd been right on schedule when we gathered down in the hotel lobby this afternoon, but then one of the sporty girls, Krystal, had to use the bathroom, and as if they were all biologically synced through the power of friendship, the other girls in her trio needed to go too. Then, just as we were about to head out, Sean had reported with the highest urgency that his phone was missing. The case was only closed when he thought to check his left coat pocket half an hour later, by which point Wang Laoshi had already helped conduct a thorough search of his room. And all of that could possibly *still* have been fine, because we'd budgeted for extra time, but then the bus had broken down halfway to the railway station.

"No, really. I'm not even exaggerating when I tell you that was the second most stressful experience I've ever had," Oliver says, rotating his seat in the row ahead so that it's facing me and Cyrus. Our group has taken up the front of the car: Daisy's curled up by the window next to Oliver, and Krystal's friends are lounging in the seats across the aisle, kicking their legs out on the footrests. It's surprisingly spacious inside, with more than enough room to walk up and down, and cleaner than I would expect any form of public transport to be—at least based on appearances. Even Cyrus looks only moderately disgusted as he sanitizes everything within a four-foot radius of him.

"The second most stressful experience?" I ask Oliver. "What was the first?"

"Other than being birthed into the world and just, like, general human existence? Probably when we had to shut down my father's winery in Australia because of the possum problem," Oliver says with a shudder. "The baby possums were having baby possums."

"Hey, I wouldn't mind keeping a baby possum as a pet," Daisy muses.

Oliver snorts. "Of course you wouldn't. I bet you'd even throw it a tea party."

"Sorry, are we meant to ignore the fact that your father owns a winery?" I demand, leaning back the same time the train eases forward, accelerating so smoothly and quietly that I don't even realize we've left the station until I see the trees flashing by the window.

"Fourteen wineries," Oliver clarifies. "But this winery was way bigger than the others. We were going to spend our summer break there last year, but after the possums took over, we had to change plans last minute and stay at one of our resorts in Sanya instead. Not even my favorite resort with the pony farm; just, like, a *regular* five-star resort. The sea views weren't bad though."

I stare at him as I digest this alarming information, and then press my fingers to my temple like I'm trying to remember something vital. "Oh my god, what is it called again?" I ask.

"The name of our winery?" Oliver says, confused.

"No, that word for when you feel bad for someone but also, at the same time, can't bring yourself to feel that sorry for them at all."

Cyrus releases a breath of laughter, then immediately hides it by pressing a fist to his lips.

"It's okay, you only need to feel *slightly* sorry for me," Oliver tells me, unbothered, and grins. "Just sorry enough to go out with me."

I raise my brows. Every time I let myself entertain the idea that Oliver and I could become actual friends, he'll say something like this, leaving me to try and figure out just how serious he's being, and whether he'll join the list of guys who stopped being nice to me the second they realized I wasn't going to hook up with them. It would be a serious shame, because despite his bad jokes and severely bourgeois tastes, Oliver Kang's kind of been growing on me. "Are you asking for a pity date?"

"I'll take whatever I can get. A pity date. A pity kiss—that's what you offered Cyrus, wasn't it?"

"Yeah, I don't really do those anymore," I inform him, with a meaningful glance at Cyrus, who's stopped laughing. "As you might be able to tell, it didn't end well the last time."

"It would be different with me," Oliver says, gesturing theatrically between us. "I can't be the only one who feels this connection we've got going on. As if our souls are bound together—"

"We barely know each other."

"We can get to know each other better right now," he says without missing a beat. "Like, for starters, what's your thing?"

"What's my *thing*?"

"You know, everyone has a thing." He shrugs and begins to point at the other members in the group, picking each of them out. "Lydia's thing is being smart and organized. Krystal's thing is volleyball. Sean's thing is—well, sleeping, and *forgetting he has pockets* . . ."

We all take a moment of silence as we remember the intensive search from earlier today.

"Daisy's thing is knitting—and probably also dancing in a field of sunshine or donating to charity or something," Oliver continues as Daisy pulls out a half-formed scarf from her bag, the pink wool unspooling over her lap, and starts finger-knitting. "And Cyrus's thing is being attractive in a cold vampire way."

Cyrus sends him a sharp, affronted look.

"What? You should be flattered," Oliver says. "Daisy, tell him I'm right."

Daisy lifts her head and nods. "Um, he's right. The vampire comparison is definitely a compliment."

"So what's your thing?" Oliver prompts.

All of them turn to me, and my thoughts nose-dive off a cliff. Because what *is* my thing? What am I meant to be? Without modeling, there's nothing special about me anymore. But that's the kind of thing you confess to your therapist after at least ten sessions together, not in the middle of a casual conversation. Plus, if I tell them the truth, they'll realize how unbearably boring I am, how my whole confident persona might as well be propped up by a few weak tentpoles, threatening to cave in under the slightest pressure.

I swallow, ignore the low, tumbling feeling in my gut, and—in an act of true desperation—glance out the window for ideas. There's not much to go off of. The sprawling compounds rush by in dark gray and brown blurs, the mountains curving in the horizon, their shapes softening with distance until it's difficult to tell where they blend in with the clouds . . . "Clouds," I say, before the silence can drag on long enough to become suspicious.

Oliver blinks. "Huh?"

Cyrus's brows furrow, and I feel my stomach twist nervously

in response. He's the only one here who knows enough about me to see straight through my lie. The only one who'd expect me to talk about modeling.

To stop him from questioning me outright, I rush to elaborate: "Cloud drawings, I mean." Like this is a very real hobby that real people most definitely have. "I just find that they're so peaceful, and there's so much you get out of drawing them. Like, artistically. And emotionally."

Cyrus stares at me for another beat, clearly trying to figure out where I'm going with this. I make myself stare back, cleanse my face of any panic, as if my palms aren't sticking to my skirt with sweat right now. *Don't say anything*, I will silently, drawing upon any mind-control powers that might be lurking dormant within me. *Don't ask about the modeling. Just accept that I love drawing clouds.*

"Remind me, what kind of clouds did you like drawing again?" Cyrus asks me, resting his chin on one hand.

This is so *not* the follow-up I was braced for, and I don't know whether to feel relieved or to start searching for the closest emergency exit on the train. Despite the utter nonchalance of his tone, there's a dangerous glint in his eyes.

I clear my throat. "Well, you know. High clouds, low clouds, medium clouds, semi-medium clouds, storm clouds..." Dammit, I'm running out of clouds. "I'm not picky."

"That's a real niche interest you've got there," Oliver comments good-naturedly, and for some reason, my relief at him buying my ridiculous lie is chased away by guilt. It'd be nice if I didn't have to choose between being myself and being liked.

"But she's *really* good at them," Cyrus jumps in, turning to smile at me. Abruptly, I remember that phrase my mom always says, one that never made sense until now: *Don't be afraid of a crying owl; it's the laughing owl you should fear.* I can handle Cyrus with his regular poker face and general air of suffering, but I have no idea what to do when Cyrus is smiling at me like that. "Leah, you have to show them your cloud drawings."

I freeze. "Oh, I mean—I didn't bring any with me. They're in my special cloud sketchbook—"

"You can draw them right here," Cyrus says, smiling still, his features positively angelic, concealing his diabolical schemes. It's middle school all over again. He just wants to see me make a complete fool of myself and laugh at my expense. "It's not like we'll be getting off this train anytime soon."

"But I don't have my art supplies," I counter, smiling back through clenched teeth. Never mind the dormant mind-control powers. I'd give anything for the power to kill with just my eyes.

"You can use this," Cyrus says at once, reaching into his bag and pulling out a black ballpoint pen with our last hotel's brand name on it. "And you can draw on my hand. I'd be honored."

I want to refuse, but Oliver's watching me with keen interest, like a child waiting to see a fireworks show for the first time.

Fighting the vicious urge to use the pen as a weapon, I snatch it from Cyrus and turn toward him. He extends his hand, his palm held open. He has the long, elegant fingers of a pianist, his skin smooth and so pale on the underside of his wrist that it's almost translucent, the purplish-blue veins as visible as creeks running through snow. I grab his arm to steady it against the movement of the train, my nails digging in with a little more force than necessary, but he doesn't flinch. Doesn't pull back. His attention remains sharp on me as I tighten my grip on the pen and press down, outlining the wobbly shape of a cloud in the center of his palm.

"There," I say. "Done."

Oliver and Daisy both peer over.

"That's so cute," Daisy says very generously, and I feel a sharp surge of affection for the girl. She's one of those people who is kind solely for the sake of being kind.

"It has personality," Oliver agrees. "Personal style is important when it comes to art."

Cyrus lifts his hand and stares down at the cloud for a long time, his lashes shadowing his eyes, focusing hard as if I've really drawn something worthy of critical analysis. Even his breathing seems to still. Then his fingers furl around the doodle. "Your art holds such potential," he tells me. "If you just added horns to it, you'd have a sheep."

If I just added horns to you, we'd have your true form, I can't help replying inside my head.

He glances past me as an attendant pushes a snack trolley down the aisle toward us, the wheels rumbling under the weight of all the bottled drinks and instant noodles. I immediately forget about him and perk up. It's only been a few hours since our last meal, but I still crane my neck to scan the trolley. This was one of my guilty pastimes when I'd force myself to go hungry for a shoot—I would stand in the middle of the grocery store aisle and simply browse through the shelves of ready-made cakes, imagining myself eating all the things I couldn't.

"You shenme xuyao de ma?" the attendant asks in Chinese, slowing down near our seats, and again, I'm surprised at how the words—which would've been a nonsensical jumble to me when I was in LA—actually clarify themselves inside my head, only because I've heard the words spoken by so many waiters and hotel staff by this point. *Is there anything you need?*

The top layer of the trolley is covered by an assortment of lemon iced tea, grape juice, and milk tea; the layer beneath it dedicated to beef jerky and sesame candy and the Choco Pies I used to crave all the time, with the soft white marshmallow filling and the crumbling cake layers.

I'm about to say yes, but Oliver turns away with a look of complete disinterest, and Daisy has already returned to her knitting. I bite my tongue, feeling stupidly self-conscious at being the only one so eager to try out a bunch of likely overpriced snacks.

Cyrus's gaze flickers in my direction, and then he tells the attendant something in Chinese. Apparently, he's asked to buy half the trolley, because she brightens and starts handing over a packet of almost every item, until Cyrus runs out of room on his lap and has to spread the mini mountain of snacks out on his tray.

"Here," Cyrus says, tossing one of the Choco Pies to me. He doesn't make any move to eat the food himself.

I stare at the pie, waiting for him to spring the trap. "What's this for?"

"You looked like you were ready to run away with those pies." He shrugs. "It would have been cruel to keep you apart."

"I was not—"

"It's the same way you were looking at the lettuce seller," he says. "There was a lot of intense squinting going on. I was expecting you to start twirling your hair and smiling unnaturally again."

I choose to ignore him as I tear open the red wrapper and take my first bite of the pie in years, the thin chocolate casing cracking under my teeth.

"This is *so* good," I say, closing my eyes with a blissful sigh.

Still, I can just imagine the look on Cyrus's face when he says, "Maybe I should give you two some time alone."

I take another slow, luxurious bite as if I'm one of those upper-class people partaking in a wine-tasting competition to prove how cultured my taste buds are, inhaling deeply and letting the marshmallow dissolve on my tongue. "You sound jealous."

"I definitely am."

"I can tell you've been single too long," I remark, matching his dry tone. "Just so we're clear, this isn't enough to get you a pity kiss from me either."

He goes quiet at that, and I feel a small thrill at having effectively shocked him into silence.

"But I *will* pay you back for the pie," I add, opening my eyes and dabbing the corner of my lips. "How much did it cost?"

"Three million yuan," he answers right away.

I stare at him. "Okay, I'll be honest: I always figured you'd become a scammer, but I didn't think it would happen quite so soon."

"You don't have to pay me back, Leah," he says, shaking his head. The train rattles through a tunnel, the darkness briefly transforming the window into a mirror, so I can see the reflection of his profile even with his face angled away from me, his gaze heavy and almost sad. "You don't owe me anything. You never will."

That must be why he's started being nice to me—or at least nicer, compared to before. Because while I've been discovering new Chinese words on this trip, Cyrus Sui has discovered a new little emotion called *guilt*.

Anger rushes down my throat, vicious and stronger than the taste of chocolate. He doesn't get to do this. He doesn't get to ruin my life and then attempt to assuage his conscience by offering me a few free snacks and vague sentences. Not after all those times I sobbed myself to sleep after I was expelled, all the dirty looks my classmates shot at me across the room, all the lunches I spent eating alone.

I don't care how guilty he feels. It'll never be enough, not without me getting my revenge.

It's almost midnight by the time we stagger into our new hotel in Anhui Province.

"I'm so tired I feel seasick, which doesn't make sense because we're on land," Oliver says with a groan, slouching against the side of the elevator, his head rested against the digital signage offering special discounts on massages. I would pay double the price for a massage right this moment.

"I'm so tired it sounds like someone's whistling off-tune in my ear," Sean complains.

"Oh, sorry—that was me," Lydia says, yawning. "I like to whistle to keep myself awake."

I'm so tired I don't have the strength to say anything. My eyes are almost as heavy as the bags weighing down on my shoulders, and my knees keep wobbling, even though I'm standing still. When the elevator arrives on the eleventh floor with a shrill *ding*, I'm ready to doze off in the middle of the corridor.

"Come on," Daisy says, tugging at my arm. She looks more alert than any of us. But then, I don't think I've ever seen her *not* alert before; it's like she's constantly braced for something to happen, even if she doesn't know what. "You can shower first."

I shake my head. Remember how to open my mouth. "You

always offer for me to shower first. You go. It takes thirty minutes just to blow-dry my hair."

We walk past countless identical doors, the sound of our rolling suitcases muffled by the maze-patterned carpet, until at last we reach our room. Daisy swipes our key card, the tiny light flashing green before letting us in, and I half drag, half kick my luggage through the entrance. I feel a little seasick too—or at least like I'm tipsy, the beige walls swaying around me. I seem to be moving on autopilot as I tug off my boots, grab a new bottle of water from the bedside table, downing half of it in a few gulps, and sink onto the couch by the balcony.

"I'll be quick," Daisy promises, pulling out her polka-dot bag of toiletries.

"No rush," I mumble. The cushions are so blissfully soft, the temperature pleasantly warm enough to forgo any blankets; maybe I could just sleep like this. Forget blow-drying my hair, or brushing my teeth. That can wait until morning—

But my eyes have barely fallen shut when Oliver's and Cyrus's voices travel from outside the room.

". . . think that *I* would want to marry you?"

"Obviously not—"

"Because I'm in very high demand, Cyrus. I shit you not, there are at least thirty people I can name who would *love* to be married to me. Hell, there was a literal prince who proposed to me when we were both only fifteen, and I was promised an extravagant wedding on a private island."

"That's hardly the point here—"

"No, but I feel like I need to make this clear to you. You shouldn't sound so disgusted—"

"You sounded disgusted too—"

"I was still *polite* about my disgust—"

I sit up, disoriented, and creep back over to the doorway. I remember hearing somewhere that exhaustion can produce vivid hallucinations, but even for a hallucination, this conversation is bizarre. Slowly, I push the door open and find Oliver and Cyrus standing apart in the dull yellow wash of the corridor, arms crossed, expressions tense.

"What's going on?" I ask, sticking my head out.

"They gave us the *honeymoon suite*," Oliver bursts out, his handsome features twisting in horror while I fight back the overwhelming urge to laugh. "It looks like Cupid hosted a massive party, got drunk, and threw up in there. Everything is all romantic and sensual. *Sensual*," he emphasizes with a shudder, like the word contains within it a whole realm of unspeakable horrors. "There are rose petals covering every surface. The towels are folded into the shape of hearts. And there's only one king-sized bed for the two of us. I need to sleep before my brain melts, and I can't—"

"So do I," Cyrus cuts in. "But your idea was terrible—"

"What's wrong with sleeping face-to-feet?" he demands. "Would you rather we fall asleep staring deep into each other's eyes, my dude?"

"I don't want your feet anywhere within a five-foot radius of my face," Cyrus says tightly.

"You see?" Oliver says to me, throwing his hands out like a defendant appealing to a jury. "This shit's impossible. And don't even get me started on that cursed bathroom wall—"

"It's made of glass," Cyrus says, also speaking to only me. "Pure glass. You can see everything on the other side of it. There might as well be no wall at all. The hotel simply doesn't seem to believe that newlywed couples would care for something as frivolous as privacy."

I've aborted any attempts to suppress my laughter by now—I double over, wheezing until my vision blurs with tears and the lines of the carpet start wobbling, my hysteria bubbling over my exhaustion.

Both of them stare at me, unamused.

"Sorry," I choke out, clutching at my stomach. "Sorry, guys. I mean, if you look at it as an opportunity to really understand each other on a deeper level . . ."

"I think we already understand each other well enough," Cyrus says. "In fact, I would argue that we understand each other a bit *too* well."

"So do I," Oliver tells me. "I could take a whole trivia quiz on him and ace it. Like how he's allergic to small talk, and refuses to drink anything except boiled water, and how he can't stop talking about you—"

Cyrus cuts him a look I'm unable to decipher, and Oliver goes quiet.

I sober up at once, leaning forward with a kind of morbid curiosity, my heart beating oddly in my chest. "He talks about me?" I ask. "What does he say? Bad stuff?" It must be. I mentally fill the sudden silence between the three of us with long lists of criticisms. Even though I've never hated myself, there are plenty of things I hate *about* myself, things I wish I could cover up with concealer like a stubborn blemish: my lazy streak, my vanity, my real laugh, my fake laugh, my inability to contribute anything interesting to a conversation, the one side of my face that's slightly wider than the other. Sometimes, it feels like I'm just waiting for other people to catch up on my flaws.

But then Oliver shakes his head. Clears his throat. "No, good stuff."

Surprise dances through me. My attention swings to Cyrus, but he's rooted to the spot, wearing such a brilliant poker face that he could win any game of cards.

"Like what?" I ask.

Oliver's gaze flickers to Cyrus as well, then back to me. "Yeah, uh, he'd kill me if I told you."

I wouldn't believe him. I wouldn't dare believe that Cyrus Sui—Number One Enemy from my childhood, Stealer of Scrunchies, Destroyer of Lives—could have anything nice to say about me to my face, let alone behind my back, except he isn't protesting outright.

Maybe it wasn't guilt alone that was making him act so weirdly nice to me, then. Maybe my plan's working already. Maybe he's actually started to like me.

"You know what?" Cyrus says abruptly, turning toward their honeymoon suite with more eagerness than even a real newlywed. "I've decided that I don't mind sleeping next to your feet, Oliver. Let's just go back inside."

"Oh, so *now* you have no problems with my feet—okay, bye, Leah," Oliver says in a rush as Cyrus seizes his elbow mid-sentence and starts guiding him away.

"Good night," Cyrus tells me without quite meeting my gaze.

Daisy's finished showering by the time I return to the room. I expect my body to call it a day and collapse on the couch again, but it feels like I've taken an extra-strong shot of espresso. All my nerves are buzzing, my mind zapped awake. It didn't mean so much to me in the moment, yet I keep going back to what Oliver said, turning it over, dissecting it:

He'd kill me if I told you.

I don't manage to fall asleep until four in the morning.

CHAPTER ELEVEN

It's a known natural phenomenon that whenever you're traveling, the rain is going to come on the day you least welcome it.

My hair is already frizzing aggressively from the damp as we gather at the foot of the Yellow Mountain. I push it back from my face for the eleventh time, blinking cold water out of my eyes. The rain isn't so heavy as to necessitate using an umbrella, but it's still heavy enough that it's wreathed the mountains in white fog and darkened the steep paths and sheer cliffs ahead of us. Even the pine trees are darker, their needle-thin leaves a shade of deep, clear green that probably predates human civilization, that might be one of the first colors to ever exist in the natural world. If it weren't for our backpacks and phones and the little flag Wang Laoshi's waving, I'd think that we had fallen through a fissure in time itself. There's an ancient beauty to everything here, from the stones that jut out like strange silhouettes in the distance to the birds calling out to one another from high in the clouds.

"The first to reach the mountaintop will be rewarded with a Michelin-star five-course meal for lunch today. You'll have your own private room and incredible views of the scenery," Wang Laoshi tells us.

"What will the rest of us get for lunch?" Oliver calls out over the rain.

"Granola bars," Wang Laoshi replies simply, which makes Oliver's eyes widen with true terror. "Now, while I'm all for the spirit of the competition, please do be careful not to slip, and look out for any falling debris . . ."

Nobody is really listening to this last part. The prospect of getting a hot meal *and* a reprieve from the rain is enough to motivate everyone to start moving. Cyrus and I are the first to rush forward, our feet pounding over the rocks.

"I see you've switched to sneakers today," Cyrus notes casually, climbing three steps at a time.

I fight a grimace as I hurry to match his strides, my calves burning from the effort. "Don't look at them too long."

"Why?"

"They're my ugly shoes."

He raises his brows. "You have designated ugly shoes?"

"I have a designated ugly everything," I tell him. "You should see my designated ugly pajamas—and by that, I mean, if you ever actually saw me in them, I'd have to bury you."

"Well, now I'm *really* curious. Though I doubt it's possible for anything to look ugly on you," he adds in the same offhand tone. He could be making a passing comment on the rain.

I stare at him. It feels like my body's internal system is malfunctioning, the wires in my brain whirring and overanalyzing those few simple words. My plan really must be working if he's handing out compliments now. But I'm still so unused to Cyrus being sweet to me that instead of responding, I stick to silence and climb onward, letting my attention drift to the dew glistening on the branches around me, the vaguely annoying pebble stuck in my shoe, anything but him.

Soon, we're so far ahead of everyone else that it feels like we're the only ones in the mountains, and by some kind of silent agreement, we both slow down, falling into step with each other.

"Can I ask you something?" Cyrus begins slowly, which ranks pretty high on the Ominous Ways to Start a Conversation List. It's second only to the dreaded *can you give me a call when you're free.*

"No," I say.

"Okay."

And he actually shuts up just like that. After a beat, I make a sound caught halfway between a snort and a sigh. "What is it?"

"Why didn't you tell the others that you're a model? Seems a lot easier than trying to pretend that you're a cloud enthusiast."

Even though I'd been more or less prepared for him to spring this question on me, my stomach judders. I do my best to focus on keeping my pace, keeping my breathing even as I reply, "How do you know I was pretending? Maybe I really am a cloud enthusiast."

"You're in luck, then," he says dryly, glancing up at the overcast sky, the thick sweep of gray settling in over the dark shine of rocks. "There are plenty of them today."

"I know. I'm thrilled."

"Visibly," he says, motioning to my face, which has probably reset itself into Ready to Kill You mode while I've been figuring out the quickest escape route from this conversation. When I don't reply, he adds, "I'm a bit surprised, that's all. If I were you, I'd be bragging about being a model any chance I got."

The truth scratches my throat. I take a deep breath. "Well, I'm not one anymore."

He whips toward me, almost misses his next step. "You're not?"

"I quit," I say. "About a month ago. Before the trip." It's more bearable this way, to get it out fast, get it over with. Whenever I was sick and my mom brewed me a cup of medicine, I would always choose to drink the bitter brown liquid in two large gulps as opposed to sipping it slowly, even if it made my eyes water.

"You quit? Why?"

I can't tell him the real reason, of course. Even just remembering the god-awful photo shoot—the supposedly *traditional* robes they forced me into, the bright red ribbons tangled around my bare arms, the harsh glare of the light as I posed for the camera like their perfect exotic model—makes my stomach turn.

"Everything was going really well until I had to do this photo shoot with a watermelon," I say mock seriously. "Bear in mind that I *hate* watermelon. It was fine at first, when they told me to pose by holding the watermelon above my head, even though the thing was, like, super heavy. Then they asked me to roll the watermelon like I was bowling, and they got pissed off when I said that it was impossible to hold it like a bowling ball, because there was nothing for me to grip, and then *I* got pissed off, so I decided that I was done, forever."

I see the exact moment when his expression slips into skepticism and then drops straight into disbelief. "Why did you feel the need to say all that?"

"What, you wanted a big story, didn't you?" I say, shrugging. "I don't have one that'll satisfy you, so I had to make something up."

He opens his mouth. Closes it. Opens it again. "Do you even hate watermelon?"

"Okay, that part's true." But I refuse to tell him why. Refuse to mention that it was the only thing I let myself eat when I was starving.

"Then what's the real reason?" he asks.

"I realized it was pointless," I say.

"What, modeling? Or life? Because I would agree—I just didn't think you were so nihilistic." He's studying me with the same intensity I've seen him wear when he's reading, like he's trying to decipher the meaning between the lines, like every word must count for something, hold some kind of weight. I don't think anyone has ever looked at me this way before. With other people, no matter how close I'm standing next to them, it feels like they're looking at me from a distance, and I'm only half there. But Cyrus's gaze pierces right through me, rooting me here, in the cold, thin air of the mountains and the soft spray of rain on my skin and the crevices in the stones underfoot.

"Everything I did was pointless," I say, shortening my strides as the mountain path cuts sharply up. "But it's all behind me now, so it's—"

"Leah, careful—"

I don't even have time to react when Cyrus pushes me to the side, the movement so sudden that my stomach swoops low, my back slamming against the trunk of a tree. It all happens in a disorienting flash of color and sound: the branches scraping my hair, the gray sky spinning above me, and Cyrus's body curving around mine, his hands firm on my shoulders. Rocks clatter sharply onto the path like shrapnel where I had been seconds before—where Cyrus stands now, facing me, taking the brunt of the impact. Yet he doesn't flinch once. Doesn't move away. Not until all the rock shards have finished falling from above.

My heart is thudding so hard I can feel the vibrations in my throat, my mind scrambling to process the facts. A fact, however improbable: *He pushed me to safety.* He shielded me, even though he had only half a second to react.

Another fact: He's injured. The edge of one of the rocks has scraped his wrist, leaving behind one long red line. Not quite deep enough to bleed, but enough to break skin.

"Are you okay?" he asks, his face bent toward me, his expression shrouded by shadows.

"Am *I* okay?" I echo, feeling as if part of me is stuck in another timeline, one that made infinitely more sense than this. "Yeah, I'm completely fine— But you—"

"Good," he says, his relief audible. His hands are still braced around me like he's scared I'll slip out of reach, and he leans closer, burying his head against the crook of my neck. His scent is stronger than the pine leaves hanging around us, or maybe I'm just more sensitive to it; all I can breathe in is the fragrance of sage. "Leah, I really . . . I really . . ." One of his hands lifts from my shoulder and braces itself against the bark of the tree behind me, his fingers clenching, nails sinking in, like it's the only thing holding him upright. His voice is hoarse. "I really . . ." He doesn't say more than that. It's as though he won't allow himself to, as though he's warring with himself on something, and to lose would cost him everything. He just repeats the words over and over, murmuring them until they're almost incomprehensible, a half-feverish jumble.

"What?" I whisper, my heart thudding faster, even though the danger is over. "Cyrus, what are you talking about?"

He steps back, and the phantom of whatever emotion had possessed him clears from his eyes. "I really—think you need to watch where you're going," he says, his voice almost normal again, save the tremor in his exhale. "Didn't you see the signs earlier? There are loose rocks everywhere, and if either of us gets killed via massive falling rock before we reach the mountaintop, we won't have a chance to win."

Of course that's what he cares about most. The rational side of my brain whirs back into action. *Winning. Securing his letter of recommendation for a spot at his dream university. His brilliant future, which involves only himself.* His concern just now had been more about the competition than me.

Still. Whatever his motivations, he *did* help me.

"Do you need something for that?" I ask, nodding at his arm. "I can head back and ask the teacher—"

"This?" He glances down to inspect the damage. "No, it's barely a scratch. Let's just keep climbing."

"You're sure you're not hurt?"

"Certain."

He says it so easily, so firmly. As firm as he'd sounded when the teacher had asked him a very similar question, two years ago: *Did someone hurt you?* But back then, there were dozens of students gathered around us on the staircase at our old school, watching with uniform expressions of shock and horror and outrage as Cyrus replied: *She did.* Two words, and I was deemed guilty. No matter how much I had protested—no matter how many times I tried to tell them the truth.

Only I knew what had really happened. I don't even remember what we were arguing about to begin with—something stupid and trivial, like all our arguments—but we were heading up the stairs from one class to another, and he was behind me, following me around as he always did to annoy me.

"Have you ever considered leaving me alone, Cyrus?" I had demanded, walking faster, taking two steps at a time in some attempt to put more distance between us. But his legs were just as long as mine, and he kept his pace without problem.

"No," he said. "It's too much fun watching you glare at me."

"When I glare at you, I'm imagining laser beams coming out of my eyes."

"See?" His voice was near my ear. "That's what makes it so fun."

"You're completely shameless," I muttered, hugging my books to my chest.

"I know."

I whipped around then, anger simmering in my throat. He looked so ridiculously pleased with himself, like infuriating me was a contest and he had just been crowned the ultimate victor. Then something fluttered out from the pages of my books. It was an ad of some kind for a lobster restaurant, printed on cheap pink paper. I only needed to take one glance at it to know who had put it there. "Are you serious? Now you're putting *trash* in my things for fun? Don't you have anything better to do?"

"The word *trash* is really subjective," he began, but I was sick of it already, sick of him. Everywhere I turned, he was there, ready to laugh at me, to pull another prank, to make my life unbearable. It was bad enough that none of the other kids really liked me, but at least they didn't go out of their way to torment me the way he did.

"Oh my god, just go, Cyrus," I snapped at him, stomping forward until we were face-to-face. He'd been unfairly blessed with another growth spurt over the summer, and he was one of the only boys in our class who was taller than me, even if it was just by an inch. "I *hate* you. I never want to see you again."

I braced myself for him to laugh in my face, because he never took anything seriously anyway, but he just blinked, frozen to the spot, something sharp flashing across his eyes like the edge of shattered glass. Then the bell rang, and he seemed a little dazed as he started to walk up the stairs again—but his feet slipped on the next step, and he stumbled. Instinctively, my hands shot out to help him, but it was too late.

Someone screamed as he fell from the top of the stairs. Their scream was so piercing that I thought he was already dead, and in my head I saw a sped-up reel of terrible images, the red-and-blue sirens of the ambulance, the puddles of blood, his parents sobbing outside the school gates.

Later, they all agreed it was a miracle that he hadn't broken any bones. He did have a concussion, but it took only two weeks for him to recover from the fall. It would take two years for me to fully recover from the fallout.

They also all agreed on this: I had pushed him.

Everyone there had witnessed it. Supposedly, we had been arguing, and in a blaze of rage, my arms had shot out to shove him down the flight of stairs. They spared no detail in describing the way my expression had twisted with fury, how I had hissed his name. Some claimed that I had insulted him outright by calling him *trash*.

It made sense to them, because of who I was.

You know that Leah girl? She was always a little weird, wasn't she? they whispered to one another in the corridors. *Didn't have a lot of friends. Wasn't really good at any of her subjects. Used to wear these hideous lumpy sweaters and invent dumb, childish games and go around nagging people to play them with her. An outcast. Nobody liked her much . . .*

They spun their own stories about why it happened. I was lovesick, obsessed with him; I'd been annoying him for years now, forcing him to hang out with me, and finally he'd stopped tolerating it and rejected me outright, and that's when I snapped.

The footage from the school's cheap security cameras only cemented my guilt. From their angle, all you could see was me marching up to him and moving forward right as he fell back. There was no other logical explanation for why Cyrus Sui had stumbled on those steps. He was one of the best students in our gym class. He never faltered, never lost his balance to something as silly as gravity; he couldn't have just *tripped* without some kind of trigger.

But none of that mattered as much as Cyrus himself accusing me of hurting him. Once the teachers heard his response, my fate was sealed.

My parents were the only ones who believed me. They defended me when the school claimed that I was violent, a threat to the other students. They comforted me when they found out that my expulsion would go straight into my records and raise the brows of any future admissions committees. My dad helped me throw out my old school uniform and began to search for a new school that would let me enroll in the middle of the year. My mom threatened to sue—the family legend goes that *I will sue* was the very first phrase she'd picked up after she immigrated to America—but even she had to admit the evidence was stacked against me, and by that point I just wanted to stop talking about it. Let my old life crumble off a cliff, let them whisper their lies behind my back. I knew I couldn't go back to that place again, not ever. My name would forever be inextricably tied to the Incident, to Cyrus, to a crime I hadn't committed. I promised myself I would never forgive him, even if he groveled at my feet.

I still refuse to forgive him, and yet—that was before the trip. Before this.

I stare at Cyrus as we pick our way up the stone steps, the familiar edges of his profile, and I think about how time is such a funny thing, running through the years like water, washing away some memories, buoying others up to the surface. But time shouldn't have the power to change someone completely, from the kind of person who would get me expelled on a false accusation to the kind of person who would protect me with their own body, bow their head the way he did, like the hurt lived inside him.

I might actually be turning into a cloud enthusiast.

The rain has settled at last by the time we reach the peak of the mountain, the sun streaming over the crags and boulders in dazzling beams of gold. A sea of clouds rolls out beneath our feet, whiter than smoke, thicker than mist, lapping against the mountain ranges. My cloud doodles couldn't possibly do it justice; it looks like the world's most gorgeous ink painting come to life, all those soft washes of blue and pale brushes of light.

There are always mountains beyond mountains, people above people, my mom would lament whenever she was in one of her philosophical moods, and I have to wonder if whoever invented the saying had been thinking of this specific place. When I squint out at the horizon, all I can see are the dark, grayish-green shapes of mountains, one outlined against the other, stretching on and on until I can't tell where the sky ends. The view is beautiful enough to distract me from the fact that we came in second. But the distraction doesn't last long.

"Damn, it feels like we're in heaven. In a non-biblical sense," Oliver remarks, standing much closer to the edge of the viewing platform than is advisable, the wind snatching at his shirt. Daisy, meanwhile, is shivering on the other side of the platform, her face white and eyes squeezed shut. "You should open your eyes, Daisy. You're missing some great views—it's not even *that* high up."

"No, thanks," Daisy squeaks out. "I think I prefer looking at the inside of my eyelids."

"Okay, how did you manage to get here before us?" I demand. "We never even saw you on the way up."

Oliver grins over his shoulder at me. "We took the cable car."

"You—" My mouth drops open as I exchange an incredulous look with Cyrus. "You did what?"

"Yeah, Wang Laoshi never said we had to get up here *by foot*, did he?" Oliver says, his smile sly. "You can't blame me for using the resources at my disposal. And you can't even accuse us of not challenging ourselves—you see these marks?" He rolls down his sleeve with a dramatic sigh, revealing four red, nail-sized crescents on the underside of his wrist. "Courtesy of Daisy. For a second back there, I thought she was secretly a werewolf."

"I'm sorry!" Daisy says in a small voice, her eyes still closed, though her complexion is more red than ashen now. "But you wouldn't stop moving around on the cable car—"

"She means I was breathing," Oliver tells us, deadpan. "I inhaled, and she told me to stay still because it was making her nervous. See? It was a *huge* challenge getting here." He pulls a puppy-dog face at me that's so ridiculous and aware of its own ridiculousness that it kind of works. "You're not going to report us to the teacher for being a bit creative, are you?"

"I guess not," I say. "I'm more annoyed we didn't think of it first."

"We *should* report you," Cyrus adds, his voice dead serious, yet I can tell he's not actually considering it. It's odd, because I'm used to people who are fake nice—or at least pretending to be nicer than they really are—in order to win you over. I don't trust most of Cate's friends for exactly that reason.

Yet Cyrus is fake mean, almost as if he wants to lower your expectations of him, to make sure you stay away.

More footsteps thud onto the platform behind us. The other teams drag themselves up one at a time; some are panting, rubbing the sweat from their foreheads despite the chilly air. Others clearly accepted defeat ages ago, and stopped for snacks on their way up. Sean is sharing a packet of prawn crackers with his teammate, both of them munching noisily and wiping their greasy fingers on their jackets.

While we wait for everyone to arrive, I spot a small, weathered fountain nestled just behind the pine trees. Fresh water trickles out from two stone statues of dragons, flowing through their open mouths and gathering in a clear pool underneath. The bottom is filled with shiny bronze and silver coins. As I watch, a young woman around my cousin's age pulls her boyfriend over to the fountain, smiling wide. He fishes a coin out from his pocket, clearly prepared for this very moment, and she clasps her fingers around it, eyes closed and head bent the way you do in prayer, then flings it into the water, where it lands with a faint splash.

"You think that's the same sacred fountain my cousin visited to bless her marriage?" I ask Cyrus.

He scans the area. "Well, it doesn't look like there's a *second* sacred fountain up here."

"Okay, give me a second." I pat my pockets for spare change. I only have one coin, but it's enough. Once the couple has left, I take their place by the edge of the fountain, feeling the smooth, cool surface of the coin against my palm. I've never really been the kind of person to visit temples or even to meditate, and as I force my eyes to close, mimicking the girl from earlier, I feel a spasm of self-consciousness, certain that I'm doing it wrong, that I look stupid, that I'm about to be made fun of. Sometimes it feels like there's an invisible comment section floating around in my brain, and with every mistake I make, every wrong thing I say, these imaginary spectators who vaguely resemble my classmates from my old schools flock forward to pass judgment . . .

Who does she think she is?

Why is she holding the coin like that? She's so weird.

She's closing her eyes? Who closes their eyes, except to sleep? I'm just embarrassed for her at this point.

Does she actually believe that praying to a fountain will do anything for her cousin's marriage?

Oh my god, look at her—she's so out of place. She literally has no idea what she's doing . . .

But then the seconds pass, and the rising wind drowns out the voices, and a strange sense of peace envelops me. It's like I'm suddenly aware of everything that exists outside my face and body: There's the air moving soft around me, pressing the silk of my shirt closer to my skin, and the steady trickle of water, and the patter of claws on stone, an animal slinking into the wilderness, the damp touch of dew, and when I breathe in it feels like I'm breathing for the first time in years.

Please, bless my cousin's marriage again, I pray, the Mandarin words coming slowly to me. *Undo whatever bad luck I might've accidentally cursed her with at the wedding.*

I'm still not wholeheartedly convinced that the fountain could help me with anything, or that the Mandarin words I chose were exactly the right ones, but I feel lighter as I let my coin sink into the water.

When I open my eyes, Cyrus is waiting behind me.

"I want to make a wish too," he explains, holding up a coin of his own.

"What are you wishing for? A glowing letter of recommendation from my aunt?"

He scoffs. "I don't need to *wish* for that. I'm going to make it happen."

"What's your wish, then?" I ask, more curious than taunting. What could Cyrus Sui possibly want in life? But he doesn't answer me, and I don't have a chance to pester him for more details. By the time he finishes with his wish, everyone's already gathered around on the platform.

"We're doing a team-building activity," Wang Laoshi announces, passing pens and paper around the group. "It's a tradition on this trip. You write an anonymous compliment to every person—"

"I've done this before," Lydia says excitedly.

I've done something like this before too at school, and I've never known how to react to the results. I'm sure the teachers mean to boost our self-esteem, but I could never stop myself from feeling along the edges of each compliment, like how you'd feel a dress to test for fake silk or frayed threads. And for every compliment I received, I could think of a way to discredit it.

You're so pretty—except they'd rescind it in seconds if they had any idea what I looked like before. Except so much of my beauty is an illusion produced by the right outfit and makeup. Except I'm never as pretty in motion.

You're so mysterious—except there's nothing really mysterious about me. It's just that I'm not very loud and open about the things I love, or I can't be sure of what I love in the first place.

But complimenting others is another story. It's so much easier to see their strengths, to speak about them sincerely, to say the things I'd be too shy to tell them out loud.

To Daisy, I write: *I know you don't consider yourself very brave, but I think you're one of the bravest people I've ever met—even if you're scared of something, you never let it stop you from doing it. I also just think you're really sweet and pretty and funny without trying, and I'm so glad the universe (or the admin team at Jiu Yin He) paired the two of us together for this trip. There's nobody else I'd rather share a fancy hotel bathroom with.*

To Oliver: *Your ego probably doesn't need this, but I have to admit that you're a lot of fun to be around, and that you're very sweet in surprising ways.*

When I get to Cyrus, I pause, my pen hovering over the paper. It seems unnecessary to write something snarky, though the temptation is there, a devil hovering over my shoulder as I chew the inside of my cheek. I ultimately settle for a casual note, neither sentimental nor taunting, simply: *Thanks for making sure I didn't get crushed by rocks back there.* Out of habit, I add a tiny heart after the sentence.

When everyone's straightened from using one another's backs as makeshift tables, we send our folded notes around and collect them in turn. I retreat to the shade to unfurl them, one by one. I'm expecting more of the same comments about how I look, because what else is there for other people to say? But the notes take me by surprise:

Your voice is so soothing—like, this is going to sound super weird, but I'd listen to an audiobook narrated by you.

I love how you always smile at everyone when you see them in the morning.

Okay, so tbh, when I first saw you I kind of expected you to be really bitchy and stuck-up . . . but you're actually incredibly thoughtful and humble and fun to be around? I'm REALLY, really sorry for ever assuming otherwise, and I hope we can be good friends!!

How are you so composed and elegant all the time?!

Then my breath catches on the next note. The ink is pressed thick in places, like the person had spent a few minutes too long deliberating over every word.

Leah. You remind me of the greatest sculptors, who can turn marble into the impression of billowing silk, the coldest stone into something soft. I suppose what I'm trying to say is that everything you touch turns beautiful. The world becomes beautiful, as long as there's you.

CHAPTER TWELVE

For the first time in a while, I wake up smiling.

I can still see yesterday's comments projected across the darkness of my eyelids. Feel them settling beneath my ribs, taking root and blossoming into warmth.

Your voice is soothing . . .

Thoughtful . . . Humble . . . Fun . . .

Everything you touch turns beautiful.

If I didn't know better, I'd think they were describing somebody else, but the compliments were written for *me*. Maybe—and it's a little easier, a little less embarrassing to let myself believe in the quiet of the hotel room, my blankets snug around my body—they're genuine. Maybe I've finally done it. Shed my past selves and emerged, skin raw and new, into a life where I could be happy and make real friends . . .

But then I open my eyes, and I realize something's wrong—mostly because I *can't* quite open them all the way. The skin around them feels swollen and tight, and as my head spins and the early-morning light drips in through the hotel curtains, the itch creeps in. And, with it, the beginnings of panic underneath my sternum.

I flip the blankets off my stomach and shuffle into the

bathroom, heart beating and blinking fast as the lights flicker on. Then I catch a glimpse of my reflection in the mirror, and I have to stifle a scream.

My hands fly to my mouth as if I'm in a tragicomic Shakespearean play: the skittish housewife who walks in on her husband kissing his decade-too-young mistress in their own bed.

Except this is infinitely worse.

A mosquito or some kind of demonic bug must have bitten me in the mountains yesterday, because there are two formidable, bright red bumps on my face—both smack in the middle of each of my eyelids, puffing them up like balloons. They're so inflamed that my features look like they've been put through a distorting filter. I haven't been this appalled by my own reflection since the days before my dramatic makeover.

"Oh my god," I whisper, touching a careful finger to my left eye, then my right, as if I can somehow wipe the hideous bumps away like a mascara stain. "Oh. My god."

"Leah?" Daisy's voice floats out from the other side of the bathroom door. "Are you brushing your teeth?"

I take a deep breath. Force my panic to stay put for a little longer, even as reality comes crashing in, all my old insecurities overriding my brief moment of peace this morning. The compliments from yesterday suddenly feel so insubstantial in comparison. "Yeah, I'm almost done—just give me a few minutes . . ." To think. To escape this hotel before anyone can see me. My eyes swing to my reflection again, half-hopeful that it might not be *as* bad from a certain distance or angle, but if anything, the bugbites only seem to be swelling up further, rendering my face nearly unrecognizable.

My stomach sinks. Even though I know that it's completely irrational and the world isn't going to end simply because I don't look super hot at present, I still have to fight the embarrassing, overwhelming urge to cry. It's the same as when Cate would post a group of us where I wasn't sucking in, or my smile was too stiff, or my hair was falling in the wrong way. That powerless, turned-inside-out feeling, the ever-present reminder that I'm not always pretty, that other, uglier versions of me exist, and nobody would ever want them.

Stop freaking out and think of solutions, I scold myself. *If not an emergency exit, then at least find a way to cover up your eyes—* which are itching so badly I'm tempted to scratch them out just to make it stop.

"Hey, um, Daisy?" I call out. "Do you have a pair of sunglasses I could borrow?" I should've brought my own pair, but I never usually wear them, because up until this morning, the lower half of my face was the weaker half.

"I'm so sorry—mine are broken," she calls back. "They fell just the other day when I was bending down to help this really sweet old woman pick up her apples . . ."

Of course that's something that would happen to her.

"Okay, that's—yeah, don't worry about it." I rub my eyes as hard as I can without damaging any vital nerves and sit down on the edge of the bathtub and try to think. As with any time I've been sick in the past, whether it was a mild sore throat or a stomachache or a scraped knee, the first person I want to call is my mom. Even if she can't give any proper medical advice, there's just something comforting about her telling me I'm okay, I'll get better, she'll look after me. But I'm too far away for that, and I remember the uncharacteristically enthusiastic voice messages she sent me yesterday night.

I spoke with your aunt today and she says she's heard some good things about your progress on the trip! Keep it up!

I'd hate to spoil her mood so soon, or admit that I'm almost considering skipping out on today's competition because the sight of my face disgusts me. No. I have to solve this on my own.

A few minutes later, I've come up with a less-than-ideal course of action. There's a mall just down the street from the hotel. If I can slip past Daisy and get to a store to buy myself a pair of sunglasses, then hurry back before everyone starts heading down for breakfast, I should be safe. After that, it'll be a matter of making sure the sunglasses stay plastered to my face until the bugbites go away.

I change quickly into the outfit I'd picked out for myself and left on the towel rack last night, zipping my jacket as high up as it'll allow and lowering the hood over my face. Then I slip through the bathroom door. I become a human shadow, the world's stealthiest spy, moving so fast across the room in three strides that I barely catch Daisy's words before I dash out into the hotel corridor.

"Leah, where are you—"

"Be right back," I yell over my shoulder in a rush. "You can get breakfast first."

I manage to make it all the way down to the lobby without bumping into anyone. But just as I'm about to flee toward the entrance, I catch sight of a familiar figure nestled in one of the plush sofas by the receptionist desk. He's reading. One leg crossed over the other, a metallic bookmark balanced between his fingertips as he flips the page slowly. He's always carrying a book with him, and never the same book twice. I glimpse the cover from a few feet away. It's a somber midnight blue, minimalistic, a translation of a Chinese text, judging from the title running down the center and the red-crowned cranes in the design. The kind of book that proclaims itself to be Very Serious—and by extension, whoever is holding it.

I try to muffle my next footsteps and slip around him, but I'm too late.

"What are you doing down here so early? And . . . why do you look like you're about to rob this hotel?"

My muscles bunch with dread. *God help me.* I consider acting like I haven't heard him, but Cyrus is already snapping his book shut and striding over toward me.

"What are *you* doing down here?" I ask before he can interrogate me any further.

"Oliver snores too loudly," he replies with a shrug. "Couldn't concentrate on the book up in our room."

"Or you didn't want to turn on the lights to read and wake him up, because as much as you hate to admit it, you're considerate like that," I counter. I can tell from the way his dark brows scrunch like I've just engaged in character assassination that I've guessed correctly.

"You still haven't answered my question, which leads me to believe that you *are* in fact about to commit a robbery—if so, all I ask is that you give me advance warning to avoid becoming an eyewitness. And if not, then you're hiding something," he says.

My gut tightens, a thousand flimsy lies falling apart inside my head before they can even reach my lips. *Screw Cyrus and his incredible observational skills.* When I don't reply, he takes a step closer and has the audacity to reach for my hood—

"Stop it," I hiss. The elevator rattles open behind me, and as the sound of English cascades toward us, panic erupts in my stomach. Desperate, I seize Cyrus by the arm and drag him around the closest corner with me. It's the only spot in the lobby that's empty—there's just a stall selling overpriced antiques that even the owner must have given up on. Nobody seems to have bothered dusting the shelves in months.

"Wow, this is all, like, really suspicious," Cyrus remarks. "Are you . . . hiding *drugs* under that hood or—"

"I got bitten by something, happy?" I tell him, twisting my head away from him.

"What? Is it poisonous?"

I freeze. Honestly, I'd been so worried about how the bumps

look that I hadn't even given thought to the actual medical implications. As if determined to validate my new fear, the itching in my eyelids intensifies to an unbearable degree. "I mean, I hope not," I say, keeping my tone as breezy as possible while I clench my fist tight to stop myself from clawing at the (possibly lethal, but whatever) bites. "I was just on my way to buy . . ."

"Medicine?"

"No. Sunglasses."

He takes a moment to digest this. "Okay. Okay, I'll judge you for that later—let me take a look first. I brought a few different creams with me in case of emergencies—"

I lurch back as far away from him as I can without knocking over a million-dollar porcelain vase from the Tang dynasty. "That's super generous of you to offer, but I'm not taking this hood off."

"Leah," he says, regarding me with what could either be affection or exasperation, as if we're playing hide-and-seek the way we used to as kids, and I'm still crouching in the corner after he's obviously already spotted me. "Come on. I promise I won't laugh."

"Oh, I don't think you're going to *laugh*." I tug my hood even lower. "I think you're going to run screaming."

"That's not going to happen. Really, Leah," he says, gentler, more serious. "At least let me look at it to ascertain that you're not dying."

"But I look so ugly right now," I whisper, my skin burning.

"Impossible," he says firmly.

It's the kind of thing any girl would dream of hearing, but it's useless, because it isn't true. I shake my head. "Don't make such bold declarations when you haven't seen my face yet."

"It's still the same face, and I've seen your face a hundred times before," he says, unfazed. "I know what you look like."

And the strange, mortifying, incredible thing is that he does. He knows what I look like with my hair styled and my lashes curled, my skin glowing from the dozen different serums I slather on at night. But he also knows what I look like from the Before times, when I would show up at school in haphazard pigtails and braces and baggy, garish shirts that would've gotten me banned from the parties I was invited to at sixteen. He knows what I look like angry, shouting across the school's oval; dozing off in the middle of class, my nose pressed against my textbooks; triumphant, eyes blazing, at the top of the world, and crawling home in defeat; sobbing and laughing until I can't breathe; hopeful, humiliated, happy. He's the only person on this trip—no, the only person I know, other than my own parents—who's seen every single form I've shape-shifted through in the past few years. He knows, and right now, it's more of a relief than anything.

I swallow. This time, when he reaches for my hood, I let him slide it back down over my head. To his credit, he doesn't laugh or scream. His expression remains subdued as his gaze roams over my face, and I wrestle away any impulse to cover myself up again, to scrutinize my own reflection in the darkness of his eyes. A beat of silence passes between us.

"Looks like a pretty typical mosquito bite," he says finally. "I'll get the cream from my room—and sunglasses—for you," he adds, the corners of his lips twitching.

"Really?"

"Yeah. Just give me a minute to run up, okay?"

All I manage to do is nod. While I wait for him in the abandoned mini museum, my hood fastened tight around my swollen face again, doubt creeps into the corners of my mind. What if this is another prank? What if he comes back not with sunglasses, but with a group of people from our trip, so they can gather around and laugh at me? It's exactly what the kids at my old schools would have done.

My heart thrums uneasily, the tension rippling down to my stomach. Maybe I should just make a run for it before he returns. Buy my own cream and my own sunglasses . . . I glance out in the direction of the lobby entrance. I have some time; I could escape if I hurried—

"Here you go."

Cyrus appears around the corner, alone, a pair of sunglasses and small white tube in his hand, extended out toward me. Just as he promised.

"What?" He laughs quietly as I take the sunglasses first, my movements slow, cautious. I'm reminded of this documentary I once watched of this horse whisperer approaching a wild mare;

he'd held out an apple and stayed very still, the way Cyrus is now, afraid to scare the creature away. "Why are you staring at me like that?"

"No reason," I say as I push the sunglasses up the bridge of my nose, still on the alert for the catch, the fine print, the open-trapdoor moment that's surely going to teach me a lesson for trusting him, but nothing comes. And I'm struck by the growing evidence that I might have been wrong before. This whole *being kind to me* thing isn't a ploy, a demonic scheme to ruin my life a second time. Cyrus Sui might not have any ulterior motive at all. As impossible as it sounds, as painful as it is to admit . . . he might actually, simply be offering me kindness because he wants to.

Cyrus grins all of a sudden, like he can't help himself. "Hey, my sunglasses look good on you."

I turn my head a fraction and see myself in the glass display. The sunglasses are bigger than anything I would've picked out for myself, the frames a little on the thicker side, the color solid black, more functional than fashionable. But privately, I like the way they look too.

CHAPTER THIRTEEN

In Shanghai, everything felt like it was sped-up.

The crowds streaming out of the subway station at five-minute intervals, swiping through emails or talking rapidly on their phones. The delivery workers rushing down the streets to drop off their next order while the food was still steaming hot. The baristas snatching empty cups from the marble counters and filling them up in a single streamlined movement. Even the elevators in our hotel were shockingly fast, the doors dinging open almost the instant you pressed the button.

That relentless rhythm eased slightly in Anhui, but when we travel from Huangshan City to Guilin, everything slows all the way back down.

There's time to stroll along the emerald banks of the rivers, to watch the cormorants soar leisurely over the karst mountains, to buy cool sugarcane juice from the spread-out stalls and shop for jade earrings. Time for the medicine Cyrus gave me to kick in, and for the swelling around my eyes to fade; by the third day, I don't really *need* his sunglasses to hide my face anymore, though I keep them on for a day longer.

The competition reaches a lull too, and it's nice just to wander through the trees and go rafting without having to worry about winning anything.

On our way down to the bamboo rafts, an old woman approaches us with flower crowns hanging around her arm. She's not the first person I've seen selling them, and most people in our group walk right past her, but I slow my steps. The crowns are beautifully woven by hand, with bursts of yellow daisies and waxflowers and camellias.

"We'll take one," Cyrus says, passing her the money.

I turn to him in surprise. "I was just looking."

"I know," he tells me, and takes his time choosing the crown with the brightest, fullest flowers, before setting it down gently on my head like this is my coronation. "My grandmother used to sell these for a living before we moved to America. It's a tough business. I would've bought myself one," he adds, following me to the edge of the water, "but I think it looks better on you."

"You have to stop being so nice to me," I tell him as I climb onto the raft, one hand holding the flower crown in place, the other grabbing the back of the bamboo chair for support.

He hops on after me, sitting gracefully down on my left. "Why?"

Because then I might not want to be enemies with you anymore, I answer silently inside my head. *Because then it's going to be much harder to go through with my plan, when everything I've done so far is to get my revenge.* "I'm not used to it."

Something shifts over his features, like the sunlight rippling off the Li River. "What are you used to, then?"

"You know. Being childhood enemies."

His smile feels like a warning, but it's not the kind that precedes a prank. It's too sincere, his voice dropping low as he says, "I'll keep being your enemy, if that's what you'd prefer." His eyes drop down too, drifting to my lips with such weight and intent that I can almost feel the ghost brush of his gaze. "I can be whatever you want me to be."

Our raft lurches off the shore, and I can't tell if the swooping in my stomach is from the rocking motion of the waters as we drift downstream, or from the way his words settle inside me.

Bamboos lean their bodies out from either side of us, their leaves skimming the surface, and the river is so clear it resembles liquid glass, reflecting all the other rafts up ahead, their shapes merging together at the edges. I can see Oliver and Daisy laughing over something; two of the girls risking everything to snap pictures, shrieking when their fingers slip and their phones almost tumble into the water; Sean leaning against his teammate's shoulder, both of them staring out at the scenery as if mesmerized.

When joy arrives, it catches me off guard.

It sneaks up slowly through my rib cage like poppies pushing through soil after the rain, and then it's there, everywhere, warmth beating in my chest, spreading down to my fingertips as I sink back in the sunlight. It's like I'm thawing. I've always been used to happiness in snatches—happiness that felt stolen, happiness that was hard-won, happiness *because*. I was only happy when someone said I was pretty, when I booked a new job, when a stranger approved of me, and then I would go home and feel the happiness seep out again, leaving behind a hollow pit in my chest.

This happiness though—it's new. It stays without asking for permission. It simply exists, like the water and the sky.

"What are you smiling at?" Cyrus asks me.

Nothing, I want to say. *Everything*.

I just shake my head, the breeze flowing past me with the river. In my peripheral vision, I can see the sun lighting up wild strands of my hair, turning it a brilliant fire-gold.

When I agreed to the trip, all I'd wanted was to run away: from the threat of the future, from everyone who expected something more from me, from the grave in my backyard where my potential had been buried, from the sadness that had leaked through my bedroom walls.

But this doesn't feel like I'm escaping—it feels like I'm returning. Like I'm reaching back in time for the person I used to be, before the tears stained my pillow and the blisters split my feet. The little girl who didn't wince at the sound of her own laughter, who plucked wild daisies and braided them in her hair, who saw a secluded garden and imagined hidden realms, who wore sparkly tiaras and waved around heart-shaped wands, picked out dresses because she loved the color pink and not just because she liked how the material clung to her body. The girl I was, the girl I had forgotten. Not an ignorant foreigner, but someone wandering through new, familiar cities.

I'm here, I think to myself again, yet what I really mean is: *I'm home.*

The longer I stay in this country, the more words I collect.

It happens naturally, as if they've been hidden in the corners of my mind this whole time, waiting for me to brush away the dust. I'm staring out at the mountains beyond the city, their highest peaks painted indigo and softening with distance, when I remember the character *shan*, followed by the characters for *rivers* and *lakes*. When a stray dog comes bounding up to us in the streets and I crouch down to stroke the soft, dappled fur on its belly, the word *keai* forms on my lips, containing within it the same character for love. I learn how to say *tao yan*, for "annoying," when Cyrus bumps against my shoulders on the escalator or steals the mango jelly from my bag at lunch, and I say it to him so often that soon it's as familiar to me as his name. I learn how to pay by *zhifu*, with a tap of the phone, and how to ask for more space by shouting *rang yi rang* in every crowd, and how to ask for more time. I learn the difference between *hai shui*, for "seawater," and *he shui*, for "drinking water," when I accidentally ask for the former at a restaurant and the waitress offers me nothing but a bewildered look in response. I learn that *shui* itself can be used as an insult, but only if there's too much of it. I learn plenty of insults and curses, thanks to the boys at the back of the bus. Under Oliver's unwanted influence, I learn a dozen pickup lines, all of which are so nauseating I do my best to forget them immediately after.

The word *guimi*—"best friend"—unfurls in my mind one evening while Daisy and I are making friendship bracelets on the carpeted floor of our hotel room, the shiny beads she'd bought at the market scattered between us. The word *kaixin*—"happiness"—trickles sweetly down my throat like the snow pear and rock sugar soup we were given for breakfast during our last day in Anhui.

And the word *mei*, for "beautiful," finds its way to me as we wander deeper and deeper into a bamboo forest. It's the kind of beautiful that sneaks up on you. One moment we're batting away leaves from the overgrown shrubbery, grumbling about the wet grass and the mud and the steep, uneven paths, and the next moment I gaze up and my breath catches. The late-afternoon light prickles through the foliage, and thousands of bamboos curve elegantly forward over a lake, their reflections blurred and distorted like watercolor. The lake itself is such a vivid, crystal blue it hardly seems real.

It feels like a scene straight out of the wuxia films my dad loves to watch after work. It wouldn't even surprise me if someone in billowing robes were to leap out from the clouds right now, sword swishing in hand; this place seems made for assassins and empresses and heroes from legends.

"You'll each be given an instant camera for the next activity,"

Wang Laoshi tells us, speaking at only half his usual volume, like he doesn't want to disrupt the peace. He sets his duffel bag down on the forest floor and begins unpacking the cameras, passing them from one person to another. "Feel free to wander around and take photos, but don't walk too far from the group. We'll all meet back here in . . ." He glances at his watch. "Let's say an hour. Once you're done, you and your teammate will need to pick out five photos to submit to me by tomorrow morning. The team with the best photo will win—and they'll get to keep their instant cameras as the prize. Got it?"

Quick, eager nods from the group. Compared to all the contests so far, this one actually sounds pretty relaxing—or at least there doesn't seem to be a significant risk of tumbling off a cliff.

The second Oliver gets his camera, he holds it up and turns it around to take a selfie. There's a soft whirring sound as the photo rolls out.

"What?" he says when he catches everyone staring at him, our judgment pronounced in the silence. Wang Laoshi appears one impulsive move and forgotten Teacher's Code of Conduct away from snatching the camera back.

"There must've been a gross misunderstanding—I don't believe the teacher was asking for photos of *you*," Cyrus says, voice flat. He's grabbed two cameras, and without a word, he walks over to me and presses one of them into my hand. "It's meant to be a photography contest. A form of art."

"My face *is* art," Oliver counters without missing a beat,

shaking the photo in the air. "It deserves critical acclaim. Don't you agree?"

Cyrus's brows rise. "Well—"

"I wasn't asking you; I was asking Leah." Oliver turns to me. "Don't *you* think my face is art?"

I search between them for the best response, my eyes flicking from Cyrus's unimpressed scowl to Oliver's expectant grin. "Art is subjective," I say diplomatically.

"So: no," Cyrus tells him.

"So: yes," Oliver says, and moves closer, his white sneakers crunching over the fallen leaves. When he's only a foot away, he lowers his head a little and winks at me. "Feel free to take a closer look if you aren't convinced."

I hold up my camera to block the space between us. "You're getting in the way of my shot, Oliver."

"You wound me." He presses both hands to his chest and gasps, as if he's really suffering from a fatal strike to the heart. "Does our love mean nothing to you? Don't you know how I feel about you?"

I snort as if he's just told a horrible joke—and it might just be that, but sometimes I find it hard to tell with Oliver. Is he flirting out of habit or boredom, or is there a chance he actually likes me? "Are you sure you're talking to the right person?"

"Certain. As certain as I am that we'd be great together. I mean, I'm hot, you're hot. Can you think of a single reason why we shouldn't—" He cuts himself off, his eyes widening at something behind me. I whirl around, but all I see is Cyrus, whose expression is perfectly neutral. "Just kidding," Oliver says in a rush, backing up so fast he almost crashes into one of the bamboos. "That was a really stupid thing to say. I'm, uh, going to continue taking pictures of my face now. See you two around."

"What was that?" I mutter to Cyrus, watching in bemusement as Oliver runs off to the other side of the clearing like he's being chased by a wolf.

"A rare moment of self-awareness, perhaps," Cyrus says with a shrug.

"Maybe," I say, raising the camera higher and squinting into the viewfinder. My experience with photography has always been limited to other people taking photos of me, telling me where to go, how to stand, how to be prettier, suck in, breathe out, stare to the side, laugh without laughing too hard, stop holding back your laughter, stop, stay still. It's a strange relief, in a way, to be totally in control for once, to see the world inside the lens without worrying how the world might see me. I snap a photo of the bamboos kissing the lake's glowing aquamarine edge, the lone pavilion waiting across the waters, a sparrow soaring through the brilliant blue of the sky at the perfect time, and slide the developed film into my pocket.

Then, as I'm adjusting the composition of my next shot, Cyrus moves into the frame.

He's straightening the collar of his jacket, even though his outfit is already perfect, not a single wrinkle to be found, and he's focused on something in the trees. His eyes are luminous under the long silk strands of his hair, so bright they could make the stars feel insecure, his mouth soft and sullen, the sharp angles of his profile stark against the deep, perennial greens of the forest. Another kind of beautiful that sneaks up on you.

I don't mean to take the photo. Or maybe I do. Maybe I want to collect this moment the way I've been collecting words throughout the trip, in case I might need it again.

I make sure to walk out of his line of sight, the photo pressed warm between my palm and my shirt like a secret, my heart beating unsteadily, before I let myself study it. The hazy, vintage quality of the instant film makes him look even more dreamlike, his hair even darker, his skin even softer and impossibly flawless. And while I doubt Oliver's selfies could ever pass for *art*, it doesn't seem so ridiculous at all to call the photo of Cyrus exactly that.

Art.

You're meant to be taking photos of nature, I remind myself, tucking the photo deep into my other pocket, knowing I'll never show it to anyone else. *Focus on the contest. If you lose this one too, you're never going to be able to fully prove to your aunt how much you've changed.*

But as I scan my surroundings, I quickly realize that everyone's photos are going to turn out very similar. They're meandering around the same few trees, their cameras pointed toward the bamboo leaves or the wildflowers growing on the banks of the lake. If I want my photos to stand out, I need to get a little more creative than that. I need to go somewhere higher, with a clearer view of the forest.

So I follow the stone steps leading up the mountain, taking two at a time. It's not long before I lose sight of the group amid the dense greenery, but I can still hear their footsteps and voices somewhere down below. They probably won't even notice I've wandered off. I keep walking, my camera out and ready, stopping every few feet or so to take a photo. The more I climb, the rougher the path becomes, twisting up and down, the blocks of stone fading into the dirt or strewn sporadically along a slope, like the people in charge of construction ran out of materials halfway through the process. In some places, the steps come to an abrupt stop, leaving me to pick my way alone through the grass, my muscles burning, sweat prickling my hairline. I have to focus most of my energy simply on not slipping.

And then I notice the silence.

I freeze, straining my ears for the sound of Oliver's loud, obnoxious laughter or Wang Laoshi scolding someone in the group for bringing too many snacks. Yet the only thing I can hear now is my own heartbeat, thudding faster and faster in my eardrums.

"It's okay," I tell myself out loud. I'd thought my voice would help steady me, clear away any fear, but it comes out small and hollow and uncertain, lost to the cool mountain air. *I couldn't have gone that far*, I finish inside my head.

But when I try to retrace my steps down the mountain, my

feet falter. I don't remember the paths branching out on the climb up. There aren't any signs to help me determine where I should go, which path will take me back and which one will only take me farther away from the group.

Suddenly, the forest feels too vast, too deep. All the bamboos look identical, and there are thousands and thousands of them, towering over my head and expanding endlessly in every direction.

The beginnings of panic buzz along my scalp with the high frequency of a fire alarm.

It's like taking a multiple-choice test, and I've never been good at those. I would always choose one of the answers at random, then doubt myself and change it, then wait ten minutes and come back to it, and change it to my original answer again. *Make an educated guess if you're stuck*, the teachers would say, but that was on the bold assumption I was educated enough to make one. Compared to algebra, I'm even less educated on the subject of navigating one's way around a forest alone.

After hesitating for a solid minute, I choose the path farthest on the left, a vaguely remembered poem about roads in a yellow wood playing over and over in my head. It's the sort of thing I'm sure Cyrus has memorized.

And at first, I'm hopeful that I've made the right choice—the path winds slowly down, and the bamboos appear to thin, offering glimpses of blue that could be the sky or the lake. But the path makes a sharp twist up again, then disappears entirely, and my stomach plummets as I find myself trapped in a labyrinth of trees. Shadows stretch out from all around me, darkening and sharpening their claws as the sun sinks behind the mountain.

I swivel my head to the left and right in desperation, but I can't even see where the steps are anymore. This part of the forest has been left to sprawl into complete wilderness.

Panic scrabbles deeper in my gut until it unearths raw, teeth-chattering fear.

Don't panic, think, I advise myself. *You still have your phone on you, right?* If I can't reach the group, then maybe they can reach me. Yes, it would mean confessing that I made the incredibly stupid mistake of wandering off by myself without telling anyone, and that I made the even more stupid mistake of walking in the wrong direction. Yes, I might disintegrate from embarrassment and never show my face to anyone in the group again. But I suppose it's better than dying by starving or freezing in a forest. The air is already noticeably colder, the day's warmth leaking out through the leaves.

I yank my sleeves farther down my wrists and pull out my phone, squinting at the dim screen. There's only one pathetic bar of signal, and it keeps appearing and disappearing like it's planning to abandon me at any moment.

Then I notice the missed calls. Seventeen of them, all from Cyrus. I don't even have time to think. I call him back at once—or try to. The reception is so flimsy that it takes three tries before the line actually connects. My fingers tremble as I press the phone to my ear.

"Leah? Where—are you?"

At the sound of his voice—so familiar, despite the static cutting into the line—an unexpected rush of emotion fills my throat. I clear it before speaking. "I think I'm lost," I tell him.

I wait for him to scoff or laugh at me or question my common sense.

But there's only a second of silence, like he's drawing in a breath. "Okay. I'll let Wang—know right—" The line won't stop glitching, his sentences fading in and out of focus, leaving me to piece his fragmented words together. ". . . and we'll figure—out. You can't be—far away if you—mobile reception—can you . . . hear—"

"Sort of," I say. "Not very well. And I don't know if I'll have a signal for long."

". . . any significant markers—can see?"

"I don't know." I scan the area, trying to identify something from all the yards of deep greens and burnt browns. "There are a lot of trees . . . There's also a . . . a rock behind me that I'm pretty sure I passed earlier—"

"Not as helpful as—was hoping." Even though half his words come out pixelated through the speaker, his sarcasm is as pronounced as if he were standing right next to me. I can practically picture him, his arms crossed, his head cocked to the side.

"Well, I'm sorry there are no giant neon arrows pointing to my head here, but it's a *forest*, Cyrus," I say, exasperated. "Its main characteristic is that it has trees."

"Describe—the rock—then . . . Be specific . . ."

"Describe the rock?" My brows furrow as I turn toward it. If the situation weren't so dire, I'd think he was playing a prank on me. "It's pretty square, as far as rocks go. About the size of Prada's straw tote bag from last season. When you stare at it from a certain angle, the surface looks shockingly like the face of a sloth."

It's hard to tell if the heavy static crackling through the phone is from the patchy reception, or just from him sighing. "Please never—get lost again."

"I have no plans to," I reassure him. "But, like, what am I supposed to do now? Describe more rocks to you?"

"Stay there. I'll come find you—"

And then the line breaks.

"Hello? Cyrus?" Cursing, I start to call him again, but the signal's gone. No matter how I angle my phone, the sign in the corner remains frozen at No Service.

Stay there, Cyrus told me. I couldn't go anywhere else if I wanted to. Now that the cold really has set in, it has a way of amplifying every ache: the painful blisters splitting open on my heel, the sharp stitch knotting my side, the cramps squeezing my muscles. So I stay standing, too exhausted to do anything productive, too alert to rest. Every hiss of the leaves or tap of the branches makes my heart startle, then sprint faster. And as the last rays of sun wash away, doubt slithers in, twisting into my gut. What if a bear or a snake or a poisonous spider attacks me before anyone comes?

In my head, the news headlines are already writing themselves: *Teen girl goes missing on trip in Guilin. Former model disappears in bamboo forest. Three-day search for high school student continues.* The local news will interview my parents, my classmates from school. *Of course we had no idea something like this would happen—we just thought it would be a fun educational trip to help her improve her Chinese,* my mom will whisper, wiping at her eyes. There might be a comment from Cate, a deep, moving tribute to our years of friendship: *I guess I liked going shopping with her.* They'll all say that I had a bright future ahead of me, since they don't know any better. If I end up dying in a horrific enough way, maybe someone will even make a documentary about me. Getting invited to a movie premiere has been on Cate's very public bucket list for years, right after kissing a royal, and I'm sure she wouldn't mind if the movie happened to be about my disappearance.

I squeeze my eyes shut against that particular depressing thought, but when I open them again, it barely makes any difference—it's as if the sky has closed its eyes too. Darkness falls over everything, sparing no inch of ground. I've never been bothered by the dark before, but I'm realizing that's just because it was never truly dark in the city. There would be the soft blue glow of my alarm clock on my bedside table, or the headlights of a passing car filtering through the curtains, or the blink of the security alarm from the ceiling, or the neighbor's porch light automatically flickering on when they returned home.

Nothing like this.

I rely on the flashlight on my phone to fend off the darkness until it drains nearly all of my battery. And then I'm rendered defenseless, shivering in the cold. My last remaining comfort is Cyrus's words, echoing through my thoughts. *I'll come find you.* It shouldn't bring me much comfort at all, given his record of getting me in trouble versus getting me out of it. But somehow, he sounded like he meant what he said. Like he was prepared to crawl from one end of the forest to the other if he had to, and if I were stranded in the ocean, he would swim through the icy depths just to search for me and carry me back to shore by himself.

So I swallow the lump in my throat, pray all the wild animals out here have an aversion to human flesh, and I wait.

CHAPTER FOURTEEN

At first I think I'm imagining it.

The soft hiss through grass. I've imagined plenty of things already, stranded here in the dark; the whisper of voices or the sound of footsteps approaching, only to look up and find nobody there.

Maybe it's just wind, I think hopefully, helplessly, even as the hissing grows louder, more distinct than anything my brain could create on its own. *God, please let it just be wind.*

But then the grass rustles, and a long, dim shape slithers closer toward me, and everything in my body boils down into one silent scream. I'm frozen, which feels almost ironic because my heart has never moved so violently inside my chest before, pushing against my rib cage like it's struggling to break free. Pure, raw fear cuts through my core as the snake stops within a few bare feet of me. A terrible mass of black scales and cold, empty eyes, its body so long I can't see where its tail ends. If I run, it might strike. If I stay, it might strike too. Every possibility seems to lead to the same horrific outcome: snake fangs piercing through my flesh, my body cold before they can find me.

They always say that your life flashes before your eyes right before you die. I'd figured that they meant the highlights: birthday parties and major coming-of-age events and rite of passages, like kissing your crush or learning to drive or the snowy Christmas you spent with your family at a cabin in the woods.

But the memories that flicker to life in my mind have no logic behind them, just a fast, confusing blur of moments I thought I'd forgotten, hurtling forward to the present . . .

History class at the second school I transferred to. A girl's called up to write something on the board, and as she brushes past my seat, her bony elbow rams into my side, hard enough to bruise. I flinch back, more from shock than pain. Oops, sorry, *she says, but I can see in the cold lines of her face that she's not, that she's been waiting for the opportunity to do this, that she's heard the rumors already. Bile fills my mouth. I pretend nothing happened—*

That's her, *they whisper at lunch. I stab my fork through the soggy spinach in my bowl without lifting it, hide my face behind the black veil of my hair. I just have to make it through these next ten minutes. My lips quiver. And then the next ten. And the next ten. Then it'll be class, and then school will be over at last, and then—*

Everyone's gathered around the table, laughing so loudly that the paintings left on the drying rack quiver. My stomach turns when I see what they're laughing at. The clay dragon figurine I'd made during our last pottery class. I'd been so proud of it, so happy while I was making it, but now all I can see is how crooked the figurine's head is, how comically large the eyes are—

Cyrus holding my lunch high over his head in the playground. Give that to me, I snap, but he just grins, black eyes glinting, and steps back, out of reach—

Cyrus chasing me across the oval, the warm, momentary press of his palm between my shoulder blades. Tag. You're it. I run after him, but the grass is still wet from the rain yesterday, and my feet slip—

Cyrus reading in the bus seat next to me, only a few days ago. He arrives at a line that makes him pause, reads it again as if to savor the words, save them for another day, and he turns around to point it out like he's just come across a rare natural phenomenon. I know that no art can be perfect, he says, but have you ever read something that so perfectly captures everything you're feeling—

Cyrus, sitting alone at dinner last night, the way I used to at school. He's in one of those moods I've come to recognize, where he retreats somewhere deep into his own brain, lost in an endless spiral of thoughts he'll never share with anyone else. He stiffens when I go to join him, then his eyes soften when he realizes it's me—

A brilliant beam of light burns through the darkness, accompanied by footsteps. Real, solid, drawing closer.

I blink fast into the sudden glare, my heart pounding.

The light sways, catching the thin silver edges of the leaves overhead, and then the snake bare inches away from me.

"Don't move," Cyrus calls out softly, the concern creasing his brows illuminated by the flashlight in his hand. His eyes find mine. "It won't attack. Just stay where you are."

I couldn't move even if I wanted to. I stand as still as I physically can, tensing muscles that I never knew existed before. My breath is clogged in my throat, my lungs contracting uselessly as I try my best not to hyperventilate. The snake slides another inch toward me, so close I can feel its scales brush against my shoes, and just when I think this is really it, these will be my final seconds on earth, and at least I won't be dying alone, not with Cyrus standing there, the snake slithers away, disappearing somewhere behind the bushes in the other direction.

"Leah?" Cyrus says, raising the flashlight. "Leah, are you—"

I don't let him finish the sentence; I rush up to him and wrap my arms tight around his body, one step short of crashing straight into him. He stiffens in surprise, but I can't bring myself to care. I can't even think past the relief melting through me, the warmth of his jacket and his breathing against my skin. *He's found me. He promised he'd find me and he did.* The fear that's been building in my bones is cleared away so suddenly I'm lightheaded as I latch on to Cyrus, a sob escaping my lips. After half a heartbeat of silence, he draws me in, anchoring me to him, his hand rubbing slow, gentle circles over my back, and maybe it's because I'd been half-certain I was about to die that I feel so wonderfully, vividly alive right now.

"It's okay," he tells me, his voice low in my ear. "You're safe."

And despite reason, despite our history, I believe it. If someone were to ask, I wouldn't be able to name anywhere safer than the arms of my childhood nemesis, in a remote bamboo forest far away from everything I've known. I would cling on longer, for as long as he'd let me, but as my pulse settles down, some sense returns.

I quickly drop my arms. Step back, angle my face to the left so he can't see my expression. I don't realize how hard I'm shivering until he unzips his jacket and wraps it around my shaking shoulders, the soft fabric falling over my body like a ghost of his embrace. It smells like him: that familiar combination of sage and sandalwood, as sweet and clean as fresh streams in spring.

"Thank you," I whisper. "How did you even manage to find me?"

A strange sense of déjà vu hits me the second the words leave my lips, and my mind skips back years into the past, to when we'd play hide-and-seek around campus. No matter how well I hid—curling up in the suffocating space of the art supply closet, silently inhaling the sharp smell of acrylic; ducking behind the rosebush in the gardens; plastering myself to the wall behind the auditorium curtains—he had always been the first to find me. It reached the point where I accused him of cheating. *There's no way you didn't open your eyes early*, I would protest when he opened the door, brushed aside the thorns, pushed away the curtains. *How did you find me that quickly?*

"I almost walked right past this area, but then I saw the rock that looks like a sloth," Cyrus says, lowering the flashlight. "I admittedly had my doubts, but the resemblance is uncanny."

"Right?"

"I mean, let's not give your rock descriptions *too* much credit," he says. "You were also shedding glitter. It was like tracking down a fairy."

I frown at him. "Shedding glitter?"

"Your top," he explains, then shines the light on his own shirt. With great mortification, I notice the glitter shimmering over the fabric from where my body was pressed to his moments ago. "Who would've thought that your impractical fashion choices would save you from an eternity of wandering through the trees?"

I wince. "I'll dust that off for you—"

"No need." His features are serious, but his eyes gleam with private amusement. "I'll just tell people that I ran into a fairy. Come on," he adds, before I can say anything else. "We should really go back before Wang Laoshi combusts from stress. He's probably getting ready to call the police—or hand in his resignation letter."

He turns around in the direction he came from, the flashlight throwing the patch of trees up ahead of us into clarity, and for a brief second, he stretches his hand out, his fingers flexing. I stare, unable to tell if he means for me to take it. If this were anyone else, it would be obvious to me. I've never had trouble reading signals before; I would know in an instant, just from how a boy looked at me, how his gaze flitted to my lips, how he walked next to me, exactly what he was thinking. But with Cyrus, everything seems to be written in Morse code. I'm still trying to decipher his body language when he slides his hand back into his pocket, the gesture quick, casual, as if nothing had happened. Maybe nothing had, and I'm just imagining things now, the way I'd imagined footsteps. Out of desperation. Out of fierce, foolish hope.

"I'm *so* glad you're not dead," Daisy tells me over the roar of the blow-dryer. It's the twentieth time she's uttered some variation of this sentiment since I returned to our hotel room approximately half an hour ago, and she's sounded fully earnest each time. When she'd flung open the door to greet me, she'd looked ready to burst into tears of relief. "We thought you'd been eaten by a bear."

"I'm really glad I'm not dead either," I say, running my fingers through the damp ends of my hair to make it dry faster. I still feel a little shaky, but only in the way where you've already woken from the bad dream and can be sure that you're safe in your bed. The warm shower has helped wash away most of the dirt and leftover adrenaline. "Sorry to make you guys worry."

"I think Cyrus was more worried than any of us," Daisy says, drawing her knees to her chest on the couch. "He was the first person to notice you were gone."

I turn the blow-dryer off, and in the sudden silence, I hear myself swallow. "He was?"

She nods. "Honestly, he looked like he was about to lose his mind if anything happened to you."

I remember that moment when he found me, how his arms had tightened around my body. It's so easy to sink into the memory—to relive every detail, from the sweetness of his scent to the hitch in his breath—that when my phone chimes from the counter, it feels like being hauled up from somewhere deep underwater. I set the blow-dryer down, then hastily pat my hands dry on a towel and open my phone to the newest message.

It's Cyrus.

can you come to my hotel room?

I stare down at the words, and my heart betrays me by skipping a stupid beat.

Then more messages pop up, sent in quick succession, like he's also just realized how his invitation sounds.

for the photos

we still need to choose the photos from today

Either he's thinking about the competition or it's a cover for what he's actually thinking about, an excuse to invite me over. I'm hoping it's the latter. I glance at the clock—there are only ten minutes left until curfew, which is when Wang Laoshi transforms from a mildly disgruntled teacher into a deeply disgruntled security guard.

This could be the moment I've been working toward the entire trip. If all goes well tonight—if I'm charming enough, pretty enough, smooth enough—I might finally be able to secure my grip on Cyrus's heart and crush it, just like I planned.

Because I definitely shouldn't be softening toward him.

Because I definitely, absolutely still want to get my revenge.

"Do you need to go somewhere?" Daisy asks.

"Cyrus's room." I let the implication fill the air. "But, like, I don't know how to get there without getting caught—I mean, it's kind of late . . ."

"I'll cover for you," Daisy says quickly. "If Wang Laoshi asks, I'll just lie and say you're asleep."

I pause in surprise. "Are you sure? Because—please don't take this the wrong way—if you don't feel comfortable lying . . ."

"Oh, I'm a great liar when I want to be," Daisy assures me. "I used to lie all the time to get out of class presentations."

I'm still making up my mind when one more message springs onto the screen.

it'll be just us btw. Oliver was called to attend his father's event across the city. he won't be back until the morning.

"Okay, I'm going," I decide. The fizzing feeling in my blood has raced upward, like soda when you shake it too hard inside the can. I smear some tinted lip balm—the one that tastes like strawberries—over my mouth, then glance down at my pale silk nightgown. It is, by most standards, a bit too flimsy to be worn out anywhere, which makes it perfect for what I'm about to do next.

"Thank you so much—I owe you," I tell Daisy on my way out, all my photos tucked into the purse in my hand.

"Hey, um, aren't you going to wear clothes?" she calls after me.

"I'm wearing them," I call back, adjusting the straps of my nightgown to loosen them further. "These *are* clothes." Kind of.

Cyrus's room is on the other side of the floor. By the time I get there, my nerves have started to fray and my self-consciousness has kicked in, and despite everything I've promised myself, it's not revenge that I'm thinking about. It's just—him. The prospect of seeing him. Of being in the same room as him. I draw my damp hair down to cover my chest and ring the doorbell, then wait for him to answer.

When he does, his reaction is subdued, but there *is* a reaction. A flash of something across his face, a breath drawn too fast. He seems to take me in all within a second, then he pulls the door wider to let me inside, reaching down to fetch a pair of slippers for me.

"Wow, nice place," I joke as I walk into an exact replica of my room in our new hotel, right down to the heavy yellow curtains and patterned carpet and two single beds.

"Thanks, I spent ages decorating," he deadpans. "Feel free to sit."

I lower myself onto the couch by the window and lean back against the crimson cushions.

His eyes widen. "Wait," he says, his voice sharp, panicked. "Not there—"

Something hard digs into my spine. I frown, turning around, and spot the corner of a small box sticking out from between the cushions, evidently stuffed there in a last-minute attempt to hide it.

"Leah," Cyrus is saying, close to pleading. "Leah, you can just leave that—"

I ignore him and pull the pastel-pink box all the way out, and for two seconds I don't register what I'm holding in my hands. Then I do, and all at once, the color spreading fiercely through Cyrus's face makes perfect sense. Silent laughter springs up inside me at the mental image of him scrambling to bury the box before I arrived, but I push it back. Raise my brows. Hold up the condoms. "What's this?" I ask, feigning ignorance, just so I can have the pleasure of watching him struggle to explain himself.

And I'm instantly rewarded with his reaction. His expression seems to race through every emotion known to mankind in the space of an inhale. He steps forward, his hands out, like he has half a mind to just snatch the box from me and burn it. "That is—" He clears his throat. I've never seen him so visibly distressed before. "That is . . . an interesting question. I promise, it's not what it—"

"Oh my god." I draw upon all the acting talent I have in my body to open my mouth in shock as I read the product description on the side. "Cyrus, what the hell? I thought you called me over here to pick out the photos for the competition together. Were you planning on hooking up tonight?"

"What? No," he says in a rush. "No, I swear—"

I lift the box higher between us. "Then?"

"It was there when we first checked into the room." He winces. "I just didn't want you to see it and assume—I wouldn't even dream of . . ."

I let him suffer for a while longer before it becomes physically impossible to maintain my fake shock. "You can relax, Cyrus," I say, cackling as I drop the condoms on the bedside table. "I was only messing with you. It's kind of cute that you felt the need to hide this from me."

His face turns an entire shade redder. "You should—we should throw them away."

"Why?" I cock my head. Grin up at him, taunting. "What if you end up needing them? Better safe than sorry, right?"

"Do you talk to all guys this way?"

"No. Just you," I say casually, sitting back down on the cushions, but I'm not teasing him. It's the truth. If he were any other guy, I would be too wary, too cautious to joke about something like this. It's almost always there, in every interaction I've had with guys since I turned pretty: the uneasiness in the pit of my stomach, the prickling dread that the conversation could take an uncomfortable turn at any second, the suspicion that while I'm thinking about them, they're thinking about my body. But with Cyrus, it's different. I might have felt tempted on numerous occasions to shove him or slam a door in his face, yet I've never felt unsafe. Somehow, I know that if I were to move closer to him right now, to press my lips to the most vulnerable spot on his neck and draw his hands down to my waist like I really, truly wanted him, he would still step back at once if I had a sudden change of heart.

Then I'm wondering how it would feel to actually do it— to kiss him. How his expression would change. Whether he would kiss me back soft and slow, or fast and urgent and breathless, if his fingers would tangle themselves into my hair or if he's the kind to touch the back of my neck . . .

Oh my god.

Don't be so weak and disgusting, Leah, I urge myself with a stern mental slap. Having feelings was not part of the plan. I should only be focused on making him want me—not wanting *him*.

"Let's look over the photos," Cyrus says, and practically leaps away from me to grab three photos from the counter. Even when he comes back and dumps his photos on the couch between us, he sits down on the farthest end of it, two feet braced firmly on the floor like he's acting out one of those in-flight safety videos. I'm not sure if I should be worried that he somehow looked inside my head just now and was scared off by the images playing there.

"You only took three photos?" I ask him. They're all of trees—not even very distinct or interesting trees, but of the planted-everywhere-in-the-suburbs variety—and they're so blurry I wonder if he'd pressed the shutter button by accident while he was walking around.

"Well, I would've taken more, but I was kind of sidetracked when my teammate disappeared in the forest," Cyrus says, examining my photos while I examine his. "Though it looks like you were busy even while you were disappearing. This one's beautiful," he adds.

I look up, and he holds the photo out to me. Birds flit between the Polaroid frame, their white wings stark against the wash of blue sky, gliding one after another over the mountains.

"This one's beautiful too," Cyrus says, pushing another photo toward me. "And this one of the lake. You know what, I think we should just choose from your photos."

"We can choose one of yours too," I tell him, just to be a good teammate.

He snorts. "You don't have to do that."

"Do what?" I say innocently.

"Deny the fact that my photos could give the average citizen car sickness," he says. "It's fine. Photography isn't really my forte."

"You don't need it to be," I say. "You already have so many things."

"As in . . . materially? Because I believe that's Oliver. Did you know he has a backup Porsche for his backup Porsche?"

"That's deeply upsetting. But I mean what Oliver was talking about on the train." I collect the five chosen photos in a neat pile and bind them together with the hair tie on my wrist. "You found your thing—your calling, your passion, whatever you want to call it—years ago. You know what you're good at, and you know what to do with it."

His expression turns thoughtful. "Maybe that's your problem."

"You're a problem," I say automatically. "Sorry. Reflex. Do go on."

"I feel like you always do things for the sake of something else," he tells me. "Am I wrong?"

"No," I say slowly. "But isn't that everyone? Isn't that, like, the point?"

"I don't love literature because I think it'll make me famous or rich somewhere down the line, or because it'll be an interesting point of conversation at a party one day," he says, and it's as if he's reciting my internal dialogue from when I was modeling, all the reasons I gave myself to keep going. Reasons that had once sounded perfectly valid to me. "I love literature because it's meaningful to me."

"Just that?" I ask in disbelief.

"Just that," he says.

"I don't really know what I like these days," I admit, except that's not entirely true. There's want bundling in my nerves, thrumming through my blood when I lock eyes with him, and I can imagine a number of things I would like to do right now.

He looks away first, twisting in the direction of the front door. "Did you hear that?" he asks.

"Hear what?"

"I think that was Wang Laoshi," he says, standing up and striding toward the entrance to peer through the peephole. "He's already patrolling the area."

We both check the time. It's already five minutes past curfew.

"Maybe you should sneak out now," Cyrus suggests. "Before it gets too late."

"What if he catches me?" I counter, which feels like a totally valid reason for me to stay in his room. To buy myself more time with him. "He's probably going to have a heart attack if he sees me leaving your room like this." I gesture down to my little silk dress, and Cyrus very deliberately shifts his gaze up to some point over my head. "And we'll *both* be in trouble."

Cyrus clears his throat. "Then—"

"Let's just wait it out until he leaves," I tell Cyrus, squinting into the peephole again. Then I stifle a yawn with the back of my hand. Now that all my adrenaline has leaked out of me, exhaustion has started pressing in on my eyelids and my brain, pulling my body to the nearest, softest thing: which happens to be the bed in the middle of the room. "Do you mind if I take a nap while we wait?" I ask Cyrus.

He blinks. "Yes. I mean—no, I don't mind. That bed's mine. Feel free to . . ." He waves toward the bed, having seemingly forgotten the English language for a few seconds.

The blankets are luxuriously soft when I slip inside them, my head sinking back against the pillows. Cyrus switches off the main lights, leaving on only the floor lamp. Then he grabs a thick, battered book from his suitcase, flipping it open to the bookmarked page, and settles down on the carpet beside me, his shoulders level with the bed.

Xindong.

Another new word I've picked up on the trip. It means, literally, that the heart is moved by something—or more often, someone. A sensation firmer than butterflies in your stomach but more fleeting than love. Throughout the trip, I've felt my heart move multiple times, and they were all because of Cyrus.

I felt it when he bent down to help me slide my heels off and apply the Band-Aid, the warmth of his fingers so gentle on my skin. I felt it when he stretched his palm out to let me draw over it. I felt it on the race up the Yellow Mountain, in those moments when he'd shielded me like it was instinct. I felt it when he offered me his sunglasses, and when he set the flower crown on my head. And again, only earlier tonight, when I saw him in the trees. But those were all light movements, small fluctuations, easy enough to dismiss.

Yet now, watching him in the soft orange light, his head bowed as he turns the page, the shift inside my chest feels permanent. It's a movement so deep it sends shock waves through my system, making my very bones ache. I'm gripped by the overpowering urge to do something reckless, to reach across the space and run my fingers through his hair.

For revenge. The old thought pushes itself forward out of habit, but it sounds weaker by the second, more like an excuse than a true plan. It's too hard to summon anger, too hard to remember why I came here and why I should want to ruin this boy's life when really, really I just want to touch him.

I shift forward, letting the blankets drop to my stomach. When my fingertips brush the space between his shoulder blades, he freezes. For a few moments, neither of us speaks. I can hear my heart thrumming faster and faster, the blood rushing through my ears, pulsing at my fingertips in the places they skim the thin cotton of his shirt, just once, lightly, before I retract my hand again.

"What are you doing?" I ask him, even though he's so obviously reading.

Very slowly, he flips another page. "Practicing gymnastics," he says, his voice sarcastic as usual, but hoarser.

I lie back on the bed, my head angled toward him. "Can you read the book out loud to me?"

"What, like a bedtime story?"

"It might help me fall asleep," I say, kicking my feet out to get comfortable. "I'd always doze off in class the second the teacher started reading something."

His laugh is quiet enough to go unnoticed, if not for the shake of his shoulders. "All right . . ." He clears his throat. *"As the train disappeared into the mist, he vowed he would never allow himself to feel any happiness again. Look what had happened to Caiyun, to Zhuji, before the fall, to him. Joy had made him mindless, complacent, disgustingly weak; it had shaken loose his heart from his bones and sold him the illusion that there could be something else for him in this life. There was nothing else. Not anymore. He shoved the blood-splattered letter deep into his coat pocket. The stars looked terribly brittle that night . . ."*

My eyelids fall shut. I don't pay attention to the story, only to the cadence of his voice filling the room. He could be reading poetry, a classic, a eulogy. If he's the one saying it, anything could sound lovely. Nestled in the warmth of the blankets, with my eyes still shut, I tell him, "You have a nice voice."

He pauses. "You must be tired."

"What?"

"When you're tired," he says, "you forget to hate me."

"I forget to hate you a lot of the time," I whisper. It slips too easily from my tongue, without warning, turned by the darkness into a confession.

He says something else then, but before my mind can latch on to it, sleep drags me down into its depths. The last thing I remember is the sound of his breathing, as soft and calming as the rustle of orange blossoms outside my childhood home.

CHAPTER FIFTEEN

We're being attacked.

They're the first words to pop into my head when I bolt upright, squinting into the dim light. My heart slams furiously against my chest as I rub my eyes, muscles bunched, searching for the source of the noise. Someone had been gasping. No, crying. Maybe a thief had broken in during the middle of the night—

But the hotel room appears undisturbed. The door is closed, the velvet curtains half-drawn over the city lights outside. The faint blue glow of the alarm clock blinks from the bedside table: 3:42 a.m. I look around more slowly, waiting for my heart to settle down again.

And then I spot Cyrus on the other bed. Only the corner of the blanket is draped over his stomach, his long legs hanging over the side, and his eyes are squeezed tight, as if in pain. A broken, helpless sound escapes his lips.

"*No . . .*" he murmurs. "No—please—"

"Cyrus?" I whisper. Wide awake now, I hop off the bed and lower myself down by his side, my mouth dry. He's lost in whatever nightmare he's having. A sliver of moonlight creeps in past the curtains, illuminating the sheen of sweat on his forehead. He's never looked so helpless before, so afraid, not even when he thought the plane was going down. "Cyrus," I say, louder, touching his shoulder.

He flinches, inhaling sharply like someone breaking through the currents right before they're about to drown, his eyes wide and disoriented. Then they find my face, and something in him changes. Goes quiet.

"Are you okay?" I ask, flicking on the night-light.

"Yes," he whispers, pulling himself up against the pillows, his knees drawn to his chest. His hair is all mussed, so long that it falls like black silk over his brows. "Sorry, I didn't mean to startle you."

"That's fine," I say, smoothing out my nightgown. Under normal circumstances, I would be more self-conscious about waking up in the middle of the night with a boy in his hotel room, but there's something about this moment that's safe, private—I feel like I could say or do anything right now and he wouldn't judge me for it. I stand up and grab one of the bottles of water from the table, twisting the cap for him before holding it out. "Here."

He accepts it gladly, and I watch the movement in his throat as he tips his head back and drinks.

"Do you have them often?" I ask, sitting down on his bed. There's only just enough room for me to avoid brushing against his legs when I turn around to face him. "The nightmares?"

"More often than I'd prefer," he says, quiet. His hands tremble faintly as he screws the cap back on. "I'm actually surprised

Oliver hasn't said anything about it. I must have woken him up a bunch of times."

"I had no idea," I tell him.

And I should really just stop there, leave it at that. I should probably even be delighted to see him suffering. But it hurts, watching him like this, his fears flooding in over his head. If I were a soldier, I would be the very first to be dismissed from the front lines or killed on the spot for my weakness, because who else would run across the battlefield to their enemy, offering up bandages instead of bullets?

"You know," I say slowly, "I get nightmares a lot too. Really vivid ones. I don't think I ever scream out or anything, but that's because I'm usually frozen inside them—like I can't move or speak. I can only wait until I wake up. When I was younger, if I had a really bad nightmare, I'd turn on all the lights in my bedroom and drink a giant glass of warm water, and then I would sing to myself under my breath. Not, like, a lullaby. But something really annoying and ridiculous, like an advertising jingle."

"An advertising jingle?" he repeats with a soft laugh, resting his cheek against his arm.

"The more obnoxious the better," I confirm, hating how much the sound of his laughter pleases me. "That way, the only thing I can hear is the jingle stuck on loop selling me crunchy chocolate cereal, instead of my own thoughts."

"I should give it a try sometime, then," he says.

"You should. Or, if that fails, you can call me," I say before I can stop myself. God help me. The desire to comfort him is so much stronger than the desire to destroy him now. "And I'll sing advertising jingles to you until they're permanently stuck in your head. I have a beautiful singing voice, you know. Very throaty."

His smile is careful, as if he doesn't want to take the offer too seriously. "Is that a threat?"

"It's a promise." I meet his surprised gaze, hold it, my heart picking up its pace inside my chest like it's in a hurry to go somewhere. He's the first to look away, the red flush of his neck visible even in the mellow light.

"I doubt you understand what you'd be signing up for here," he says quietly. "It takes forever for me to go back to sleep once I've woken from a bad dream. A lot of the time, I lie wide awake until morning, just—thinking. Thinking about things I shouldn't."

"Like?"

He hesitates. Starts to say something. Stops again before it can get past his lips. "Mostly, the things I regret," he tells me. "The things I should have done differently, or shouldn't have said. Terrible mistakes I've made. The measures I could have taken to prevent my parents from splitting—"

"Your parents split?" I ask, shock rippling through me. I had seen them together a few times at school, when they were coming to pick Cyrus up or attend the annual school concert or one of his piano recitals. I'd never spoken to either of them, but even from afar, they seemed the perfect match. His mother was beautiful in that elegant, timeless way that could have made her a star in another age. His father was popular among the teachers, with a booming voice and laugh and a rotation of tailored suits. They seemed *happy*, holding hands as they strolled across the football field, down the wide corridors where the preschoolers' fingerprint art was on display.

"It happened right after you left," Cyrus explains, the words coming slowly, like he's piecing them together out loud for the very first time. "The official split, at least. They'd been fighting long before that. That was actually why I started to get into reading. Whenever I heard their voices rise, I'd quickly grab a book and go to my room and it would help me escape into this other world where I could pretend to be someone else.

"But even then, even though I hated it when they were mad at each other, it was like—you know how people say that growing up, they thought it was normal to have candy for breakfast, or to skip school whenever it rained, because that's simply what their family did, and they had no other point of reference? I thought it was normal for your parents to fight at home almost every night. For them to throw things and slam doors and scream at each other for hours on end. I asked my dad about it once, and he said that my mom was only angry at him because she loved him. Because it meant that she cared. He said that was the secret to a relationship: You had to keep things interesting, even if that meant getting on their nerves. So maybe I should've seen it coming, but I didn't—when they told me it wasn't working out anymore, I wasn't even sad at first. I was purely stunned." He scoffs, shaking his head. "Stupid, right?"

"No. You couldn't have seen it coming," I say firmly, my chest aching for him. "You were so young."

His eyes are exquisitely dark, desolate. "But I keep thinking that if only I had—I don't know, maybe everything would have turned out better. I wouldn't have made things so difficult for them. They argued about me more than they argued about any other topic. Whether I should be spending more time practicing piano, or if I was spending *too* much time on the piano. Whether I should sign up for summer camp or stay home, and if I did, then who was going to cook for me and look after me. Whether I should pick Chinese or French as my language elective. And it might seem ridiculous, but part of the reason why I want to get into Stanford so badly is because that was one of the only things they ever agreed on. It meant something to them. I still remember sitting with them on the couch together one night, and it was so . . . unusually peaceful. They were both in a good mood for once, and my dad was holding my mom's hand, and we were sharing these bowls of roasted sunflower seeds, and they started talking about the future . . . They met at Stanford, you know that?"

I shake my head, wide-eyed. "No. I didn't."

"Yeah, when they first started dating, my mom was getting her PhD—her mentor at the time was Dr. Linda Shen, who was basically my mom's idol—and my dad was getting his master's degree because he'd taken some time off from his studies to work. So they were both telling me about it, how beautiful the campus was, the places they'd go to get lunch together, and my dad said he thought Stanford would be perfect for me. It was close to home, and familiar, and it'd be, like, this family thing, if we all went there . . ."

That's why. Now it all makes perfect, painful sense. The determined glint in his eyes whenever he spoke about Stanford, the strange intensity in his voice, even his obsession with getting a recommendation letter from my aunt. It's not just about his dreams for the future—it's his dreams for his family.

"I keep imagining it," Cyrus says, swallowing. "I imagine calling my parents to tell them I was accepted, that Dr. Linda Shen herself wants me at Stanford, and they're both so excited about it that they start talking to each other again, and maybe they remember how and why they fell in love in the first place. Maybe then . . . Maybe I could fix it."

"Cyrus, that's—" My voice catches, and for some reason, I feel like I could cry. "It's not up to you to fix your parents' marriage."

"But I was the one who ruined it in the first place." His expression remains even, almost calm, yet his fingers tighten into a fist. "They were happy, before they had me. Sometimes," he says, very quiet, "I think I ruin everything I touch."

Yes, you do, the vindictive voice in my head whispers, but it's more distant than ever, as if sounding from a thousand miles away. I grab his hand, unfurling his fist, and tug it toward me, letting it rest on my exposed knee, right where the hem of my silk nightgown ends. His fingertips are so warm that the heat spreads upward through me, curling inside my ribs. My skin itches pleasantly with the sensation, and I have to steady myself for a moment before speaking. "See?" I say, soft. "You haven't ruined me."

He stares down at the place where his hand burns against my leg like he's still deep in a dream, then up at me. "Haven't I?" he whispers.

Part of me wants to say that he has. That my life was ruined once by him when I was expelled from my old school, and again, by myself, when I gave up modeling. It's the same part of me that was convinced my life was already over, destroyed beyond repair. That while everyone else was moving on, I was moving in circles. But now, alone in this room with him, the night breeze sighing against the windows, the sweet song of crickets filling the air, the press of his palm like a salve, nothing feels entirely ruined. How could it be, if I ended up here?

"Don't overestimate yourself, Cyrus," I tell him with a faint smile, as if everything inside me hasn't reoriented itself to his touch. His thumb shifts, just slightly, probably by accident, and it sends a shock of electricity coursing through my veins. I lick my lips. My mouth is dry, my throat tight with all the things I want, and suddenly I'm scared that I've gone too far with this little revenge plan of mine, that everything's slipping out of my control. I'd wanted his heart, but I hadn't wanted to give away mine.

I stand up. Turn around. "I should head back to my room—"

"Wait," he says, a hitch in his voice. "Don't go."

I whirl back toward him in surprise.

"You . . . You might wake people up if you leave now," he says. "You can keep sleeping on the other bed until early morning and slip out before the group starts heading down for breakfast. Oliver won't be back until then anyway."

"Is that the real reason?" I ask him.

He goes still, alarm flashing in and out of his eyes. "What?"

"Are you really scared of waking people up? Or are you just scared of sleeping alone after a nightmare?"

"Maybe," he says, more easily than I would've expected.

I pretend to think it over, pretend I'm not giddy as I hop back onto the bed, drawing the covers up to my chest. But I can no longer pretend that I don't have any feelings for Cyrus Sui.

"What. The. Hell."

I nearly fall out of bed at the sudden slam of the door, the familiar voice that shouldn't be here. Or wait, no, I shouldn't be here. This isn't my hotel room. This isn't even my *bed*. I look up, my disorientation fading, blankets tumbling down around me, and find Oliver standing just a few feet away. His bag hangs off his shoulder, his jacket still on, his brows lifted so high they're at risk of leaving his forehead. On the other bed, Cyrus is also slowly blinking awake, rubbing his eyes.

"Wow," Oliver says, apparently unable to utter anything except exclamatory sounds. "Wow, wow, wow. Wow."

"Okay," I say, checking to make sure that the straps of my nightgown haven't slipped down my shoulders before sitting up. "This isn't how it—"

"*Wow.*"

"Have you recovered yet?" I demand.

"Nope. I may never recover," Oliver says. "I was not prepared to come back to this."

"We were just looking over photos," I say as righteously as I can while very much aware that this scene looks like it belongs to the front page of a tabloid.

Oliver's brows climb up even higher. "While you were asleep?"

"Before we fell asleep. Wang Laoshi was outside and I was stuck here, so Cyrus gave me his bed to take a nap . . ." I clear my throat, unable to look at Cyrus without reliving everything from last night, the quiet intimacy of the darkness and the vulnerability in his voice and the odd beat of my heart. "We didn't expect you to be back so early."

"I didn't expect to be back so early either," Oliver says, shrugging off his bag and leather jacket in one movement, "but it appears my dad's new driver is a street racer. Or just someone who doesn't believe in traffic lights."

"What event did you have to attend anyway?" I ask, hoping to divert his attention from the fact that I'm now climbing slowly out of the bed. "Did your family open up another winery?"

"No, this was for his client's new art gallery. My dad wanted me there to charm all the guests. Well, *supposedly*, but the old man gets bored out of his mind at these things so I think he just wanted some company— Hang on." He narrows his eyes. "Don't change the subject. What were you two doing the whole night?"

"*Nothing.* I told you, we were looking at photos, and then we fell asleep. The end." I nudge one of the slippers on the floor toward me with my toe. "Can you just let me go back to my room and act like this never happened?"

"I'll let you go back to your room," Oliver says. "But you should know that I'm not a good actor."

True to his warning, Oliver maintains a thoroughly scandalized expression all throughout the morning, from when we bump into each other again at the breakfast buffet to when everyone regroups in the hotel lobby to when we pile into the bus for our next stop.

"Can you quit looking at me like that?" I ask, crossing my legs in the seat beside him.

He drops the scandalized face but only to peer over at me with unabashed curiosity. "You're not sitting with Cyrus?"

"No," I say. "I thought I'd talk to you." Ever since I returned to my own room, where Daisy was waiting, wide-eyed and looking ready to burst with questions, I've spent the whole morning untangling my feelings in the daylight. And though I can't guess at what might be going through Cyrus's head after last night, I can be certain, at least, of what I want.

Oliver flashes me a grin. "And whatever did I do to deserve this honor?"

"I'm going to ask you a very obnoxious question," I begin as the bus rumbles onto the road. "But I need you to answer me honestly."

"Sure. Honesty is one of my best traits," Oliver says. "Along with my good looks, natural charisma, impeccable style, shiny hair, and melodic voice, of course."

"Okay, no comments on any of that—"

"Because there's no need to comment on what's objectively true," Oliver says, nodding in understanding. "I get it."

Just ask him. Say it. I take a deep breath and choose the most direct route possible: "Do you like me, Oliver?"

He pauses. Stares at me for what might be a full minute. "*Like* you, as in a let's-make-out way?"

"Not really the wording I would've chosen, but yeah. Romantically. Not just as friends."

Another pause. His voice is light when he asks: "Do you want me to like you?" As if he's asking whether I want him to grab me a soda.

"I mean . . . it would be nice if you liked me as a friend, because despite my initial reservations, I like you like that a lot,"

I say carefully, and brace myself for the fallout, my fingers gripping the seat belt. Maybe he'll ask me to go sit somewhere else on the bus. Or maybe he'll just spend the rest of the ride in sullen silence and never speak to me again, because what's the point, if I don't see him as a potential boyfriend?

But the warmth doesn't fade from his eyes. "If you don't want me to like you in that way, then I won't."

"Seriously?" I twist around in my seat to face him, my relief mingling with surprise. "How does that even work? You can't just switch your feelings on and off. You don't decide to like someone; you simply do."

"What can I say? It's a tough skill to master, but I've mastered it," he says with a shrug. "This may be very hard to believe, seeing how totally cool and in control of my emotions I am now, but I used to fall in love way too easily. Like, I would fall in love with the attendant who helped add ice to my drink in the airport lounge. I'd fall for a stranger who held the door open for me once, or a guy in my class because he waved at me in the halls, or a cute girl handing out flyers for the local animal shelter, or a waiter who swatted a fly away from my meal and smiled when our eyes met. And I would act on it. I'd ask for their number and buy them flowers—I didn't have any game like I do now, just stupid sincerity." He looks away, out at the blurred sweep of trees, and turns quiet.

"But they never loved me back, and you kind of get sick of the whole unrequited love thing after a while, you feel me? There are only so many angsty, depressing love songs you can listen to before you start feeling a bit pathetic. So I got my shit together and stopped falling so deep that I can't help myself up when I need to. I still have my little crushes because it keeps things interesting, but I don't actually, like, *like* anyone until I'm certain they'll like me too. And I was never certain with you."

My heart pinches. Even though this is the confirmation I was after, I still can't help imagining him years ago, offering up his heart on open palms to people who dropped it or tossed it aside.

"What about the prince?" I ask.

"Right, yeah. That guy." Oliver glances back over at me and makes an unimpressed face. "Forgot to mention the part where he was after my dad's money because he'd spent all his royal savings on a massive emu farm, and then he got bitten by an emu and decided he wanted nothing to do with them anymore. Not really what I'd consider boyfriend material, let alone husband material. Plus, he wasn't even that hot."

I wrinkle my nose. "You can do so much better."

For the first time, I think I glimpse the self-doubt underneath the lacquer of his brash confidence, the active effort it requires to smile all the time, to keep everything light and make everyone laugh. "We'll see. But hey," he says, holding up three fingers like he's making an oath, "I promise I won't fall for you. You're, like, a bro. Like, a very pretty bro, who I'm into platonically, and whose house I might crash at in the future, once you're married and I'm named the most eligible bachelor of the century."

"I would love that," I tell him earnestly, bumping his shoulder with mine. "I don't have any other guy friends. You'll be the only one."

"Damn, I feel special, then. But, like, really? You have *no* other guy friends?"

"None," I admit. Before, when I wasn't pretty, it was like I didn't even exist to guys, unless it was as the punch line of all their cruel jokes. And then once I turned pretty, I was only a girl to them, apparently too dumb and too different to join in on their important conversations. They would discuss my body openly like it was a debate topic and feign interest just to withdraw it the second it became clear I wasn't willing to sleep with them, and even when we did hang out, their eyes never stayed on my face. The nicer ones got girlfriends, and their girlfriends warned them to keep their distance from me, until our every exchange felt monitored, morally wrong somehow, and it just wasn't worth the trouble anymore. Cyrus wasn't like the rest of them, but he was never a friend to begin with.

As if reading my mind, Oliver asks, "What about Cyrus? Or— Oh." His brows rise. "I'm guessing you wouldn't have any problems with *him* liking you in a let's-make-out way."

"Okay, still not warming up to that phrase. But it's . . . complicated between us," I say, which feels like a severe understatement. "We have a long history. I just didn't want to accidentally lead you on."

"Wow," he says, blowing out a breath.

"Wow, what?"

"I have to admit, you're kind of different from what I thought." He peers over at me. "Like, you're hot, obviously, but you're also thoughtful and brave and mature and nice even when you don't need to be, which is, like, actually really rare these days. And I swear I'm not just saying that. Cyrus is a lucky guy."

"Oh shush," I say, like this might not be one of the kindest arrangements of words anyone has ever gifted me with. *Maybe I can be all those things*, a new, hopeful voice inside me whispers. *Maybe I already am. Maybe I don't have to be the outcast, or the model—I can just focus on being a good person surrounded by other good people in beautiful places, and that's more than enough.*

"Yes, sure thing," Oliver says, then winks at me. "Well, you can rest assured there's no boy drama here." He raises a fist like he's making an invisible toast. "To friendship."

I have to laugh as I mimic the gesture, clinking my fake champagne glass against his, my chest warm with affection. "To friendship."

CHAPTER SIXTEEN

Friendship is the last thing on my mind when I hop off the bus.

Cyrus is waiting there on the stone pavement, and as our gazes meet for the first time since I snuck out of his hotel room this morning, he smiles at me, sincere and almost shy. It's the kind of smile that makes you forget everything. The sun. The sky. Gravity. Every major and minor hurt I've ever endured. Every name that isn't his.

At least for a second.

Because in the daylight, it's easier to pretend the intimacy of last night was only a spell, an embarrassing mistake made in the moment. Easier for the old doubts to creep in, to remember the Incident and all the years of pain that preceded this, why I owe it to my younger self to at least keep my revenge plan on the table. Even if my heart can't quite make up its mind about Cyrus, I shouldn't let myself weaken.

But something is going to happen between us today—of this, I'm entirely certain. There's a rhythm to these things, like the melody leading into a chorus.

I'm just not certain if it's a blessing or a curse that we're given half an hour to explore the village we're visiting on our own. Right now, it might actually be easier to have a contest to win, something to focus on, anything that could distract me from the hot, jittery feeling inside me. If there are butterflies in my stomach, their wings must be on fire.

Revenge or desire? Since when did the two feel so similar?

"Should we go?" Cyrus asks me.

I glance around us. The others have started to split off down the bridges and canals and winding streets, where red lanterns swing from the eaves. "Okay," I say. I don't ask where to; I don't really care.

We walk without talking for an impressively long period of time, past the houses with golden *'fu'* characters pasted over the front doors, the bikes resting against gray tile walls, the wooden planks propped up by uneven stone steps, the floral dresses left out to dry in the warm breeze. But Cyrus doesn't even seem to register his surroundings. His expression has retreated inward, his shoulders tight. A few times, he sucks in a breath, as if on the verge of saying something, but then he snaps his mouth shut again.

He could be getting ready to confess that he's a vampire, my brain volunteers. *Or he could have caught you looking at him like you want to lick his neck—*

I do not want to lick his neck, I argue, kicking an innocent pebble in protest.

I'm your brain, my brain reminds me. *You can't hide anything from me. And it's painfully obvious how attracted you are to Cyrus, even though you should really cut that out and refocus on the part where you reject him in the most humiliating fashion—of course, you'd need him to actually say that he likes you first—*

I tell my brain to shut up.

But just when I think I can't take the silence anymore, Cyrus says quietly, "I didn't mean it, you know."

"What?"

We turn into an empty alley, and he slows down, the sunlight spilling soft over his skin, illuminating every subtle detail. The way he pauses to swallow, his throat pulsing. The nervous shift of his fingers before he slides his hands into his pockets. The intensity in his gaze, his beautiful features entirely serious. "I never meant to lie about you pushing me," he says, his voice very soft, just audible over the calls of birds in the distance. "Much less get you kicked out of the school. It was all my fault. I was concussed and everything happened so fast, I wasn't thinking properly—when the teacher asked if someone had hurt me, my first instinct was to say that you did, because I *was* hurt, but it had nothing to do with the fall itself. I just— It's so mortifying, but when you told me you never wanted to see me again, I was at a complete loss. I'd never experienced such pain before in my life. And I knew I had screwed up, and I was the only person to blame for the whole mess."

"What?" I say again, like we're back at my cousin's wedding, and he's speaking in Mandarin faster than I can understand. I might be able to recognize a few words here and there, but strung together, none of them make any sense.

"I never wanted you to hate me," he whispers. "I never wanted you to leave. I only meant to tease you until you truly noticed me. I would wait every day for the moment you walked into class with your polka-dot socks and your cute sweaters and pigtails—it was like my day didn't even begin until I saw you. I loved the games you invented and the stories you came up with and your laugh, how it bubbled out of you and you could hear it from down the corridor. All I could think about was you, all the time, and how funny and sweet and beautiful you were—"

"*Beautiful?*" I repeat, staring at him. "Are you sure you're not remembering someone else?" He has to be—he can't possibly be describing the version of me I hate the most, the version I've tried to kill off, the one I'm so embarrassed of I can't even bring myself to look at old photos without wincing.

"I thought you were the most beautiful girl I'd ever seen," he says, somehow without an ounce of sarcasm. "You've always been beautiful—beautiful like the stars are, like Shanghai is. I could never get sick of looking at you. But back then I just . . . I didn't know what I could possibly do to make you so much as look my way, and again, it's awful, but I thought—I thought that was simply how it worked. My own father had told me that being in love meant fighting with each other all the time, and I was foolish and naive enough to believe him. Only later did I realize how completely, utterly wrong he was—and how wrong *I* was to have resorted to tricks and childish teasing when I should've just gone for it. Treated you like you were precious and perfect because you always have been."

"There's no way," I say, shaking my head fast. I would actually be less stunned if he revealed that he's a vampire. "There's— I mean, how? Literally, how? I don't even know what you're talking about—"

"I tried to tell you in other ways," he says, a pleading edge to his words. "I wanted to leave flowers in your locker for Valentine's Day, but I was so allergic to them that I never got to properly place them inside, and all I'd managed to achieve was attracting bees. I would make up these ridiculous excuses just to talk to you, and I'd deliberately leave my homework unfinished so I could ask to look at yours. I would join in on your games, thinking I could impress you if I won them all. But I kept messing up, like always. Everything I did to pull you closer only ended up pushing you further away. And then you were gone—" He takes a deep breath, resting one shoulder against the gray-tiled wall, like it's costing him everything to stand here and keep speaking. "I swear, I begged the teachers to change their minds. I did everything I could to convince them that it had been a huge mistake, but they thought I was only lying to cover for you because I felt bad. And everybody else was so certain they had seen you push me . . ."

I stare at him. I stare and stare and attempt to wrestle my thoughts into order but I can't, everything's changed irrevocably, and I don't even know what to say except: "You never apologized."

Now it's his turn to blink in rapid confusion. "I did. I must have apologized thirty, forty times over in my letter . . . I wrote it so many times I ran out of ink."

"Letter?" The ground seems to wobble beneath my feet, my mind racing faster and faster like a bullet train, threatening to throw me right off its tracks. "What letter?"

"I wrote you a letter," he says.

"You did *what*? It's the twenty-first century, Cyrus. The human race is alarmingly close to developing literal mind-reading technology. You couldn't have just gotten out your phone and *texted* me?"

"You blocked my number," he points out.

A very good point. I clamp my teeth together.

"Besides, I—I thought a letter would be more sincere than sending a simple text. I begged you to give me a chance to explain everything, but then you never replied, and I figured you just didn't want to hear from me at all, which would have been entirely fair . . ." Understanding trickles into his expression the same time I feel it wash over me. "You never received it."

"No," I whisper. "It must have gotten lost in the mail or something—I had no idea—"

"I was deeply, truly sorry then, and I'm sorry now," he says, and I can see it written like a confession in his eyes, their darkness as lucid as a cloudless night, clear enough for you to map out every constellation. "I know I won't ever be able to make it up to you, no matter what I do, but I needed to tell you. I needed you to understand how I felt. How I feel."

"But what about the wedding?" I demand. "You didn't apologize then. You weren't even being *nice* to me when you saw me there."

He huffs out a self-mocking laugh. "Do you know how nervous I was that day? It was all I could do to look you in the eye, Leah. I was so scared—scared you'd simply take one glance at me and leave before I had the chance to talk to you. Scared that if I came across as too nice all of a sudden, you'd assume I had some kind of evil plan or that I was playing another prank. I mean, at that point, we hadn't seen each other in two whole years. Imagine if I confessed to you then what I'm confessing to you now. You wouldn't have believed me for a second and I'd have ruined any hopes of ever being your friend or—or something more."

I'm stunned. He knows me in ways I wouldn't have thought anyone ever could, or would ever even bother to. It's like he's reached into my brain and peered at the mess there and gently untangled everything.

He knows me so well. And I don't know him nearly as well as I thought.

"I—" There are too many emotions crashing through my chest. I nearly expect my rib cage to crack open from the force of them: anger and relief and disbelief and giddy joy and, finally, a snap back to anger. "*Seriously*, Cyrus. What the actual hell? How could you— I don't even— Why would you tell me and then— just—" I twist around on my heel, breathing hard, and march away from him down the alley before I can do something stupid. Like throttle him. Or kiss him.

Within seconds, I hear his footsteps chasing after me, echoing over the cobbled stones. "Leah. Wait—"

I don't plan to, but my feet resist all executive orders and slow down on their own, letting him catch up to me. I fold my arms across my chest and make the mistake of lifting my head to meet his achingly earnest gaze.

"Are you mad at me?" he asks, his brows drawing together.

"No," I snap. "Not at all."

"You very clearly are," he says.

"I'm not. There's nothing to be mad about."

"Leah—"

"Look, you can't just *say* things like that, Cyrus." The words burst out of my mouth before I can stop them. I wave my hands about in the air, my composure shattering. "You can't, unless you're absolutely certain you want to be with someone and you're in love with them—"

"I am."

The world freezes.

My heart, the willow trees, the green waters in the canals, the sparrows perched on the tiled roofs. All of it stops right there and then, and the only thing that restarts is the fierce, uneven pulse in my ears, thudding harder and harder, building into a deafening roar.

"You're in love with me?" I whisper. "Since when?"

His smile is wry. "Only the past seven years."

And I think about the people who first discovered that the earth was not at the center of the universe, that you would not fall off if you sailed too far across the ocean, that fires could be built from kindling to give us light and warmth, that stars would live and die just as we do. The initial shock of the revelation, and the aftershock as everything they'd once thought to be true was destroyed and rearranged. "I . . . This whole time?" I ask him, almost afraid to believe it.

"Of course," he says, watching me intently, his dark eyes serious, his hair tousled and soft around the sharp lines of his face. "There's never been anybody else for me. There never will be."

I'm not sure how any of this is happening. I'm not even sure I'm breathing.

"I can stop talking about it if that's what you want," he goes on. "I can promise to never bring this up again. But I meant it when I said that I can be whatever you want me to be: whether that's an enemy for you to curse and hold a grudge against for the rest of your life; a friend you can trust to accompany you anywhere and drive you safely back home, the one you can call at any hour of the night and tell all your secrets to; or the person you fall for, who will always wear a jacket so you don't have to bring yours, who will be the first to find you when you're lost and alone, who will remind you how heart-wrenchingly, unfathomably beautiful you are even on days when you don't feel it. The only thing I ask is that we don't ever become strangers, because I really—" He breaks off. Clenches his jaw, fighting against some ineffable emotion. "I don't think I could bear it, Leah. I don't think my heart would be able to survive it."

He's gazing at me, waiting, hoping, imploring, and this should be the perfect chance to execute the final step of my plan. It's our last full day here, my last opportunity to do so before the trip comes to an end. He's at my mercy, just like I always wanted. If I reject him right now, tell him that I hate him, that I'll never forgive him for what he did, the consequences will be devastating. He'll suffer terribly, and the image of it—the inevitable hurt on his face, like an open wound, his cheeks tinged red with humiliation—should send a thrill of satisfaction racing through me, but when I open my mouth to deliver the fatal blow, nothing comes out.

Nothing comes out, because his lips are on mine, crushing the distance between us, and instead of pushing him away like I should, like I'd planned to, I pull him closer, one hand guiding him forward by the nape of his neck, the other cupping his face, letting my fingertips linger against the hot shell of his ear, teasing, tapping a faint beat in rhythm with his pounding heart. *I can always break it later*, I reassure myself, a half thought that crumbles when his mouth parts, soft and slow and slightly stunned, and I can sense his disbelief when he inhales. And even though he's far from the first boy I've kissed, it feels as if he is; the others simply don't count compared to him. He kisses me not like he wants to own me, but like he's mine, and he's desperate to prove it.

"You have to know how much I wanted this," he whispers, his breathing unsteady, his voice thick and hoarse the way it is when you've just woken from sleeping too long. "Qin ai de."

I recognize the words. "Did you just call me your worst enemy?"

He smiles against my lips. "I was lying."

"What?"

"Qin ai de doesn't mean *my worst enemy*," he says. "It means *my love*."

I barely let him finish speaking. I kiss him harder, my thoughts all tangled up like lace ribbons in the collar of his shirt, in the feel of his arms, and the shadowed corner of the alley just a few yards away, where we would be free to do whatever we wanted—

"Oh damn."

Oliver's voice cuts through the air, snipping the ribbons of my thoughts in half, and I release Cyrus reluctantly, my eyes opening to the sight of his swollen lips and dark glare.

"I swear that guy is everywhere," Cyrus mutters to me, adjusting his clothes.

"I know," I whisper back as I turn around. "He's basically omnipresent."

"Sorry," Oliver calls out to us as he walks over, his grin only half-sheepish. "I didn't mean to interrupt. We should be heading back to the group now though. If you want to continue later, then by all means, go for it. Since I just won two hundred dollars, I'll even be extra generous and steer clear of our hotel room tonight until curfew."

"Two hundred dollars?" I repeat with a frown. "For what?"

"Yeah, so, um, there's kind of a running bet in the group about whether you two would get together," he says cheerily, following us back down the alley. "And, you know, being the genius that I am, I figured early on that it was a win-win situation if I bet on it happening. If you didn't like Cyrus, then maybe I'd have a shot with you. And if you did like him, then I'd make some extra money."

"Why are those the only two possibilities?" Cyrus demands, sidestepping a manhole that Oliver marches right over.

Oliver throws him an incredulous glance. "Let's face it, bro, it's not as if there was any chance *you* didn't like *her*. Like, you can barely stand up when you're in her presence. You look at her like you're seeing the moon for the first time or some shit. It's kind of disgustingly obvious."

"Thanks for that," Cyrus says, but despite the self-consciousness creeping into his voice, he doesn't deny any of it.

"Anytime, bro."

I have to bite the inside of my cheek to stop from smiling too wide.

The most memorable conversation I've ever had with Cate Addison took place shortly after I kissed Adam, the popular quarterback.

We were lounging across the chairs in the cafeteria with her friends—because in my mind they were always first and foremost *her* friends, even if we all went out to brunch and the movies and parties together on a regular basis—when I told her.

"We kissed before lunch," I said. "Or, well, he kissed me, and I went along with it." And then I waited eagerly for her reaction. It was ridiculous, but that was the main reason I'd let Adam kiss me in the first place—so I could talk about it with Cate afterward. In those early days, I kept hoping for a breakthrough, something that would allow us to really, truly bond and giggle and whisper together like best friends in movies. Sometimes I just wanted proof that she actually *liked* me, and wasn't keeping me around because I made for a nice prop in her social circle.

Cate had glanced up briefly from her blueberry bagel. "Um, who?"

This was after Adam had been texting me for weeks on end—they were mostly emojis, which I had mixed feelings about—and had delivered a bouquet of doughnuts straight to my doorstep. "Adam," I clarified anyway.

"Oh. Cool," she replied, then held up her phone to show me something in her shopping cart. "Hey, do you think this dress looks cheap?"

It was all very anticlimactic, and I'm sure Cate had forgotten what we were talking about by the end of lunch. But I remember every detail from that exchange because it was from then on that I vowed to stop getting my hopes up. To stop wanting *more*—from others, for myself. I had people to sit with at lunch, people who were nice to me, a relatively secure position on the social ladder, and that was enough.

So I'm not expecting much when I tell Daisy in a restaurant bathroom that I kissed Cyrus.

She almost drops the paper towel in her hand. "You did *what?*" she asks, whirling around to face me, eyes wide. "Oh my god, when? Are you guys together now?"

And maybe I hadn't managed to throw my hope away completely, because when I start talking, every unimportant detail spilling from me in an excited rush, Daisy nodding fast and clapping a hand over her mouth at all the right parts, I feel it rising up beneath my ribs. The delight of finding a real, true friend, someone you can talk to about anything, no matter how serious or silly.

"I'm so happy for you," Daisy gushes, then pauses, scanning my face like a bridesmaid seeing the bride in her wedding gown for the very first time. "Are you happy it happened?"

"I . . . don't know," I confess. Now that the initial giddiness from the kiss has had time to settle, and my brain cells aren't being compromised by my hormones, more questions have popped up. Do I still go through with my revenge plan? Do I make him my boyfriend? Are we dating now, or are we something else?

"What do you mean, you don't know?" Daisy asks.

"There's just a lot for me to process," I say. "It happened so suddenly and it wasn't what I expected and . . . I'm still not sure where to go from here."

She doesn't push me for details, but she does offer me a gentle smile in the mirror. "Well, if you ever want to talk about it— I'm here."

"Thank you," I tell her, which feels too light, insufficient. It means more than she could possibly know.

As Daisy finishes drying her hands, I unzip my makeup bag and start gently dusting powder around my nose and cheeks. Out of the corner of my eye, I notice her watching.

"Where did you learn to do that?" she asks.

"What? This?" I swish the brush I'm holding in midair.

"Yeah. Your makeup is perfect all the time," she says, her voice half-curious, half-admiring, which takes me by surprise. I've only ever seen her barefaced, and I'd figured from our first night in Shanghai that she simply wasn't interested in makeup.

"I've had a ton of practice," I tell her, then hesitate, unsure how to word my next offer without sounding like I'm making a rude suggestion or pushing her into something she isn't comfortable with. "Do you want me to do your makeup for you? Just for fun?"

She flushes. "Oh, I was just curious. You don't have to— I mean, it's probably a lot of trouble, and your products look pretty expensive—"

"I literally dream of doing my sister's makeup," I assure her, pulling her closer to the mirror and angling her face toward the vanity lights with my free hand.

"You have a sister?" she says.

"Not at all. Which is why this is a dream come true for me," I say as I examine her features up close. They're softer than mine, doll-like and sweet, so I go for a more natural look, dipping my brush into the warm browns and baby pinks in my palette.

"I've attempted to do my own makeup before," Daisy tells me, closing her eyes to let me dab concealer below her brow bone. "Emphasis on *attempt*. But I swear it just made me look even worse, and I almost poked my eye out with the mascara wand. I just . . . I don't know how to do the things that others girls seem to do so effortlessly," she says, her voice small. "I don't know how to pose for photos, or curl my hair, or walk in high heels. I've asked my mom before, but she's very practical—not in a bad way or anything, but she'd tell me to just go read or study instead of wasting time trying to look nice."

"Well, you do already look nice, and you don't *need* to know how to do this," I say, smudging blush in a circular motion over her cheeks. "But if you want to, I can teach you. Also, for what it's worth . . ." I hesitate. Do I break the illusion? Ditch the false image I've crafted of being naturally confident, naturally beautiful? It feels safe, is the thing. It's something I can hide behind, so nobody can ever mock me like they did at my old schools. But how can I ever be truly loved and known if I'm always hiding?

So before I can lose my nerve, I push myself to go on. "I didn't know how to do those things either. It took a *lot* of trial and error—if you'd met me two years ago, you wouldn't even think I was the same person."

She blinks, stunned, like she hadn't even thought it possible, but there's no trace of mockery in her features. "Really?"

"Really."

A brief beat of silence.

"Leah?" she says, meeting my eyes in the mirror.

"Yeah?"

"When I first saw you, I thought you would hate me," she admits.

"I get that a lot," I say with a snort. "It's just my face, unfortunately."

"No, no," she says quickly. "It's my problem; I tend to assume that everyone hates me. There might be some deep-seated childhood trauma there, but what I'm getting at is, you have this . . . this cold, unapproachable aura—"

"Like an icicle," I put in. "Or an abandoned house."

"Like the green-tongue Popsicles I've always loved."

I set the blush back down by the sink and cast her a bemused look. "The what?"

"Lü she tou," she says. "It looks like a regular green Popsicle, but it's made of jelly, so when it melts, it turns soft. Sorry, I know that doesn't sound super appealing, but I promise it's amazing. Anyone who's ever given it a try ends up coming back for more."

"That was probably the strangest and nicest compliment I've ever gotten," I say, my laughter bouncing off the gilded bathroom walls, all my discarded hopes finding their way back to me. "Thank you."

"Anytime."

CHAPTER SEVENTEEN

From morning all the way to the evening, I contemplate the great Cyrus dilemma.

The more I think about it, the less sense it makes. How could he have been in love with me this entire time? It feels like a fabricated tale, a myth on par with Santa or unicorns—or worse, like a practical joke.

And yes, sure, he'd looked and sounded sincere when he was making his sweet declarations. Maybe even *he* believes he means it. But the same thing has happened with a lot of guys in the past, and without exception, they turned around and proved themselves to be liars, or changed their minds about me. How can I trust Cyrus not to do the same?

I'm so distracted that I can't even bring myself to admire the scenery. I know, objectively, that it's gorgeous: the Sun and Moon Pagodas shine side by side over the waters, glowing gold and silver, perfect twins in structure. But there's a difference between knowing something and caring about it, and right now, I could hardly care less where we are, if we were in a literal empty room or standing before one of the Wonders of the World. All my thoughts are narrowed in on the boy beside me.

"Why?" I ask Cyrus as we stroll along the lakeside. It's the first time we've been alone since the kiss in the alley, and during that time, I've created a questionnaire to help determine if his feelings are real. It'd be preferable if I could inspect his thoughts with a microscope, but until technology catches up, this will have to do.

He looks over at me, the waters glittering behind him. "Hm?"

"Why do you even like me?" I ask him, striving to keep my voice light, cool, nonchalant. It's just a question. Just something that's been eating away at me for the past, oh, I don't know, six and a half hours. No big deal.

Cyrus's voice is serious and deep as gravity when he slides his long fingers through mine, intertwining them like a vow, and says, "Why not? It's very easy to fall in love with you, Leah. The easiest thing in the world."

I feel the throb of my heart, the movement reverberating throughout my whole body. How desperately I want to believe him. To accept the words without hesitation.

"I'm not really sure when, exactly, it clicked," he continues, his thumb grazing over the underside of my wrist, gently leading me around a crack in the pavement. "I don't think I even realized I liked you until later. I just knew that I noticed you a lot from the beginning. Like how you would wear a different scrunchie every day of the week, or how you'd always pick out the tomatoes from your sandwiches, or how you were far from a teacher's pet, but you still made sure to thank the teachers at the end of the lesson. I found it fascinating, because you had this very intimidating face, but then you would laugh," he says softly, "and it was like you were glowing."

I bite my tongue, overwhelmed by a riot of sensation, inside me and all around me: the breeze riffling my hair, the distant laughter eddying around the banks, the firs bathed in green lights, the bright smattering of stars in the sky above. Every word he's saying.

"You really mean that?" I ask him, searching his face carefully for lies, warning signs, any damning evidence that might suggest otherwise.

"Yes," he says, with infinite patience. "Of course."

"You actually like me?" I confirm again, just in case. I'm aware that I'm being annoying now, but I can't help myself. "As a person."

"I do. Why is that so hard to believe?"

"I mean, it wouldn't be, if you said you were attracted to me. I'd totally get it. But you're saying you had this huge crush on me," I emphasize, raising my brows with incredulity. "Since *seven years ago.*"

He shakes his head, and my heart stops. *I knew it*, the cruel, ever-present voice in my head declares at once, the voice that sounds like every kid who's ever bullied me. *I knew it was a lie. He doesn't love you after all. Nobody ever will.*

But as tourists squeeze forward to take photos of the shining lake, he turns away from the scenery to face me. "Do you know the Mandarin word for *crush*?"

I frown. "No. What?"

"*Anlian*," he says. "*An* for 'darkness.' *Lian* for 'love.' I always thought it was poetic—that when you secretly have feelings for someone, you love them in the darkness. But there's this other word. *Minglian*. *Ming* for—"

"'Light,'" I finish for him, recognizing the character. It's the same word for bright, or luminous, the way the twin pagodas glow against the night sky.

"So it's not anlian," he says, his eyes dark and intent on me, and though the rest of his sentence goes unspoken, I hear it as clearly as if he had whispered it into my ear: *I don't love you in the darkness; I love you in the light.*

It feels like there's light in my very veins, blazing through my chest and burning away all the years of loneliness before him. And for just a few seconds, my skepticism takes a break, and the voices in my head go quiet.

"Leah. Do you have a moment?"

I glance back over my shoulder, squinting past the tides of people to find Wang Laoshi waving me forward. There's a woman I've never seen before standing next to him—too old to be a student, too young to be a teacher, one of those bulky, professional cameras hanging around her neck. Her makeup is so perfect that it looks photoshopped, and when she smiles at me, I can't help noticing how well her shade of lipstick suits her complexion. It's a dark cherry tint, no gloss, sophisticated but not overdramatic.

"This is Pei Jie," Wang Laoshi introduces us, raising his voice to be heard above the crowds. "She's a photographer for Sima Studio. She noticed you earlier and is offering to take a few free photos of you as part of a promotional campaign they're doing—we would also be able to use them at Jiu Yin He to promote our Journey to the East program for future students." He clears his throat. "Now, it's entirely up to you whether you agree to it or not. I thought it might be a worthwhile experience, and you should have enough time before we gather for tonight's show, but I know not everyone enjoys—or is used to—getting their photo taken . . ."

I almost laugh at the irony. *If only you knew how many photos I've had taken of me.*

"You're very pretty," Pei Jie tells me in Chinese. She goes on to gush about something I can't entirely understand, but I hear the words *model*, and *perfect*, and *beautiful*, and it's like she's plucked them straight out of my old dreams for the future. But they're *old* dreams for a reason. Abandoned, expired. Once upon a time, I would've jumped at this kind of opportunity to prove myself. Now, though, I hesitate.

Before I can respond, Pei Jie holds out her camera and starts scrolling through the photos she's taken in the past. There are dozens of different styles—girls reclining on velvet couches in crimson qipaos, their lips painted crimson to match; smiling sweetly and hugging bouquets of flowers to their chests; leaning, bored, against a brick wall with lollipops in their mouths, their plaid skirts and button-down shirts designed for an alternate world where school uniforms are actually meant to be flattering; posing against an ice-blue backdrop in a stunning ball gown, pearls spilling down the sides. And though the girls themselves are all completely different from one another, she manages to capture their best features.

"Do you want to?" Cyrus asks me quietly, stepping closer to my side. "Don't feel like you have to say yes."

I squeeze his hand, my gratitude too deep to be arranged into words. Even though he couldn't possibly know the real reason for my reluctance, he still sensed it. "I think it's fine," I tell him. "I want to give it a try."

He scans my face for another beat. "Are you sure?"

I nod and turn to Pei Jie. "Okay, let's do it."

"Amazing. I promise it'll be quick—these photos are going to turn out *great*." She starts to usher me forward down the street, waving for Cyrus to follow. "Your boyfriend can watch," she adds, and then, in a whisper just to me, like we're gossiping at the back of a classroom: "Zhen shi ge shuaige ya." Thanks to my exchange with the lettuce seller, I understand the word for *handsome* in an instant.

"I guess he *is* handsome," I allow, neither confirming nor denying the *boyfriend* comment.

She nods discreetly to the girls in the crowd as they pass Cyrus, many of them doing double takes or elbowing their friends when their eyes land on his face. "You often see girls who are much prettier than their boyfriends, but he's the perfect fit for you."

I wonder what she'd say if she saw the girl I was before walking on the street next to him. If she'd still think we were a perfect fit, or if she'd assume, like my classmates had, that I was the one obsessed with him and he was only tolerating my presence.

We turn the corner near a cluster of shops selling jade pendants and grilled squid. Then she guides me down a short flight of stairs, through a somewhat sketchy, dimly lit corridor that opens up to the cornflower-blue walls of a makeup studio. It's instantly familiar to me: the clothing racks bursting with satin and tulle and silk, the vanity mirrors set up in rows of three, the eyebrow pencils and lipstick-smeared cotton swabs lying out on dressing tables, the dolled-up girls assessing their glossy reflections with varying degrees of satisfaction and scrutiny.

"Sit here," Pei Jie says, pulling me toward the empty table in the middle. She yells something to one of the makeup artists, who's testing out brushes on her wrist, then pats my shoulder. In the mirror, I lock eyes with Cyrus, who stands patiently off to the side, hands in his pockets. He offers me a small, encouraging smile, like he can detect the shakiness spreading through my muscles, and I breathe in. Remind myself that it won't be the same as last time. If I need to, I can always leave.

"Have you ever tried on traditional clothing before?" Pei Jie asks. "I think it would look incredible on you; your features are so well suited for it."

I don't know how to answer her, if what I had worn for that awful photo shoot would even count. The memory rattles against the back of my skull like a monster in a closet, flashes of white-hot lights and bloodred tassels, the sick feeling pooling in my stomach. I draw in another tight breath. Shake my head.

"Well, now is the perfect chance." Pei Jie waves at another woman and points to an elaborate set of scarlet-and-gold robes hanging over the dressing room door. "Prepare to be amazed," she says.

Shortly after I made up my mind to turn pretty, I fell down the rabbit hole of makeover videos.

It was the closest thing to love at first sight I've ever experienced. I would sit cross-legged in my bedroom, the stuffed orange giraffe my mom had brought back from a business trip for me squashed against my stomach, and watch every makeover video I could find on the internet. I wasn't just obsessed with seeing the results, which filled me with the same sense of wonder and awe as pulling back the window shades just in time to catch a brilliant sunset, but the process itself. How a few swipes of mascara, a flattering dress, and some nice hair extensions could transform a person into a completely new version of themselves. The girls were already beautiful at the start, but by the end of the video, you could tell that they felt it too.

That was the feeling I chased in the first few photo shoots I did. I wanted to be astonished by my reflection in the mirror, to see myself in a new way. I wanted to be completely, irrefutably happy with how I looked, even though it seemed an impossible task: You stare at your own face long enough and you'll inevitably find something to hate about it.

But for every occasion where modeling succeeded in making me feel beautiful, radiant, valued, like the girls in the makeover videos, there were a dozen more occasions where it made me feel like I was nothing. I soon learned to lower my expectations, to brace myself for the moment the makeup artist stepped back, prepare for the possibility that I would have to redo my eyeliner myself because they weren't sure how to work with the shape.

I brace myself now as I slowly open my eyes, the shadows from my false lashes skimming the very edges of my vision. I had been too nervous to look while the makeup artist brushed my face with powders and slid pin after pin into my hair, but I feel my chest expand, my jaw releasing its grip as I blink and blink again at the person in the mirror.

"You like it?" Pei Jie asks.

I nod fast, the amber beads in my headpiece rattling like music. I've never looked this way before, but I also look more like myself than I ever have in the past; the tiny gems glued below my lash line make my eyes that much brighter, more alive, the rose blush dusted along my nose and cheekbones blending naturally into my skin, the vermilion tint enhancing the bow shape of my lips. It's makeup that doesn't try to alter my features or hide them or exaggerate them to near-satirical proportions. And suddenly there's an embarrassing knot in my throat, delight and gratitude and raw relief at being seen, and I have to swallow hard to speak. "What do you think?" I ask Cyrus, standing up and twirling before him, the fabric of my robes swishing past my ankles.

He doesn't reply. He's too busy staring, his eyes wide and transfixed, like he's not sure I'm real.

"I think you've left him speechless," Pei Jie says to me, laughing.

Cyrus flushes, and takes a tentative step closer. "You're incredible," he breathes.

"This is going to sound silly, but I feel like a princess," I admit, touching the delicate silk sash around my waist. "Like, I want to drink from a fancy teacup and then take a bath filled with rose petals and walk very slowly down the stairs where my lover awaits below."

"You should've spoken sooner about the rose petals; Oliver and I collected a whole basket of them at our last hotel room. I'm definitely free to wait below a flight of stairs though," he says. "I can wait as long as you'd like."

I roll my eyes, but I'm smiling.

With the swift, determined steps of someone on a mission, Pei Jie leads us out into the night again, glancing behind her shoulder every few seconds to check that I haven't tripped over the long layers of my skirts or gotten lost in the crowds. Instead of heading in the direction we came from, we walk farther down the street, where the architecture starts to draw inspiration from ancient China, designed with stone carvings and crimson pillars and curved roofs. It's like existing in two time periods at once. Outside the noodle restaurants and pagoda-style art galleries are the cool white haloes of ring lights, where live-streamers are broadcasting themselves singing or talking animatedly about whatever makeup products they're holding.

"This spot is good," Pei Jie declares, fiddling with the lens on her camera as we stop outside a hotel that could pass for a palace. Crimson lanterns tumble from the gold-lit eaves, and scholar's rocks pose artfully outside the double gates. "You stay where you are."

The people are more scattered here, most of them also trying to get pretty pictures. A girl a few yards away is attempting to teach her boyfriend how to take photos of her, gesturing with increasing desperation for him to angle the camera higher, until she finally gives up, switches to selfie mode, and turns him into a human phone-stand while she records herself.

"Start walking toward me now," Pei Jie instructs while Cyrus finds a safe spot behind the camera to watch. "Slowly. Move your left hand a little, like you're brushing your hair but not actually brushing it. Look over there—you see that lantern on your right, by the door? Keep looking. Lower your shoulder. Your other shoulder. Keep your chin down. Okay, yes, good! Now hold—"

I stumble over some of the instructions at first, partly because it's been a while since I had to do this, and partly because of my

Mandarin skills. But I guess posing is a pretty universal thing, because even if some of her tips sail straight over my head and splatter on the ground behind me, I soon ease into the rhythm of it. I bring my hand to my cheek as if I'm suffering from a toothache, but in a high-fashion way. I tighten my abdominal muscles and arch my back. I wave my broad sleeves in the air and place one foot gracefully in front of the other and look up, look left, look pretty.

A few tourists stop to stare as they pass us, but I don't get the same self-conscious, ready-to-hide feeling I used to. It's like my brain has undergone a makeover too, those dark spots of doubt brushed away and replaced by almost obnoxiously optimistic thoughts. *Maybe they're staring because they also think this style suits me. Maybe they're admiring how the pins glow in my hair. Maybe they too want to experience the thrill of spinning around in traditional robes. Maybe they're trying to figure out how much a photo shoot like this costs.*

"You're doing such an amazing job," Pei Jie calls out to me a few dozen different angles later, the camera clicking furiously. "Have you ever modeled before?"

I swallow. "No," I say, but the lie worms its way down my throat and sharpens its teeth to gnaw at my stomach.

"Well, maybe it's something you should consider," she says, lowering the camera to inspect the last couple of photos. "All right, I think we're finished here. Thank you *so* much for agreeing to this—I can't wait for you to see how they turn out. We'll do some retouching and send the final files through to Wang Laoshi—I've already added him on WeChat..." She starts going into what I assume to be the technical things, and that's where my Mandarin fails me and I have to revert to smiling and nodding and hoping that she hasn't slipped in a question about whether I'd be happy to sell her a vital organ.

But I understand exactly what she says as I turn to go, only because I've heard the same words from my friends and relatives before, always meant to be encouraging, to steer me toward the right place in life: "It'd be such a waste if you weren't a model."

Before, I would've given those words all the weight in the world. I would've let myself become convinced that, yes, being a model is the only way for me, if that's what other people think. But a new, exhilarating thought pushes up in resistance: *It's not for them to decide.* I *could* be a model, but I could be a thousand other things, lead other lives, follow new paths and find my way forward. I can't know exactly where I'll end up, but I don't have to let them choose for me.

I walk without looking back. The farther I go, the lighter I feel.

CHAPTER EIGHTEEN

It takes far less time to remove the elaborate wig and robes than it took to put them on, but most of the evening is already gone when I join Cyrus outside the studio.

The last time I brought a boy along to one of my photo shoots—and only because he'd insisted that he was interested—he had gotten bored and wandered off halfway through. When I went to find him, he'd snuck into some other photo shoot for a lingerie ad, his eyes glued to the models who were older and prettier than I was, as if he'd completely forgotten that I existed. He looked at them the same way he would look at me when he wanted to kiss me, and I was suddenly nauseated that I'd ever let him kiss me at all.

A small part of me had expected Cyrus to grow bored of the photo shoot too, but he's waiting right there by the door, patient as ever, my purse hanging around his shoulder.

Tenderness blazes through me, warming the empty space between my ribs.

"Thanks for holding my bag," I tell him, reaching over to take it from him.

"It's an honor to hold your bag," he says. "And it's so light I barely felt it."

I laugh as we wander over to the quieter parts of the lake, where the lights are dim enough to see the pearlescent shimmer of the moon above us, and the trees are dense enough to drape their leaves around us like curtains. "Okay, you don't have to pretend. I know that thing's ridiculously heavy."

"I *was* starting to wonder if your hobbies included carrying bricks in your purse."

"Yeah, those are my only two passions in life," I agree sarcastically. "Drawing clouds and carrying bricks around."

But his expression turns thoughtful, as if I've just uttered something profound. "You know, you looked happy earlier, doing the photo shoot. It's none of my business, of course, but I suppose I'm still trying to understand why you gave it up if it was something you loved so much."

I stop walking. Glance up at him. I can tell that he means it—that he's really trying, his eyes dark and earnest as they study me. And my lie from earlier scrabbles its way back up, itching inside my throat. "I don't know if I loved it," I say slowly. Because was it really love if it ate away at you? If it felt like trying to hold on to a fanged creature while it sucked the blood from your hand? All I know is that I had to let go before it killed me. "It just stopped being worth it."

"What do you mean?"

"It's kind of hard to explain, but modeling is different from, like, gardening or knitting," I say, rubbing my arms. "It's not this skill that you can separate from yourself. It's *you*; you're the product. It's your appearance that they're selling. So when you get criticism, it's always going to be personal, and it's very often about things you can't control: They'll tell you that you're not tall enough, or you're not striking enough, or you stand out too much. I mean, I've had someone say straight to my face at an audition that I simply wasn't attractive. Not even, like, a specific feature. Just everything about me."

I can feel his eyes on me, and I falter. *Am I really doing this?* Am I really about to tell him the truth, spit out the hot stone of shame that's been burning inside me this whole time? It's my last defense against him. Once I say it, I realize, there'll be no going back. I'll have trusted him with everything, and it'll be entirely up to him what he wishes to do with it. He might like me less after I tell him. He might not understand.

But there's nobody else in the world I can imagine sharing this with. Nobody else I *want* to confess to, as terrifying as it feels, as high the risk is.

So I take a deep breath, like I'm about to dive headfirst into the ocean, and continue, knowing as I do that it's really a lost cause now. I might as well be offering him my heart on my palms, holding out hope he'll be tender with it.

"It's really twisted, but it's like, the more worthless they make you feel, the more determined you are to prove your worth to them. I tried to take on all their criticism and change myself. They told me to tone my legs, so I did those stupid diets and threw myself into my workouts. They told me I had to grow my platform, so I made all these social media posts and obsessed over my numbers and wore myself out trying to keep up with the trends. But I still didn't have that mainstream appeal they were after, and it took me forever to figure out what they actually meant by *mainstream*."

Because it was also what the boys who dated me really wanted, even if they didn't directly admit it. They'd whisper things like, *You're the first Asian girl I've ever been with*, or, *You're so gorgeous—I can't believe you're Chinese*, as if I was meant to feel special or grateful to be some kind of exception, and once their interest in me fizzled out, they would turn their attention back to the gorgeous blonde girls in our class. I looked nothing like them, and I never would.

"I regret it now," I say bitterly, "but I did whatever I could to blend in. I copied their makeup style that wasn't suited for me at all, and I never volunteered my Chinese name if I could help it. Even if I was never going to be mainstream, I—I just wanted to be closer to it. I felt like I had to, or else nobody would want me. Then all of a sudden, people were saying that it was trendy to be Asian. It was *cool*. I booked more jobs within a couple months than I had in a full year. And then they asked me to do a photo shoot for this magazine—I don't know if you've heard of *Amalia*—"

"The one with the hot-pink logo?" he asks. "I think I've seen it before."

"That's the one. It has a pretty good reputation, so obviously

I said yes. I was genuinely excited going in; I thought that it was my moment. That I would become, like, a real, proper model after I did it, and everything would be worth it, because that's how it goes in the movies, right?"

I don't realize I'm tugging at my hair until I feel the pain prickling my scalp. I force my fingers back down to my side, my gut churning as the memories bubble up like acid. This is the part I've blocked out. The part I haven't even let myself think about for too long.

"You don't have to explain anymore," Cyrus says softly.

"No, it's okay." And it really is. For once, I just want to be honest about all the ways it hurts. I could never have done that, before. When you sign up for this industry, you give up more than just your image and your name; you give up your ability to cry out to the people who are hurting you.

You're told to put your head down. Stick it out. Grit your teeth until they break. Shut up and be grateful. Remember that you're living out every girl's dream, and nobody wants to hear about the nights you lie awake hurting, so hungry you could gnaw on your own hand. Because there's a literal line of people waiting to replace you the moment you tire, and they're all prettier than you, or prettier in a different way, and they won't complain.

"From the second I walked into that photo shoot, everything felt off," I say, finding my voice again. "The whole theme was meant to tie back to ancient China, but I was the only person there who was even Chinese. And then the backdrop just looked . . . It looked like someone with the *vaguest* idea of where Asia was on a map had thrown it together overnight, and the clothes they asked me to put on were supposed to be traditional robes, but they didn't even remotely resemble what I was wearing earlier tonight, and the skirt was so much shorter than I was comfortable with, and I just felt so—exposed. In every way."

"Leah, I'm sorry," Cyrus tells me, his features tight, like he's in pain thinking about it. "I'm so sorry you had to go through that. You shouldn't have had to."

When he pulls me to his chest, I feel something inside me fissure.

Everything I've been forcing back, every memory I've buried, all the hate I've harbored, the blame I bore. *I'm so sorry you had to go through that.* Here, at last—someone to understand and smooth my hair with his palm and hold me tight, tight enough that the memories retreat to the edges and I let myself sink into him. I never even told my parents exactly why I left. I didn't tell anyone, because I thought, foolishly, that I could digest the shard of glass in my stomach given enough time.

"I just couldn't do it anymore," I whisper against his shirt. "The day after the photo shoot, I woke up and I thought: *I can't go on like this.* And that was it. I couldn't. I didn't have the strength to." I swallow. "Does that make me weak?"

After all, there was a certain narrative prevalent in the documentaries I watched: the rise and fall and inevitable rise again of the hero. The shocking pain of the fall itself was only relevant because it paved the way for their return to the spotlight, their grand victory. Everyone loves an underdog, so long as they ultimately win in the end. Otherwise, the story isn't complete.

But for every singer or actor or model who's achieved the kind of breathtaking ascent people dream of, how many have simply disappeared like me? Quit halfway through? Changed courses?

"No," Cyrus says, his fingers threading through my hair. "No, you're not weak at all. If something costs more than it's worth, you let it go. If anybody dares make you feel bad for it, then screw them."

I make a sound that's part sob, part laugh, and it feels like a page turning. Like stepping out into the summer rain, letting the water run down my face and wash everything away.

CHAPTER NINETEEN

My whole body feels lighter as we join the others in the stands for the night show.

Impression of Liu Sanjie: A Folk Song Story. It's set entirely outside, the sheer scale of it shocking, unlike anything I've been to before. The stage is the Li River itself, the twelve peaks of the mountains behind it forming the natural backdrop. A soft breeze floats through the gathered crowds, people squishing into the front rows of the green-shrouded terraces, some already getting their cameras out.

There's not much room left, but Cyrus shifts back, giving me more space to stretch out my legs. Which is a very nice, chivalrous thing to do, except I don't really want any space from him.

"Are you cold?" he asks me.

"Not cold enough to need a jacket," I say, and lean toward him, my head resting against the crook of his neck. "This is good."

What I mean is: This is perfect. It feels like the grand finale—the last night of the trip, the last part of the competition. We just have to write an essay describing tonight's show, and then it'll all be over.

The night deepens, turning everything into shades of blue.

The moonlight shines down over the water like a spotlight, and the mist rolls in over the river, and I'm mesmerized. It's like the show is the world, or the world is a show; performers float in on rafts, seemingly descend from the sky dressed in silver and silk, the music rising like the hills.

It's a love story, I soon realize. A girl sings to her lover from across the river, her movements in trained harmony with the dancers around her, her voice floating up to us, clear and sweet and luminous. Then the scene changes to gold, the performers rowing forward with hundreds of fishing lights.

I'm so transfixed that I don't notice the whispers in the beginning. Not until they pick up over the music, spreading fast. Not until I hear my name.

". . . god, what was she . . ."

". . . thought she looked familiar . . ."

I sit up straight, alert, and squint around. Most people in the crowd are still watching the dancers, but then I see Sean holding up his phone, whispering furiously to the girl sitting next to him, who shakes her head. Then they both look straight at me. The hairs on my arms stand up. They're all looking at me—practically everyone in our group. It's dark here in the stands, but I swear I can see the disbelief in their expressions.

Cyrus turns around and frowns. "What's going on?" he whispers to me.

I shake my head, my stomach tightening.

And that's when I spot the photo displayed on Sean's phone, right as he flips it over to show it to someone else. A violent buzzing fills my skull, as if a swarm of wasps have suddenly rushed in through my ears.

It's me.

It's me, but not how I would ever want to be seen. Me with bright, bright red lipstick and heavy blue eyeliner and cheap tassels draped over my skin. That nightmare of a photo shoot, the very thing I had confided to Cyrus less than an hour ago. It makes my aunt's comment about me at the wedding seem almost generous. *Ignorant foreigner.* Because who else would agree to a photo shoot like that? I hate that girl, hate that photo, and it should've stayed buried in the past, but it's here again, haunting me. Of course. No matter how hard I run, I can never escape the versions of myself I used to be.

But that doesn't explain *how* people found those photos of me, unless—

As if in tune with the dread roiling through me, the music in the background changes, the string instruments shrieking, the drums clapping louder.

I jerk away from Cyrus. "Did you tell them?" I whisper.

"What?" His eyes are wide, but I don't know if it's from confusion or guilt. If it's only an act.

"The photo shoot," I say, my voice trembling. Even my hands are shaking, the stands swaying beneath me, everything cracking apart. There's nothing for me to hold on to, nothing to steady my heart against. I want to vomit. "You—you're the only person I told."

"Of course I didn't," he says quickly. "You know I wouldn't."

Do I really? Once the voice sneaks into my thoughts, I can't shake it out. I'd wanted to think that Cyrus was different from the other guys. I'd been so willing to trust him, to accept his apology about the past, to hand my heart over to him. But it's like I've been doused with freezing water, left gasping as the chill sets into my stomach. My mind spins with images of the boys I've been with before: the unexpected flash of the camera when I leaned in to kiss one of them, documenting a private moment so they could share it with their friends; the boy who bragged about making out with me before my lipstick had even dried on his mouth; the ones who only remembered to text me back when I posted a pretty photo of myself in a tight dress. All the boys who'd charm me and kiss me and lose interest right after, the thrill of the chase expired.

What if Cyrus isn't any different? What if his kindness was a ploy all along, his tenderness something I'd made up inside my head just because I wanted him? More questions crowd forth, racing one another toward the worst-case scenario.

It's all just too much of a coincidence. I'd offered him the one piece of my life I've hidden from everyone else—and almost right away, this happens.

"Leah," Cyrus says, but I can barely hear him over the loud, incessant buzzing in my eardrums. "Leah, please—"

"Why should I trust you?" I demand. Oh my god, I think I'm really, actually going to be sick. I'm so *stupid*. If I weren't about to burst into tears, I'd laugh at myself, at everything I was thinking a few minutes ago, fantasizing about a grand love story with the boy who's already proven himself capable of destroying my life. Such naivete, such disgusting *optimism*, thinking I'd finally found someone who knew me, who would protect me, keep my secrets safe.

I should've known better.

Then Sean holds his phone up, his eyes locking with mine, the accusation in them clear. "Leah, is this you?"

Everyone from our group is watching me. Waiting for an explanation, or maybe simply waiting for me to confirm that I am a terrible person, a fake, a sellout, a slut, someone complicit in the fetishization of their culture. Even Oliver is frowning at the photos, his mouth puckered with what must be distaste or pure disgust. A recent memory rises like a sepia-toned scene from an old film: laughing in the bus seat next to him, our fists raised in mock toast, *to friendship.*

Now there's no mock toast, just self-mockery. *What* friendship? These people barely know me; we've only spent a total of two weeks together. Traveling on the same tight schedule to the same pretty places might have bred the illusion of intimacy and comradery, but that can't change the age-old curse: The more people know about me, the less they like me.

"I—I didn't want to do it," I try to explain, and I'm talking too loud now, but it's like I've lost control over my mouth, lost the ability to breathe. "I really didn't—I mean, it's me but I—"

A woman from higher up in the crowds shushes me, silencing my desperate attempts to win over the jury after the verdict has already been reached.

It's like the Incident all over again.

But it feels like I'm the one falling from the stairs, the ground giving way underneath me, the breathless, terrifying tumble and the violent, rib-cracking jolt of the landing. So much for fresh slates, new beginnings, shots in the dark at happiness. I can feel all the layers that had sloughed off hardening around my heart again.

I stumble onto my feet. Squeeze past the people in the stands, mumbling apologies under my breath. I have no idea where I'm going. My feet are moving on their own, faster and faster, taking me up the stairs, to the exit, back out onto the road, my heels clapping against the stone pavement. I can't think about anything except the fact that I need to leave. Now.

There's a sharp, sour feeling stuffed in the back of my throat and nose, like when you choke on a mouthful of water, and the more I try to blink away the tears, the harder they press against my eyes, until finally, the invisible rope that's been tying me together snaps, and everything goes blurry. The pale light of the moon wobbles in my vision, the stars streaking silver across the sky, and I'm still walking, hugging my arms around myself, crying so hard that I can't even breathe.

My whole body heaves as the tears trickle down my chin, the taste of salt seeping into my mouth.

I'm alone, I realize. I'm so hopelessly, utterly alone—the road ahead is empty, and around me there's nothing but rice paddies rippling in the breeze like the waves of the sea, the dark streams running between them, and the layered, indigo shadows of the mountains. I can never see the people from this trip again. I'll have to buy an early plane ticket to LA and run back to my parents and—

And then what?

There's nothing for me.

I repeat the words in my head, and then out loud, sobbing them over and over to myself like I'm trying to build up immunity, but it cuts deep enough to bleed each time. Hurts in new, different ways. *There's nothing for me. There's nothing for me anywhere. There's nothing left.* I wasn't good enough at the only thing I'm good at. Everything I did was for nothing. Everything I gave up just landed me here, alone at the very bottom.

I wipe my eyes roughly with my sleeve, my ribs aching, the weeds tickling my bare ankles. I'm walking so fast that I almost don't notice the cow crossing the road.

I stop, rub my eyes again, my surprise freezing my tears in place. The cow stares serenely back at me under a trickle of moonlight, its large brown eyes following me as I step forward. It occurs to me that I've never really seen a cow up close before, and there's something majestic about the way it lifts its heavy head to the stars, the gloss of its deep brown fur. It's chewing grass, its mouth moving in a slow rhythm, like it has all the time it needs.

And for a moment, I forget that my world is ending.

"Hello," I say softly, through sniffles.

The cow's ears flicker toward the sound of my voice. Another breeze ruffles the paddies, their surfaces darkening with movement, and the night air turns cooler, the scent of it sweet and laced with Osmanthus. The landscape flows around the creature like a poem, and I'm stunned by how readily my heart makes room for beauty, even at a time like this.

"Did my cow startle you?" An elderly woman walks over from the same place the cow had appeared, wisps of silvery-white hair floating around her bun. She has the sort of face you would stop to ask for directions in a foreign city: Her broad features are kind, her eyes crinkling when she says, "Don't be afraid. She doesn't like to bite people."

"I—I know. I'm not afraid of her," I say in Chinese, reaching out to the cow. She meets me halfway, bumping her nose gently against my hand, her fur so much softer than I expected, and warm, as if she had been lying down in a sunny orchard just before.

"Then why are you crying?" the woman asks.

My throat threatens to close up again. I could blame it on something else, anything: allergies, a sad movie I watched, a silly argument with a friend. But it's like I've forgotten how to lie and act nonchalant, or maybe I've just never been good at indifference. The instinct—the impulse—to tell the truth is overwhelming. "Because I failed."

"You failed?" she repeats, her voice free of judgment. There's only concern and more patience than I deserve. "At what?"

"Everything," I say tearily, not even bothering to hold together the last cracks in my composure anymore. I fumble for the right words in Chinese. "My life. I—I have no idea what to do or where to go. Everyone else has their own talents, like a sport or an instrument or a subject in school, and they're all heading off to college with some idea of what they want, and it's like they were all made for something. But I'm not smart enough, and I'm not athletic, and I'm not particularly likable, and I'm not that funny or interesting, and I don't even have a five-day plan, let alone a five-year plan. Maybe I'll never be better than this," I whisper, still patting the cow. It's the closest thing to comfort that I have right now. "Maybe I'm just not cut out for anything."

If I were the woman, and a stranger had just given me this deeply depressing speech while using my cow as their emotional support animal, I would probably be fleeing into the distance.

But she smiles at me, and with a sharp pang, I remember how my nainai would smile across the dinner table at me while I ate the chicken soup noodles she'd cooked, like I was the most precious thing she had ever seen. Like the simple fact that I existed was a joy.

"It'll work out," she tells me.

My voice trembles. "But—what if it doesn't?"

"Look at the sky," she says.

"What?"

"Look at the sky," she repeats steadily.

I do, and at first I have no idea what I'm meant to be looking at. There's nothing. But then the sky opens up. The stars are brighter than I've ever seen them, like pinpricks in the velvet darkness, letting the light in. Entire constellations lie above me, endless, eternal, and there's a feeling I can't name stirring deep inside my chest, like reaching the bridge of your favorite song. The fresh gash of the memory doesn't disappear from my mind, but it's just one star of many, glistening in the night.

Slowly, I breathe out.

"Leah?"

I spin around at the sound of Daisy's voice. She's stopped a yard away from me, her arm half-outstretched, hesitant, like she's not sure what to do next, but maybe that's just because I'm standing next to a cow. Then she sees the tears dampening my face or maybe just the look in my eyes and she rushes forward.

The old woman steps politely to the side, leading the cow out of the way.

"Are you okay?" Daisy asks, squeezing my hand.

I'd been expecting plenty of questions, from *Why **didn't** you* *tell us you were a model?* to *What the hell were you thinking when you did that photo shoot?* But not this one.

"Why—why are you here?" My voice catches.

"What?" She looks confused by my confusion.

"That photo shoot . . . you saw it, everyone saw it. And I'm not even a model anymore," I babble, aware that I'm probably making zero sense. "You don't gain anything out of being friends with me, so why did you follow me?"

Daisy stares at me, stunned. Then, very slowly, she says, "Leah, have you never had a real friend before?"

A real friend. My mind browses through the years and comes back empty-handed. *You have plenty of people you hang out with at school*, I try to remind myself. *Hundreds of numbers in your phone. People who compliment you all the time and invite you to things.* But how many of them can I actually call? Someone like Cate would drop me in a heartbeat if I ever made a scene the way I did just now. With her, everything is conditional, transactional.

"No, not really," I whisper. It's so humiliating to admit that I can't even look at her when I say it. The mirage is gone now, the beauty filter switched off, the makeup removed. It doesn't matter how pretty or popular I make myself—I'm always going to be the girl nobody wanted to sit with at lunch.

"Okay, well, now you do," Daisy says. She sounds more sure of herself than I've ever heard her, and I jerk my head up in surprise. "I don't know exactly what you've experienced in the past," she goes on, louder, raising her voice for the first time since we met at the airport, "and there are a lot of horrible people and horrible situations, but you can't keep holding on to that for the rest of your life. You have to believe that there are people who will genuinely like you, and care about you, and worry over you when something's wrong."

I swallow thickly. "I . . . I'm just . . ." Bone-tired. Unbelievably, extraordinarily sad. Guilty. Betrayed. Heartbroken, heart-shattered, heartsick. All of the above, and yet, that still wouldn't even begin to cover it. Every emotion I've ever pushed down in the past few years has reappeared, breaking past my ribs.

"Also, for what it's worth," Daisy adds, "Sean's an asshole."

"Sean?" I repeat, confused.

"He kept insisting that he recognized you from somewhere, and then he basically stalked you online for proof . . ."

I barely hear the rest of what she says. "*Sean* was the one who found the photo shoot?" I ask, my pulse skipping.

She nods.

"Not Cyrus?"

"Cyrus?" Her brows scrunch. "No, I don't think any of us have even spoken to him since lunch."

"You're certain?"

"Certain . . . that he didn't find the photo shoot?" Daisy asks, looking bewildered that I'm even confirming this with her. "Of course he didn't. You should've seen him after you ran off—he was . . . Well, let's just say that I don't think you should be worried about anyone spreading those photos around."

The wasps in my head finally go still. It had been instinct to distrust him. Instinct to assume the worst. If you were to suffer a blow to your stomach every time you walked down a road, you would automatically start tensing before you've even taken the first step, bracing for the pain. You wouldn't dare believe that one day, you'll be able to walk right down, and someone will be waiting at the end of it, smiling gently up at you.

"I need to talk to him," I say, but not before I pull Daisy into a tight hug. She's so much shorter than I am that I'm scared of crushing her, but she hugs me back just as hard, pressing her head to my shoulder. "Thank you," I whisper. "For coming after me. For being on my side."

"I'll always be on your side," she says, and I believe it.

CHAPTER TWENTY

Our itinerary doesn't really plan for private conversations after you dramatically run off into the night.

I'm forced to chew on my words all the way from the final scene of the performance to the bus ride back to the hotel. But instead of heading back to my room, I follow Cyrus to his.

"Yeah, I just remembered I needed to go . . . buy another winery," Oliver says when he sees me enter, and he promptly disappears, leaving the two of us alone.

Cyrus stares at me in the silence, and I have no idea what he's thinking, where or how this will end, so I speak first. "I made a snap assumption back there," I begin, shifting my weight from one foot to the other. "The wrong assumption. I—I didn't even give you a chance to explain, and I should have."

"Leah," he says, so tenderly I think I might burst into tears again. "You've considered me your enemy for years, and I'll never be able to make up for what happened. You thought what any person would have thought. I wouldn't expect you to go from hating me to trusting me completely right away—I would want the chance to win your trust slowly, bit by bit, if I had the honor. I'm honestly . . ." He releases a shaky breath, and for the first time tonight, I see the rush of emotions in his eyes. "I'm honestly shocked that you came back. Shocked, and very, very glad. I didn't think you ever would."

It feels like someone's grabbed hold of my heart and pulled.

Cyrus, who blamed himself for not recognizing a bad situation when he was in the thick of it, and then trained himself to assume the worst of every situation. Cyrus, who thinks that everything he touches will burn and fade to embers, who thinks that everyone is destined to leave him in the end. Cyrus, who always rejects people before they have the chance to reject him, who's afraid to be happy for fear of the day the happiness is taken away from him, who doesn't think he deserves happiness to begin with.

"Who else would I go to?" I say, smiling.

There's a loud rumbling noise outside, followed by a hiss and sharp whistling. We both whirl toward it at the same time, and Cyrus yanks back the curtains right as a brilliant array of colors explode across the night.

Fireworks.

"Look," Cyrus says, leading me forward by the wrist.

A breath of pure delighted laughter escapes my lips, and we almost trip over ourselves as we fumble with the lock on the balcony door, my hotel slippers shuffling against the carpet, and then we're rushing out into the crisp, cold air, leaning over the railings to stare in wonder as another *boom* fills the sky with sound and bright, dazzling gold. More colors shower over the horizon: the most vivid pops of green and blazes of red and stars of silver, lighting up the city.

All around the hotel, for six floors down and as far as I can see, other travelers have hurried out onto their balconies to watch the fireworks too. Fathers balance their toddlers high up on their shoulders for a better view, happy couples wrap their arms around each other, mothers usher their children over from the bedroom. A gray-haired woman shakily retrieves her phone to start recording, maybe to send to her partner or her grandchildren. I don't know any of them, and they might be traveling for a family holiday or a honeymoon or a business trip, and they could be from the neighboring town or halfway across the world, but we're all standing here right now. And my heart swells at the silly, simple, human fact that when we stumble upon something beautiful, our first instinct is to show it to the people we love. It's what we do with pretty seashells on a beach, a radiant sunset, a rare bird flitting through the trees, a herd of wild horses grazing in the countryside. *Look*, we say, saving these little pieces of beauty for each other. *Do you see it too? Isn't the world such a strange, lovely, breathtaking place?*

"I think the fireworks are for a wedding happening nearby," Cyrus says.

"Well, good for them, and great for us," I say.

Cyrus gives me a sidelong smile. "Let's just hope nobody accidentally curses the bride and the groom."

I raise the hand he isn't holding to make a threatening motion at him. "Oh my god, if you bring that up again, I swear—"

But he grabs it too and easily locks both my wrists in his grip, tugging me forward until I'm inches away from him, close enough to watch the yellow light of the fireworks through the reflection in his eyes.

And suddenly I remember the note from the Yellow Mountain, written by a steady, careful hand. *You remind me of the greatest sculptors, who can turn marble into the impression of billowing silk, the coldest stone into something soft. I suppose what I'm trying to say is that everything you touch turns beautiful. The world becomes beautiful, as long as there's you.*

It really is beautiful, I think to myself as I lean in to kiss him.

Before the sun has even risen, I slide out of bed, the mattress creaking behind me. Then I shrug off my pajamas and zip up my sundress, fumbling around in the dim light as quietly as possible to avoid waking Daisy. I can already feel the anticipation building beneath my bones as I brush my hair and teeth and spritz perfume just behind my ear. It's the same eager flutter I would get on the morning of Christmas or my birthday, when I had everything in the world to look forward to, even if I didn't know what was going to happen yet.

A cool breeze fans my skin as I step outside, ruffling the hem of my dress.

Dew glistens on the wild grass around me, and the clouds

burn gold and pink on the horizon, the early mist softening all that it touches: the wind chimes tinkling from the hotel's overhanging eaves, the cobbled path leading into town, the sloping, layered lines of the rice terraces. Guilin at dawn looks like something out of a dream. It's so beautiful that my breath catches, that my throat aches a little from it.

And then I see him.

He's waiting on a stone bridge, the canal flowing beneath him. His dark hair is wind-rumpled, his shirt loosely buttoned, and the surreal, dreamlike sensation intensifies. When our eyes meet, a small, surprised smile comes to life on his face, like he can't believe I'm joining him.

"Where do you want to go?" he asks as he makes his way toward me.

"Here is perfect," I say. Right now, I can't think of a single place on earth I would prefer to this.

We both stop at the foot of the bridge, and for a few moments we're silent, the kind of silence that's as natural and seamless as breathing. It's enough to simply be standing together, just the two of us, staring at the clear waters and the jade mountains.

"I don't think I'm ready to leave," I admit.

"I'm not either," he tells me. "But you can always come back. We can always come back."

"Seriously?" I grin, pushing my hair back. "You're ready to take another trip with me so soon?"

"Who else is going to haggle over lettuce for me?"

"I can show you how," I say, pretending to deliberate over the serious matter. "Though it might depend on the person you're bargaining with. It just works a lot better if they're attracted to you. That way, all you have to do is look at them like this . . ." I spin around and angle my face so I'm gazing up at him under my lashes. "And lower your voice. Lean over and pout a bit . . . Trust me, it's *very* persuasive."

He stares back at me, his eyes wide and almost dazed.

"Don't you agree?" I add, leaning close, the words whispered against the shell of his ear.

I hear his sharp inhale.

I'm laughing as I pull away, delighted and nearly lightheaded to know the effect I have on him, to see the blush rubbing off his complexion like smeared lipstick.

He still looks half-drunk when he catches my wrist and tugs me close to him again. Some of my laughter dissolves at the heated, intense look in his gaze. "You know, I've had fantasies about this," he murmurs.

"About being taught how to flirt your way into getting cheaper vegetables?" I ask. I'm fighting with every muscle in my body to maintain my composure, but I sound breathless, even to myself. I sound like I'm asking him to kiss me without speaking the words aloud. "You should've told me earlier. I'd be happy to teach you in more depth."

"About you," he says, swallowing. "About being next to you."

"And? Do I live up to your fantasy?" I say it teasingly, yet my heart thuds as I wait for his answer. I never have in the past. For every guy who's claimed to like me, I was just something nice for them to think about, my eyes and my hips and my legs, prettier on posters and in magazines than in real life. Of course they all noticed me. Of course they all left in the end.

Cyrus shakes his head. "No fantasy could ever live up to you," he whispers. "Nothing can compare to how it feels to look up and see you there. Even though I thought of you every day after you left, my imagination has proven to be painfully inadequate when it comes to the sound of your laughter, or how your brows furrow when you're focused, or the way you steady yourself before entering a room. And you're going to make fun of me for saying it, but part of me is worried," he says, dropping his gaze to the white glimmer of water, "that this is just a spell. This whole trip has been so strange and wonderful and unexpected . . . It's like there's magic here, and I can't stop myself from worrying that when we leave this place, the magic will disappear for you, and none of it will be real anymore."

It does feel like there's magic here, in the whispers of the Osmanthus trees and the rose light curving over the tiled roofs. But there's no way to separate it from the boy standing at the end of the bridge with me as the sun climbs up, who's now watching me with a tenderness I wouldn't have believed existed before him. *I could love him anywhere, in any city, any season*, I think to myself. I can easily envision us coming back together, maybe a year or two from now, strolling down the Bund at night, lost in Shanghai's brilliant array of lights, or taking photos in the ancient water towns, his hand intertwined with mine. Just as I can envision us in LA, riding our bikes along the coast, packing strawberries and croissants into picnic baskets, lounging on the couch at his house.

The only thing I can't envision is no longer wanting him.

"How could this not be real anymore?" I ask, mapping out the line of his jaw with my fingertips.

He shivers at my touch, then—like he can't bear the remaining distance between us anymore, can't quite control himself—he pulls me in, his body bracketing mine, until I can feel how fast his heart is beating, how shaky his breathing is.

"I agree with you," he says hoarsely, his hand warm and gentle over the back of my head, and everything in me turns into molten gold, as if I've drunk the dawn air. I let him hold me as tight as I'm holding on to this moment and all the moments that have come before it, leading up to us. I have no intention of moving for years.

"You agree with me?" I barely remember to ask. "On what?"

"Here is perfect."

CHAPTER TWENTY-ONE

Packing for the trip had been an exercise in spatial awareness.

Every dress was carefully folded and tucked into laundry bags, every pair of socks squeezed strategically into the remaining gaps, every compartment utilized to its full potential. Packing for the plane ride home, on the other hand, is more a challenge to see how much I can stuff into a single suitcase without it exploding.

"Um, I admire your ambition, Leah, but I feel like this isn't going to work," Daisy tells me, cross-legged on the hotel bed. When Cyrus walked me back to my room half an hour ago, she was already wide awake and dressed, her bags prepared by the doorstep. *I'm physically incapable of packing at the very last minute*, she had explained as she triple-checked the bathroom for any forgotten items. *Like, the stress would render me immobile.* "That zipper looks like it's about to go on strike."

"It's fine. I'll just give it a motivational speech and promise it a raise that'll never materialize." I wipe the sweat from my brow, sit down on the bulging suitcase with all my weight, and yank at the zipper again. It doesn't budge.

"How did you even bring so many outfits with you?" Daisy asks with what sounds like genuine amazement. She points at one of the jackets threatening to escape from the suitcase. "I barely remember seeing you wear that."

"I—definitely—did," I say, panting, as I shove the jacket back in with the monstrous mass of dirty laundry and boots and eye shadow palettes. "I wore it one morning—for breakfast."

She hops off the bed and crouches down next to me to inspect my luggage, the way a doctor might examine a dying patient. "Maybe . . . we can both try standing on it," she says skeptically.

"You think that would do the trick?"

"I think it would be better if a hippo stood on it, but we don't exactly have the resources—or the time."

From outside, I can hear the rumbling of other suitcases being pushed down the corridor, the thud of doors slamming shut. Wang Laoshi had commanded us to meet in the lobby at nine thirty—exactly three minutes from now.

"Oh my god. Wait. I just remembered I have a boyfriend," I say, a ridiculous smile leaping to my face as I whip my phone out. "I'll ask him to help. "

"Good thinking," Daisy says, nodding sagely. "This is, like, one of the only times a boyfriend comes in handy."

A knock comes mere moments later, and there Cyrus is, entering the room with his sleeves rolled up like someone conjured from my sweetest fantasies.

"This suitcase over here?" he asks as I stand up to make room for him. Daisy excuses herself, sliding out the door with a wink over her shoulder and a motion to meet downstairs later.

"Yeah." I lean back against the wall, watching him with the simple, exquisite pleasure of knowing I don't have to pretend I'm looking somewhere else. "If you can get it to close, I will be eternally grateful."

He glances over at me, the corner of his mouth lifting. "Eternally grateful how?"

"I'll . . ." I consider it for a beat. "I'll buy you a sticker."

"That's your definition of eternal gratitude?"

"A really cute sticker, with little stars on it," I specify. "I mean, you can't expect me to offer you my life's savings in exchange for zipping up a suitcase. Unless you have something else in mind."

"I do," he says immediately. "I want another one of your cloud doodles."

I burst out laughing, but he doesn't seem to be joking.

"Okay, fine, then," I say, still laughing. "I promise you one wonky cloud doodle."

Satisfied, he turns his attention back to the suitcase and pushes down from above with one hand while pulling the zipper with another. Miraculously, the zipper cooperates, and nothing explodes. Within seconds, he has the suitcase propped upright, and wheels it toward me.

And as I take it, I feel that shift deep inside my chest, like my heart has moved just to make more room for him. *Xindong*. Gazing up at him, his dark eyes and quiet smile, I'm not sure my heart will ever be still again.

Once all the suitcases have been wheeled out and our key cards deposited at the front desk, Wang Laoshi claps his hands to get our attention.

"I've spent most of last night reading your essays and tallying up the scores," Wang Laoshi begins. "There were a few essays that were . . . surprisingly moving." His eyes land on me, and I blink, hardly daring to believe that he's talking about my essay. I can barely even remember what I wrote—something about a girl getting lost in a bamboo forest, a metaphor and memory combined. I worked on it after the fireworks show, my head light and my chest full, trying not to be distracted by Cyrus playing with my hair, and submitted it just two minutes before the deadline.

"I'm happy to say that we have a winner . . ." Wang Laoshi continues. "It was *very* close. Whether you're first place or not, I've witnessed firsthand the progress you've made in your Chinese, and while there's always room for improvement, you should all be rather proud of yourselves." He pauses, blinks, his usually stern expression softening for just a moment. "Now, on to the results—drumroll, please."

We all oblige, drumming our fingers on our suitcases, and then Oliver really gets into it and starts mimicking an entire orchestra all by himself, complete with trumpet and bass and what might be a teeny triangle, and Wang Laoshi hurries ahead to announce the results before the hotel staff can kick us out of the lobby.

"The winners are . . ."

I exchange a look with Cyrus, try to lock my nerves up in a steel trap inside my stomach. I know for a fact that we can't be *last*, but that's all I really know. After everything I've already collected from this trip, every new memory and shot of joy I've downed, it feels almost greedy to want more. But my hopes of getting into a decent college are riding on this.

"Leah and Cyrus," Wang Laoshi says, smiling over at us.

My heart soars. The rest of the group bursts into applause that's definitely too loud for an indoor setting, and I throw my arms around Cyrus's neck without thinking.

"We won," I squeal. "We *won*."

"We did," he says, laughing, his hand coming up to rest over the small of my back like there's nobody else around. "I told you we would, didn't I?"

"You know what we should do to celebrate?" I ask him.

He pulls back just slightly to tilt his head, his eyes gleaming. "Are you asking me out?"

"Maybe," I tease. "There *is* a nice restaurant I've always wanted to try down the street from my house . . ."

"Let's go there," he says instantly.

"Cyrus, you don't even know what restaurant it is—"

"Doesn't matter," he tells me, "as long as I'm going with you."

It strikes me then it's all coming to an end—the competition is over, and in only a matter of hours, we'll be leaving. There's an ache in my chest, but it's a happy ache, like the car ride home after a party, when your feet are sore from dancing and your cheeks are stiff from laughing the whole night.

The first thing Cyrus does when we settle into our seats on the plane is start wiping everything. The folding tray. The screen. Every inch of the seat belt. It just goes to show how quickly one's brain can be rewired, because more than anything else, I'm impressed by how thorough he is. *If we were to ever move in together, our house would be so neat*, the delusional voice in my head sings.

"Can you please wipe down my seat too?" I ask him.

He raises his brows but immediately tears open another pack of alcohol wipes and cleans the armrest between us. "I see you've been influenced."

"I have," I say shamelessly. "Full credit to you. Maybe you should be an influencer."

"For sanitizers?"

"See, you've already found your niche," I tell him. "And with that pretty face"—I reach out and tip his chin up on one hand—"you could sell anything."

His complexion turns a lovely, irresistible shade of pink, his smile shy, and I decide that I'll never stop thinking of ways to make him blush.

"You know, it's really lucky that we got seated next to each other twice," I remark as smiling attendants hurry up and down the aisles, double-checking the overhead bins to make sure that no suitcases are going to tumble out halfway, calling politely for a man to straighten his seat before takeoff. "Like, what are the chances?"

Cyrus hesitates. "I . . . have a confession to make," he says.

"Oh?"

"Two confessions, actually," he amends. Clears his throat. "Though I suppose you could consider them to be connected."

"All right, I have no idea where this is going, but I'm listening."

"I wasn't actually meant to sit next to you on the plane ride to Shanghai," he says. "My original seat was four rows away, and I had to bribe this extremely disgruntled college student into swapping with me. Also . . . I was hoping you would be at your cousin's wedding. I did plan to find Dr. Linda Shen, of course—that letter of recommendation is really important to me. But when I said there was someone I needed to see, I was talking about you."

I blink, very nearly certain that he's kidding.

"I'm not kidding," Cyrus says, and his eyes are serious, tentative even, searching mine for some kind of reaction. "None of it was an accident."

"You did all that . . . for me?" I whisper. My heart leans all the way forward, close to toppling right out my chest.

"Of course," he says.

Maybe, another day, I'll find the right words in either English or Chinese to tell him everything I'm feeling, how grateful I am that we came here together, how happy I am whenever I'm with him, how close I'd been to losing hope before he found his way to me. But a lump fills my throat, and for now I can only lean against him, squeeze his hand tight as the plane begins slowly backing away from the gate.

I must nod off at some point, because when I open my eyes again, we're already above the clouds and Cyrus's fingers are laced firmly through mine. I'm still not sure where I'll end up a month from now, or a year, or half a life, whether I'll find something I love as much as I love this moment, and whether it'll last. But all I have to do is look out at the sky, that deep, lovely, endless blue, and remember that no matter where I end up, joy will never be too far out of reach.

EPILOGUE

We're the first family to pull up outside the Jiu Yin He front gates.

"You know, we probably didn't need to leave our house an entire *hour* early. The GPS said it'd take fifteen minutes with heavy traffic," I tell my mom as she shuts the car door behind her and struts her way down the empty lane in her brand-new Michael Kors pumps. Most of her outfit is new, from the pearl-studded earrings to the sharp blazer vest, selected just for this occasion. Yesterday, I'd caught her unveiling one of the fancy face masks she'd been saving ever since her colleague brought them back from her business trip to Seoul. She hadn't even put in that much effort for my cousin's wedding. She probably hadn't put in that much effort for her *own* wedding.

"Well, we couldn't risk being late, could we? Not when you're the star of the show," my mom says, beaming wide at me. From the way she's been gushing about it, you'd think I'd won the Nobel Peace Prize, not a competition hosted by a Chinese school.

I exchange an amused glance with my dad before we both follow along. A single poster—small enough that you'd miss it if you weren't paying careful attention—has been pasted onto the school's brick walls. *Welcome, Parents! This Way to the Journey to the East Afternoon Tea* is printed out in Chinese block text, with arrows pointing the way forward.

The venue is basically a gym that's been repurposed for this afternoon's event. Plastic chairs have been set up in tidy rows along the basketball court, and there are a few scattered tables offering cold chicken-and-avocado sandwiches and plastic cups of orange juice, but my mom's beaming at the place like it's a grand concert hall.

"Do you have your speech memorized?" my mom asks me, nodding toward the microphone stand up front.

"Don't worry, I've got it," I assure her. I have the speech so well memorized that although it'd be exaggerating to say I could recite it in my sleep, I'm pretty confident I could recite it first thing upon waking. But then the gym doors swing open again, and I momentarily lose the ability to remember anything when I see Cyrus walk in.

His eyes go right to me, like I'm the only reason he's here, and I have to contain myself from running straight over and throwing my arms around him.

"That boy again," my mom mutters under her breath, but she doesn't stop me from moving to his side, which I'm taking as a good sign. Improvement. She'd been too preoccupied to recognize Cyrus as my childhood enemy at my cousin's wedding, but she'd definitely noticed him when she'd gone to pick me up at the airport. Likely because he was holding my hand. I'd spent the entire car ride home explaining to her that we were good now, that he was and always had been good, really, I swear, he made me happy. And just when I thought she might accuse me of losing my mind, she'd simply smiled in a resigned sort of way.

It all sounds very bizarre to me, considering how much you hated him before, she'd confessed as the car crawled along the highway, *but I can tell you're happy, which is what matters most.* She'd glanced at me again in the rearview mirror. *Something's different about you, baobei—I can feel it. Just like how before you left, I could tell how unhappy you were. You hid it well enough, but your smiles were always forced, your laughter strained. It's like you were making yourself go through all the motions without feeling anything, and I . . . I couldn't bear to see you that way. Now, though,* she said softly, *when you talk about him, when you talk about Shanghai . . . Your happiness is real. It's practically radiating off you.*

That was three weeks ago.

Three blissful weeks, and the happiness has stayed, made a home inside my heart. With every day that I've spent with Cyrus since, I've uncovered something new about him. I learn all the books he keeps on the shelf beside his bed, Chinese and English titles mixed together, his favorites annotated so thoroughly he might as well have written another novel within the novel. I take note of the bag he carries to school these days—cream canvas, sturdy, practical—and the expensive fine-liners he keeps in his pencil case, his only "luxury purchase." I laugh at his playlist the first time he drives me home (*Cyrus, what kind of retro shit is this?*), but he knows I'm just teasing and he knows exactly how to shut me up, because when he parks two houses down the street, he gazes over at me in the darkness, and his hands find the nape of my neck and he pulls me toward him. Pauses for a few seconds, simply holding me there, until I think my heart might explode and his lips finally find mine with that awful retro song still playing in the background, but it's sort of grown on me by the time we reach the last chorus.

I experience the rare thrill of discovering what he's like when he's in love and it's no longer a secret. The second we're alone together anywhere—in an elevator that moves at half the speed of the ones in Shanghai, in the empty corner of the bookstore he frequents on weekends, in the parking lot behind the mall— he's drawing me to his chest, his fingers sliding over my waist, and it's so natural, so right, it's like I've loved him my whole life. Everything feels natural with him. Like how he kisses me when we're waiting at the traffic lights and when we're halfway through the door, or how he keeps a protective arm around me through every crowd, how I nuzzle against his shoulder while he's browsing through takeout options for dinner, my legs dangling off the love seat. *Xiaolongbao, sushi, or hot pot tonight?* he asks. *Anything sounds good*, I say, but I'm secretly craving xiaolongbao, the crab roe kind, and I can't conceal my delight when that's exactly what arrives as if he's read my mind.

I still wear makeup when I want to, but on nights where I get tired of how heavy the products feel on my skin, or in the mornings when I'm simply too lazy to spend ten minutes blending out my eye shadow, I choose to go without it. In the beginning, my face feels raw and tender and exposed, but Cyrus reassures me, *It's nothing I haven't seen before*, then points to his own face: *Look, I'm not wearing any makeup either.* He tells me I'm pretty like it's what everyone else is thinking, and the miracle of it all is I know he means it.

"Miss me?" Cyrus asks, grinning, as I join him at the front of the gym.

"I saw you only, like, sixteen hours ago," I point out.

"Right," he says, his grin widening. "Not that you're keeping count or anything."

I roll my eyes, but I doubt it's convincing when the corners of my lips keep twitching upward. "Definitely not."

"I missed you too," he tells me, leaning closer, his breath tantalizingly warm against my neck. Then he rights himself again, all serious, the picture of the perfect student as more families and teachers start trickling indoors.

I catch sight of Daisy entering with her parents, who I've already met twice now at her house and who refused to let me leave without bringing a full basket of homegrown plums and two containers of frozen pork dumplings with me. I wave at her dramatically, as if I'm stranded on a remote island and trying to capture the attention of a passing helicopter. It's the kind of thing I'd be too embarrassed to do around Cate and her friends, but Daisy matches my enthusiasm and mouths, *Good luck*.

Once the seats have all been filled, the gym falls quiet, and Wang Laoshi comes up to the microphone for his opening speech while Cyrus and I wait in the wings behind him.

". . . very honored to be partnering with the Department of East Asian Languages and Cultures at Stanford . . . Please welcome . . ."

"Nervous about the speech?" Cyrus whispers to me.

No, I'm about to say, and it would be true if my aunt didn't make her entrance right at that moment. She's dressed in regal black from head to toe, and she steps forward without haste, barely acknowledging the crowd's applause for her, as if this is an ordinary part of her daily routine, or possibly even a downgrade from the celebrity treatment she's accustomed to.

I swallow, my stomach clenching. The Chinese characters from my speech swirl around inside my head. *It's okay, you can do this. You're prepared. You can redeem yourself.*

". . . the winners from the competition, Leah Zhang and Cyrus Sui."

Cyrus squeezes my hand twice, and I let myself focus on the warm, familiar pressure, the scent of his cologne.

Then we're walking out together, the bright gym lights spilling around us.

I take the microphone first. Hold it too close, my fingers quivering. I can hear my breaths in the static, feel the weight of my aunt's gaze from the other end of the stage.

"Welcome, parents, students, and teachers," I begin in slow, careful Chinese, hoping they can't detect the shakiness in my voice. "I have to be honest—when my mom first signed me up for this trip, I didn't particularly want to go . . ."

As I go on, my voice strengthens, my words coming out smoother, clearer, acquiring their own cadence, and I remind myself that this isn't a completely foreign language. It's the language of my mother's hometown, the language spoken by my father and his father before him, the language I breathed in for a fortnight, the melody of my surroundings.

It helps that the audience is generous, welcoming. They laugh at all my bad jokes and listen with rapt attention as I describe parts of the trip they already know—the beauty of Shanghai at night, the long train rides, the bustling markets, the steep, rainy climb up the Yellow Mountain, the serenity of the bamboo forest.

"So I want to thank my parents," I finish, my eyes finding their proud faces in the front row. "Thank you for sending me on this trip, for everything you've done, for being patient with me when I lost my way and waiting with open arms when I found my way back. And thank you to my family at large for tolerating my terrible blunders and for watching me grow. I've learned language, in its purest form, is really about understanding each other, seeing the heart of what the other person is trying to say. I hope there'll be more chances for you to understand me, and for me to understand you better . . ."

I brace myself as I glance in my aunt's direction. It strikes me suddenly how much she resembles my own mother; something about the structure of her jaw, the intelligent arch of her brows. The resemblance is stronger than ever when her severe features finally soften, and she offers me a faint, approving smile.

Afterward, we stroll through the city together, my hand in his.

At the end of the road, I take out the Polaroid camera we won on the trip with my free hand, and snap a quick photo when he isn't looking. When the film finishes developing in my hand, half the frame is filled with sunlight. There's so much sunlight in every photo I take of him. Like the sun is all I can see when he's with me. It makes his features look softer, burns the strands of his hair gold like alchemy in motion, bathing him in its glow. In this photo, the sun is coming down directly from above him like a halo, the white-purple flare of it flashing just above his head.

"It's so nice here," I say, though we're technically not anywhere in particular. I have no idea what street we're on, only that it's beautiful as the sun sinks lower, a soft, dreamy haze washing over the palm trees and high-rise apartments.

It's the same LA I've grown up in, but it feels different, maybe because I am, and these days I find myself falling in love with the city all over again. Through brunches with Daisy at Brent's Bakery, where their fresh sourdough loaves are so chewy, with the perfect kick of tanginess, that we always end up buying a second loaf and sharing it on the way home, munching happily as we walk; through pottery classes, also with Daisy, even though we're both horrible at it and we gift each other with the world's wonkiest mugs when we're done; through karaoke nights organized in the Journey to the East group chat and entirely paid for by Oliver('s father), whose off-key belting to classic Chinese ballads is almost as fun as trying to convince Cyrus to sing, which he adamantly refuses to through afternoon teas with my parents at their favorite dim sum restaurant, where I'm a little too pleased to show off the characters I can read on the paper menu. This is how I fill my days now: food and full-body laughter, instead of counting calories and keeping a tally of my mistakes. Doing things because of how they make me feel rather than how they might sound.

Nothing's perfect, but everything's wonderful.

We walk for miles, content in each other's company, stopping to point out a pretty flower or a squirrel in the trees. Soon, the evening chill creeps in. I try my best not to notice it, but my feet feel frozen in my sandals.

Without question or comment, Cyrus shrugs off his jacket and drapes it around my shoulders.

"How did you know I was freezing?" I ask, turning to him in wonder.

"Because I know you," he says simply.

"You love me," I say. I can't pinpoint when it stopped being a question, and when it started to feel like a simple fact. There are 6,479 miles between Shanghai and Los Angeles. The sun will come up tomorrow. You can never go wrong with a well-fitted black dress. And he loves me.

"Of course I do," he murmurs against my hair.

We keep walking, and I don't ask him where we're going, and I don't even care, as long as I'm with him.

ACKNOWLEDGMENTS

All my thanks to the wonderful, talented people who made this book possible:

A huge thank-you to my agent, Kathleen Rushall—I can't believe it's already been over four years since our first call, and what a journey it's been since. I wish there were enough words to express my love and awe and gratitude for you. Thank you for everything you've done. Thank you to everyone at Andrea Brown Literary Agency for your dedication and expertise.

Thank you to Maya Marlette, my phenomenal editor. You bring so much joy to the process of shaping an idea into a book, and I mean it wholeheartedly when I say it's an absolute delight to work with someone as warm, passionate, and brilliant as you. Thank you to the fantastic Maeve Norton and Taylor Yingshi for the absolute dream of a cover. Thank you to the incredible team at Scholastic for all your support: Elizabeth Whiting, Caroline Noll, Melanie Wann, Dan Moser, Jarad Waxman, Jody Stigliano, Jackie Rubin, Nikki Mutch, Savannah D'Amico, Kelsey Albertson, Lori Benton, John Pels, Rachel Feld, Erin Berger, Greyson Corley, Amanda Book, Seale Ballenger, Duaa Ali, Janell Harris, Michael Strouse, Emily Heddleson, Lizette Serrano, Maisha Johnson, Meredith Wardell, and Sabrina

Montenigro. My endless thanks to David Levithan, Ellie Berger, and Leslie Garych.

Thank you to Taryn Fagerness at Taryn Fagerness Agency for your insight, enthusiasm, and hard work. It's so surreal to see my stories translated, and I'm deeply grateful for the opportunities that have come my way because of you.

Thank you to everyone in the United States and abroad who has helped me bring this book to readers. Thank you to the librarians, booksellers, teachers, and book bloggers for all that you do.

Thank you to my friends, both the ones I've known since my awkward teen years and the ones I've been lucky enough to meet along the way. I am amazed every day to be surrounded by such smart, generous, witty, kind, and extraordinary people.

To my parents—thank you for giving me everything I have. Thank you for your patience and your unwavering faith in me. Thank you for always posting about my new releases on WeChat and sorry for all the giant boxes of books lying around the house.

Thank you to my sister, Alyssa, for keeping me humble and keeping me sane. I honestly don't know what I'd do without you.

Thank you, a thousand times over, from the bottom of my heart, to my readers. You've made all my childhood dreams come true. What a rare privilege it is to say, *There's a story I want to tell*, and have someone willing to listen.

ABOUT THE AUTHOR

Photo by HIMO

Ann Liang is the *New York Times*, *USA Today*, and Indie bestselling author of critically acclaimed young adult and adult fiction. Her books have been sold in over twenty foreign territories. Her work has been featured on *Good Morning America* as a GMA Book Club pick, and on the *Today* show, *Cosmopolitan*, *PEOPLE*, *Harper's Bazaar*, and more. Born in Beijing, she grew up traveling back and forth between China and Australia, but somehow ended up with an American accent. She now lives in Melbourne, where she can be found making overambitious to-do lists and having profound conversations with her pet labradoodle about who's a good dog. You can find her on Instagram at @annliangwrites, or by visiting her website, annliang.com.